THE *NEW*
HOTEL
SCARBADOS

To

Caroline

Mark Harland.

THE *NEW* HOTEL SCARBADOS

A novel set in Scarborough, North Yorkshire

MARK HARLAND

Published by MVH Publishing 2025

A CIP catalogue record for this book is available from the British Library.

ISBN 978-1-7397547-7-8 (Paperback)
ISBN 978-1-7397547-8-5 (ePub)

Typeset by Clare Brayshaw

Manufacturer: York Publishing Services Ltd
64 Hallfield Road, Layerthorpe, York YO31 7ZQ
Tel: 01904 431213 | Email: enquiries@yps-publishing.co.uk
Website: www.yps-publishing.co.uk

Represented by: Authorised Rep Compliance Ltd.
Ground Floor, 71 Lower Baggot Street, Dublin D02 P593, Ireland
www.arccompliance.com

AUTHOR'S NOTE & ACKNOWLEDGEMENTS

Writing the "Scarbados Trilogy" over the last eighteen months has been something of an adventure for me – not to mention a monumental trip down memory lane.

I have revisited lots of my old haunts as a very young boy to try and recapture those moments that were so special in my childhood. Scarborough is a great place for children to grow up in and many of those experiences came flooding back as I put pen to paper – or rather fingers to keyboard.

At the same time, as the stories and plots progressed, I wanted to try and look forward to what might unfold as Scarborough's future. I am utterly convinced that the town's destiny as a premier resort is guaranteed – provided that its trustees, the people who live and work here, nurture and protect their heritage. There is no other town in England quite like "Scarbados" and it is worthy of the utmost care and attention.

I should like to take the opportunity to thank everyone who assisted me in this endeavour – in particular, Barbara Ralph, Susan Hullah, Allan Richardson, Mike Davis and the superb team of people at YPS – York Publishing Services.

Mark Harland
Scarborough
North Yorkshire

FOREWORD

For the Fishburn family, originally from Hull, life seemed like a moving travelator that never stopped. After twenty years as a senior steward on the Hull to Zeebrugge ferry, the MV Pride of Bruges, redundancy had hit Peter Fishburn and his family hard. When a legacy left to his wife Mandy from a distant and reclusive aunt came out of the blue, the chance to change the family's future was too good to miss.

With the Covid epidemic still gripping the country, their options were limited. However, when family discussions pointed the way forward, the Fishburns "upped sticks" and moved up the coast to purchase a small run-down hotel near to the famous Peasholm Park, in Scarborough. It was called the Wendover. When informed it had a chequered history they decided to change its name to the catchy Hotel Scarbados. They never looked back, the only upset being that Mandy didn't settle in Scarborough and eventually returned to Hull to live with her sister. An opportunistic and ambitious magazine editor, Pamela Hesketh, soon ingratiated herself into the business and the lonely and hapless Peter soon fell for her charms.

There followed a sequence of fortuitous events that could not possibly have been predicted. In less than a year of trading they were in a position to bid for a much larger hotel, the Clifftop, which was back on the market after being used for some years by the Home Office to house refugees. They were the only bidders but Peter, son Jamie and daughters Millie and Lucy, all leapt at the opportunity with alacrity. In turn, they changed its name to the Hotel Koala to give it a fresh look and a new identity. They were soon joined by the scheming Pamela who had to finally reveal her true colours. She was now a Director and on the Board of Best Eastern Hotels, a dynamic and almost predatory company, financed by overseas money, that was keen to acquire promising assets in the booming hospitality industry.

Pamela Hesketh eventually managed to purchase Mandy Fishburn's shares in the Hotel Koala and it was only a matter of time before she recommended to the Board of Best Eastern Hotels that they bought at least a fifty percent stake. This made Peter and Pamela cash rich and, with his family's blessing, he made a bid to buy back the former Hotel Scarbados. His bid at auction was successful and the hope was to take the youngest daughter, Lucy, and their two labradoodles with him. The recent revelation that his former Belgian mistress, Stephanie van Gelder, had borne their love child, ripped Peter's heart strings to shreds. Grabbing the bull and his emotions by the horns, he invited Stephanie and the daughter he had never seen, to visit Scarbados. He promised to meet them at St. Pancras Station in London if they travelled by Eurostar.

That was just a couple of weeks earlier and the trip was fixed for the Easter school holiday when young Natalie, now aged ten, would be off school. Thus the story resumes in this the final book in the trilogy, "*The* New *Hotel Scarbados.*"

Now read on …

1.

'It'll be fine, Dad, trust me. Just chill.'

His eldest daughter Millie's words of encouragement reverberated around Peter's head all the way from York to Kings Cross, a journey of two hours. In reality he was a nervous wreck. As the train passed by the Emirates Football Stadium and started to slow down, he knew that in just a few minutes his train would arrive. Then, a couple of minutes walk away, was St. Pancras – the London Terminus for the Eurostar. Peter was grateful that his train arrived at Platform 8 which was the nearest one to St. Pancras. His legs felt like jelly as he walked past Platform "nine and three quarters," so beloved by fans of Harry Potter and the Hogwarts Express. Crossing the pedestrianised square he made for one of the many entrances into one of London's finest architectural wonders. He hadn't been there before and its splendour took him unawares. Was this England in the twenty-first century? It was Victorian art at its best. There was nowhere else in Europe quite like it, so he thought. A little Belgian girl was about to educate him.

Peter stared up at the electronic information board. He sighed.

'The Eurostar arrival from Brussels is delayed by one hour.'

This was not what he wanted to hear. It meant another sixty minutes of anticipation and nervousness verging on dread. How would Stephanie behave towards him? How

1

would Natalie, his own flesh and blood, react to meeting her father for the first time? He dived into a COSTA COFFEE and tried to take his mind off the situation. He failed totally. He decided to call Millie on his mobile. She was always cool and sensible.

'Dad, calm down. Just be you, OK. When you think about it, they are going to be as nervous as you, aren't they? Go for it, Dad, and Facetime me later OK when you've settled into the hotel. Don't forget. Lucy and Jamie will be here too.'

She was right. He got himself a flat white, grabbed a free copy of *The Metro* and tried to settle down and watch the world go by through a window with a good view of the concourse. How many fathers in their late fifties would be lucky enough to take advice from a daughter instead of handing it out? Not many, he thought, as he reflected on what a wonderful and mature young lady his daughter had become and she was barely twenty-one. One day she would become a wife and mother herself – but not yet, please God. Right now he needed her. He was brought out of his daydream when his iPhone pinged once. It must be a WhatsApp or a Facebook message. The words 'Just one ping' reminded him of Sean Connery in the movie *The Hunt for Red October* – one of his favourites which he never tired of watching. It was probably Millie who had forgotten to tell him something. He depressed the blue button and within a second was staring straight into the face of a little girl. She was Lucy's double – it was Natalie! Instantly his nerves departed. He just melted.

'Hello Papa – it's me – Natalie.'

It had been Stephanie's idea. She thought it would break the ice early. She was right there.

'How are you today, Papa?'

Within a few seconds she passed the phone back to her mother, her English vocabulary temporarily expended.

'Hi Peter. I thought that would surprise you …'

'Oh wow, Stephanie, that almost floored me. But how nice of you to …'

'Pete, we are delayed by almost one hour. The train is leaving a place called Cheriton so we are now in Kent – the Garden of England I think you once called it. Are you at St. Pancras already?'

'Yes I'm here, don't worry.'

'And how long will it take us to get to "Scarbados" as you keep calling it?'

'We're not going there today. We're having a couple of nights in a hotel in London. Tomorrow, I want to show Natalie Buckingham Palace, the London Eye and …'

It had been yet another brilliant idea of Millie's.

'Get to know Natalie slowly, Dad.'

She was always right was Millie.

It would prove to be the longest hour of Peter's life but when the moment of reunion came it was easy and comfortable – thanks to Stephanie's brilliant idea of the Facetime call. As she and Natalie came through Immigration at the UK BORDER Peter could spot little Natalie's pink anorak from fifty metres away. Mutual recognition was swift and Natalie broke free from her mother and positively raced the short distance to her father. She buried her face in Peter's midriff and clung to him like a limpet on the hull of the Pride of Bruges. Eventually she looked up at him and said 'Hello Papa' with just a hint of a continental accent. Peter melted like snowflakes in May and looked down. She was Lucy's double. Two massive tears ran down his cheeks, one port one starboard. Stephanie just smiled and embraced him when Natalie finally let go.

It was a short walk back to Kings Cross and the taxi rank. Natalie had seen black London taxis on TV and films but today she was actually going to ride in one. Wow! She was so excited and jumped in as soon as Peter had opened the huge door and lifted in their cases.

'Where to Guv'nor?'

'Claridges, please.'

Peter knew this was going to cost him an arm and a leg but what the heck. He'd bought back the Hotel Scarbados for a lot less than he thought and he wanted the occasion to be a memorable one. In any case the plan was for the girls to fly back to Belgium a week later, possibly from Manchester. They might never come to London again, although he hoped that they would, preferably as a proper little family but he kept that thought up his sleeve for the time being.

'Pete, why did the taxi driver call you Governor? Don't tell me that you're the Governor of Scarbados already?'

They both laughed to the bewilderment of Natalie. She thought all adults said funny things and she hadn't even been to Yorkshire yet!

'No, I'm not a Governor yet but we did have a High Commissioner, from Barbados, staying with us. He's going to come back again soon, when the cricket season starts.'

The look on Stephanie's face was one of those "I'm not sure if you're joking" looks.

'We're nearly here Guv. Traffic's light, surprisingly. You were lucky to get into Claridges, Sir. It's always full at Easter. Let me lift your bags out, Sir.'

Peter paid the driver in cash with a generous tip and a bell-hop arrived with one of those smart luggage trolleys. Five minutes later and they were in their small but immaculately furnished family suites comprising two en-suite bedrooms with a sitting room twixt the two. Peter hadn't been sure what type of rooms to book. He didn't want to make any assumptions with the sleeping arrangements. Perhaps liberties could be offered but not taken? He hoped he'd got it right.

After unpacking they had tea and cakes delivered by room service and held a little conference.

'OK Natalie, now you get to choose.'

Stephanie translated the tricky bits into Flemish to make things jog along easily. Peter continued.

'Where shall we go to eat later? We can stay in the Hotel if you're tired or we can …'

'Pizza! Pizza Express! A Margherita with extra cheese and mushrooms please.'

'Er, OK, but I don't know how far …'

''Papa, I saw one on the way here, only three hundred metres away. Please …'

'Pete, she doesn't miss a trick I'm telling you – as you'll come to learn.'

'She's a vegetarian too, hence the choice of Margherita pizza. Where the heck they get these ideas from I just don't know – school probably.'

Peter just sighed and almost surrendered to the inevitable. It looks like Natalie and Lucy were twins already and they hadn't even met yet.

'OK the Pizza Express it is. But let's Facetime your half-sisters and brother first shall we? They're dying to meet you.' Peter reached for his iPhone and dialled Millie's number.

'Millie, I want you to meet Stephanie and Natalie. He swept the camera lens towards them and everyone waved. Then it was Lucy's turn. She smiled and then pointed the lens at a cute little doggie on her lap.

'And this is AlfieBoy. You can be his Mum too if you like.'

And they hadn't even got to Scarbados yet.

2.

They all had an absolute ball in London the next day. A ride on the London Underground to Green Park was Natalie's first ride on such a train – apart from the "Chunnel" of course. They got off at the exit next to the famous Ritz Hotel and walked into the Park itself. At this time of year there were still no proper leaves on the trees, just a few buds, so visibility all the way south to Buckingham Palace was good.

'Papa, why isn't there a flag on the roof? Our Royal Palaces always fly a flag.'

Fortunately Peter knew the answer although he was floored that Natalie should even have asked him that question. Like Stephanie had remarked the previous afternoon – 'she doesn't miss a trick, as you'll find out.'

'It's because the King isn't in residence, meaning he's not there at the moment. If he was there then the flag would be flying.'

'So why isn't he there? It's his house now isn't it?'

'Well it's Easter so he's probably at Windsor Castle instead.'

'Can we go there too, Papa? I want to see lots of castles? How many are there?'

''Er well no, sorry, it's too far away. Maybe we can come another time. We can go and see some some smaller castles when we get to Yorkshire.'

'Natalie, stop pestering your father. She can be a little minx when she gets a bee in her bonnet, Peter.'

Actually, Peter was rather enjoying the reparti with a little girl – something he hadn't done for almost a decade when a younger Lucy had the same enquiring mind.

'Tell you what, let's go to Madame Tussauds shall we and look at all the waxwork figures – see how many we can recognise!'

The queue to enter was quite long as London was full of tourists but it moved quite quickly. Thankfully Peter had booked their tickets online for the London Eye as they had to be booked in advance like airline tickets. No sooner had they got into their designated gondola when it started to rain, not heavily, but enough to create drops that ran down the outside of the giant plastic bubbles. It was almost surreal and Natalie clicked away with her smart-phone and added pictures of the River Thames and the Houses of Parliament. She was so excited. She jabbered away in Flemish to her mother.

'Natalie, I told you. Try to speak in English all the time while you're here in England please. If you don't know the English word then ask me. OK?'

'Yes, Mama.'

That was yesterday. After two nights at Claridges which almost emptied Peter's wallet, they were now at Kings Cross ready to board the East Coast Main Line train to York. Peter stared up at the electronic departure board. They were booked on the twelve noon train to Edinburgh via Peterborough and York. The "Azuma" train's departure was going to leave from Platform 0 and the train was "on time" according to the up to date information. Peter was baffled – where the heck was Platform 0? It didn't make sense. He was just about to ask the gentlemen stood next to him who looked equally baffled, when Stephanie suddenly exclaimed.

'Where's she gone. Where's Natalie?'

'She was here a minute ago. For God's sake, the train leaves in ten minutes. We're cutting it fine already thanks to the heavy traffic. There she is over there. Look!'

Her hi-viz pink jacket gave her away. She was lined up outside Platform nine and three quarters taking selfies with the Hogwarts Express sign in the background.'

Like Queen Victoria, Stephanie was not amused.

'Please don't do that again. Your father was having kittens.'

The expression was totally lost on Natalie who looked suitably sheepish. They found Platform 0 to the far right of the concourse beyond Platform 1. They made it with four minutes to spare but the helpful conductor had more bad news for them.

'First Class seats are at the front of the train, Sir. Move along quickly now please.'

They were about halfway down the platform heading for Coach A when an announcement caused them a little concern. The Tannoy boomed out around them.

'The twelve noon train to Edinburgh from Platform Zero will be departing in two minutes. Passengers travelling on this train should board now.'

Another conductor ushered them into an open carriage door marked Coach E.

'Let me help you with these bags, Sir. Quickly please, Sir. Thank you.'

Less than sixty seconds later the electric doors closed behind them with a "whoosh" and a metallic click. They were still four whole coaches away from where they needed to be. Peter led the way forward pulling his own fairly small wheeled case. Behind him Natalie pulled her own little case and behind her Stephanie trailed her own somewhat larger case. Peter reached the end of the carriage and was just about to the press the yellow "OPEN" button when he heard his phone ringing in his breast pocket of his jacket. He was not happy. What a bonkers time for anybody to make a call, not that anyone would know his situation at that moment. It was Lucy!

'Hi Dad. Just checking you're on the train and it's on time and …'

'Lucy, we're fine. Call you in five, I promise.'

He stuffed his iPhone back into his pocket and continued his trek towards the front of the train and the comparative refuge of First Class. The train was rammed with students going back home from Uni for the Easter Holidays. They had to step over umpteen rucksacks, several guitar cases and what he swore blind was a double bass case. Thank goodness students couldn't afford to play golf he thought to himself. He spoke too soon as he tripped over a sand wedge that had slid out of a golf bag from the overhead rack. They finally made it to Coach A.

'Phew! Sorry about that girls. It was just bad luck that First Class is at the front of the train. Sometimes it's at the rear. You don't know for sure until you actually board the train.'

It was Stephanie's turn to be fraught.

'Why are your English trains so crowded? And why don't they use double-decker trains like on Belgian Railways? I thought you Brits invented the damned things? You'd have thought that …'

'Because we have lots of tunnels that's why. You lot don't have any because the land is flat. No hills no tunnels OK. Got it?'

It was their first little tiff, in front of Natalie anyway. No matter. Natalie broke the awkward silence.

'Papa, don't forget to call Lucy back.'

In fact, in the hassle of having to walk through four carriages and disengaging himself from the straps of musical instrument cases and rucksacks, not to mention the mushrooming bruise from the Ben Sayers sand wedge on his starboard knee, he had forgotten all about Lucy.

'Yes, all right Natalie. Let's just settle down first shall we? Oh look here comes the complimentary drinks trolley. The stewardess, a brunette in her early twenties, looked towards Natalie.

'Noo, what ken I get ya, honey? Just take your pick from the trolley. Coffee or tea for you Madam? And you Sir?'

Natalie was totally floored by the the broad Midlothian lilt and Stephanie wasn't far behind.

'Papa, where does that girl come from? Not England!'

'No, she's from Scotland, probably Edinburgh. That's where this train is going and it stops there.'

'There's a big castle there too isn't there? Can we go there as well please?'

'It's a long way away. Maybe another time OK?'

Peter urgently needed a distraction. It came unexpectedly when his phone rang again. It was Lucy – again.'

'Dad, what's wrong? You didn't call back like you said you would. You promised.'

'Sorry, love. It's been a bit hectic but we're well on the way now. We've just got coffees and some Scottish shortbread and …'

'Can I speak to Natalie please, Dad?'

There then followed a full ten minute conversation, limited by Natalie's English, about AlfieBoy's age, state of health, sleeping habits, eating habits and his favourite walks. The call was brought to an abrupt halt when the train entered a tunnel and the signal was lost.

'And that, my dear Stephanie, is why we don't have double-decker trains in England. Got it?'

3.

The rest of the journey to Scarborough, with a change of trains at York, was thankfully comparatively uneventful. Before the train reached Malton it slowed down considerably to navigate a section of the route known as the Kirkham Curves and the overly curious Natalie immediately noticed.

'Papa, why is the train stopping?'

'It's not stopping. Look over there on the other side of the river– another castle for you!'

'That's not a castle. Nobody can live there. There's no roof.'

The ruins of Kirkham Abbey were all that remained of the original structure built in the eleven hundreds. Managed by English Heritage it was a favourite spot for riverside picnics.

'Papa, can we come back here one day with AlfieBoy?'

Peter didn't know what to say. The whole question of whether they would come back again had still not been discussed. Already she wanted to come back again – next time with a dog she still hadn't even seen in real life yet. He glanced at Stephanie who just looked at him, smiled and said nothing.

Disembarking at Scarborough thirty minutes later they joined the short queue for a Station Taxi. Millie had offered to collect them in the family estate but Peter had declined. She might be busier than she thought. He was right there.

'Where to pal? Which hotel?'

"The Koala please, on the North side.'

'Where, mate? The Koala? Never heard of it.'

'It's the old Clifftop Hotel on the ..'

'Got it! Sorry, I can't get used to the new name. I saw the story in the Scarborough News. The new owners have erected massive neon-lit koalas on it. How the heck they got planning permission for them God only knows. It's the same old story – it's who you know not what you know!'

Peter was tempted to tell him that the Head of Planning had formally switched the lights on but decided to keep that up his sleeve. The driver took the shortest route and was quick to deliver his passengers and return to the station as a train was due in from Hull in ten minutes' time. Easter was always busy in Scarbados.

Millie, Jamie, Lucy, Sebbie and little AlfieBoy were in the hotel's car park to greet them. They all started to wave as soon as the white diesel Mercedes turned off the road and slowed to a halt within a few feet of the hotel's rear entrance. Millie and Jamie were very apprehensive. How were they supposed to greet the woman who had been their father's mistress for years on the other side of the North Sea? There was no protocol for this. In the event Lucy solved the dilemma by hugging her little half-sister almost to death as soon as she got out of the taxi.

'Hello Natalie. And this is AlfieBoy. Here, give him a treat.'

'She emptied not just one but two doggie treats from a packet and put them in the palm of Natalie's hand.'

The grateful AlfieBoy accepted both with one swirl of his tongue. He had no idea who this new little lady was but one thing was sure. They were now friends for life. Millie and Jamie had had a little chat prior to their arrival and had agreed to maintain a little formality. After all, Stephanie had been their father's "knock off" for over a decade. Jamie went forward first.

'Welcome to Scarborough, Stephanie. I hope you enjoy your stay with us.' He shook hands rather stiffly. Then it was Millie's turn.

'Yes indeed. Welcome to our home and Scarborough and …'

'Don't you mean Scarbados? Your father has briefed me well.'

They all laughed. There was no more ice to break. Natalie rushed at Jamie and Millie in a little group hug. Until now she had been a lone and lonely child who of necessity had spent a long time with her grandmother. And now, suddenly, she had three siblings. For her it was like Christmas Day.

'Oh yes and this is Sebbie – AlfieBoy's father.'

Natalie gave Sebbie two treats as well. She wanted to be best friends with both of them. Jamie assumed the role of hotel porter and took the new arrivals' cases to the lift in the lobby. As soon as they were in the lift heading for the top floor, Millie gestured to her father.

'Dad, a quick word on our own please. Let's pop into the dining room with a coffee OK?'

Peter could see immediately that work had been done on transforming the smaller, second dining room into the Four Seasons Restaurant. The work wasn't complete but it was well on the way and the "Spring" theme was already on display. Somebody, or some people, had been busy. On the walls were paintings and prints of rural Yorkshire depicting flocks of sheep, lambs and drystone walls. Daffodils, the overriding symbol of Spring, were everywhere in little posies. Much of the artwork had been bought at a local "Affordable Art" auction and none of the acquisitions had cost more than fifty pounds. There were prints of orchards showing profusions of pink blossoms, not just in Yorkshire, but across the whole country. It was meant to attract visitors and diners from whichever part of the country they came from.

OK, Dad, while the girls are upstairs and out of earshot, I'll tell you that I've allocated two adjacent rooms on the top floor for Stephanie and Natalie. I didn't think they would like to be too far apart. After all, Natalie is only ten. It just so happens that Stephanie has Pamela's old room by the way. And don't worry I went through it like a spy de-bugging it for security reasons. There won't be any earrings or lingerie anywhere trust me.'

'Millie, for goodness sake …'

'Dad, on the subject of Pamela, she has now moved into an apartment in Sandpiper Heights as she promised she would. She wanted to leave the coast totally clear for you. Perhaps it was guilt, who knows, but she's not all bad you know.'

Peter swallowed hard. Recent memories of his months long dalliance with Pamela were still raw but now he had to look to the future.

'So, what else has been happening while I've been away? Jamie's new restaurant project looks to be well under way doesn't it? Any idea when his Chef's Diploma will be completed? It can't be long now, can it surely? And will he pass?'

'Don't worry on that score, Dad. I had coffee with Samantha Lyon, his tutor, last week. He's on target for a top grade. The course finishes in about five weeks. The blank space on the wall over there is where he intends to hang his framed Certificate, by the way. A nice touch I thought. Samantha also thought that a formal presentation on the launch night for the Four Seasons might also be a nice touch. What d'ya reckon?'

'That sounds great, love. Any other news?'

'Yes, the Home Office's Solicitors were on the phone, as were the Auctioneers who handled the sale. There's the little matter of the buyers' premium to settle apparently – ten per cent of the hammer price – forty-two thousand five hundred quid.'

'What? You're joking. I'll call Clive as soon as ...'

'I already have done. He said he'd speak with Arthur Price and get in knocked down to five per cent. They're old school chums apparently. It's still the old story – it's who you know not what you know.'

'Even so, twenty-two grand for less than two minutes work with a gavel is absolutely staggering when you think about it, isn't it?'

'Dad, be realistic, you've got what you wanted. The Hotel Scarbados is now yours. It will take at least a few weeks, if not months, for completion. You know what lawyers are like, not to mention the Land Registry. At least the buggers are back at their desks now and not working from home. And by the way, when do you plan on moving back there? And are you planning on taking just Lucy and the dogs or will two others be joining you? You know where I'm coming from.'

'Millie, it's a bit early for that decision yet. Stephanie and I are only just beginning to rekindle our relationship.'

'Mmm, well be careful, that's all I'm saying.'

'Did anything interesting come in the post while I was away?'

'Quite a few things actually. I saved this until last.'

A glossy exotic postcard was handed over postmarked Dubai with a cruise liner in the foreground amid a backdrop of palm trees. It was from his ex-wife Mandy.

'Gorgeous here. How are you all managing without me? Mam xx

4.

Mandy's postcard from Dubai, or more accurately the words she wrote on it, coursed through Peter's mind for hours. What on Earth did she mean *'How are you all managing without me?'* What a brass neck she had. She had effectively abandoned her family and gone home to Hull and Bingo with as many cruises to warmer foreign climes as possible. No doubt she was living the high life on the high seas together with her sister Gwen. She had fallen on her financial feet with almost no input from herself. Oh well, no matter. His own immediate future was more important to him. Millie was right. He had to be careful. Stephanie and his, or rather their, daughter were only here in Scarborough for a week. That was the understood arrangement and the seven days would fly by quickly. Don't holidays always do that? The girls were still upstairs changing and settling in when Jamie came into the room.

'Hi Jamie, oh there you are. What scrumptious nosh are you cooking up for us all tonight?'

'I'm not! Didn't Millie tell you? In case your trains were delayed we've booked a table for seven people at the Lucky Dragon at seven o'clock. We can walk, I thought, and the new girls can get a bit of a sea view on the way. Yes?'

'I suppose so, yes. Seven? There's only six of us surely?'

'No seven, I've invited Chloe to join us. She can meet your, er, friend Stephanie and my new half-sister at the same time. Can't she?'

'Well yes, of course. You don't seem terribly chuffed to me.'

'Look, Dad, let's face it this isn't easy is it? I've had to explain to Chloe that, out of the blue, I have a new sibling as a result of my father's extra-curricular social activities that none of us knew about ten years ago. Can you see where I'm coming from?'

'You're right, Jamie, I'm sorry. I've taken a few things, and people, for granted. Let's just go out and have a nice meal. Chloe is easy company and talks happily with just about everyone doesn't she?'

'Yes, she'll be a sort of a catalyst, her word not mine. But don't eat too much. We're all invited to the Ritson's for Sunday lunch tomorrow and you know how hospitable they are.'

'What? Nobody told me?'

'Dad, I heard Millie tell you days ago. You've had your head up your backside ever since you heard about Stephanie and Natalie. The trip to London seems to have propelled you into a world of make-believe. You need to get a grip. You have major decisions ahead. Get it right. Anyway, let's have a "boys only" beer before we go out shall we? I'll get a couple of tins of your favourite Wold Gold beer out of the fridge. You get the glasses.'

Not for the first time Peter reflected on what fabulous kids he had. His son, not yet twenty-one was giving him advice and not the other way round. Obviously Jamie and his sister Millie and been talking.

'Right then, is everybody just about ready? There's a cool wind off the sea. Mam always said that Easters were cold and that's why the tradition of Easter bonnets came about. Of course it might just be an old wive's tale. You know what she was like.'

They set off on foot with the younger girls, Lucy and Natalie, about twenty yards ahead. Natalie wanted to know why AlfieBoy wasn't coming with them. Perhaps the rules regarding dogs in Belgium were slightly more liberal? Both Sebbie and AlfieBoy were curled up back in their baskets hard asleep. Tomorrow they would be having an outing to the old Hotel Scarbados – they just didn't know it yet. Peter pointed towards the ruins of Scarborough Castle as they walked the several hundred yards on the cliff-tops towards the Lucky Dragon Chinese Restaurant. Lucy was in high spirits.

'Jamie, I hope you told the restaurant in advance that Natalie is a vegetarian too.'

'Nobody told me, Lucy. I'm sure it'll be fine as the chef always looks after you!'

Although Stephanie had taken her daughter to a Chinese Restaurant before, in Ostend near the railway station, this was their first attempt at using chopsticks. It caused great hilarity all round but as soon a Natalie asked 'can we come here again Papa?' it once again raised the vexed question; what if there wasn't going to be another time? It just sowed the seeds of confusion and doubt in Peter's mind even more. Why was life so complicated? His anyway.

Tired after a day's travelling, Peter, Stephanie and Natalie retired to bed as soon as they got back to the Koala around nine-thirty. Millie made a hot chocolate drink for the remaining three of them. It was time they had a quiet talk amongst themselves. Jamie opened the discussion.

'Listen you two, while we're on our own we need to have a serious talk. Agreed?

The girls nodded but Lucy alone seemed uncharacteristically quiet. It was time for her big brother to step in.

'You look miles away Lucy. Are you all right?'

'Yes and no. It's been a shock to find that I have a little sister but I already feel as if we've grown up together. And she just loves AlfieBoy, she really does. Apparently her grandmother used to have a little doggie, a Chihuahua from her description but when she died not so long ago the poor little thing had to be re-homed and she never saw it again. The dog was called Bandito being as the Chihuahua is a Mexican breed. She was almost in tears trying to explain it to me. Stephanie had to step in as interpreter when she stumbled a bit. That's why Natalie feels so at home here with us and our two doggies.'

'The fact that she doesn't have a father figure back in Belgium won't help either' chirped up Millie.

'Here she has her natural father plus an older brother in you, Jamie. Look, in a week's time they'll both be back in their natural home. What happens after that?'

'Is Dad going to ask them to stay longer or what? If he asks them to stay permanently what the heck happens then? It'll take weeks, months even, to sort that out. Natalie is back at school in Bruges soon. Then there's the summer term next which might not be the same as here?'

'Stephanie seems a nice, attractive and warm lady I'll give you that. No wonder Dad fell for her – especially when the ferry had those extra refurbs in Antwerp. What do they say about sailors? Any port in a storm?'

'Well there must have been quite a few storms in the North Sea, that's all I can say.'

Jamie sounded a trifle trite. Millie came to her father's defence.

'That's not very fair, Jamie. You know how moody Mam could be sometimes, menopausal even. In fact maybe that was the cause. Her sister, our Aunty Gwen, wasn't a good influence either – always dragging her out to bingo and spending Mam's money on gin and tonics. Sometimes he hardly got to see her when he was on leave in between voyages. Anyway, that's water under the bridge now. Let's look at the possibilities shall we?'

Lucy looked puzzled and even more taciturn than earlier.

'What do you mean by the possibilities?'

'OK option one. Stephanie and Natalie have a nice holiday here with us and then fly back to Belgium in a week's time. She and Dad just remain good friends and after that it's Christmas cards, birthday cards and occasionally a phone call see how Natalie's doing at school – that sort of stuff.

Option two. Dad suggests that they come over again in the summer holidays for a much longer stay, a month or two even. Dad and you, Lucy, will be firmly settled in back at the Hotel Scarbados by then, please God, because he'll drive us all nuts if he stays here.

Option three. He bites the bullet now, or very soon anyway, and asks Stephanie to sever all ties in Belgium, turn round within a few weeks, and join him and you Lucy …'

'And Sebbie and AlfieBoy. You keep forgetting them. That's not fair!'

'Sorry, Lucy, of course. But you'll be busy with your vet's studies by then won't you? Dad will have to find extra staff just to run the Hotel Scarbados as a B & B guest house, let alone a hotel. It's not as easy as you think, as we've all found out. Now, as it happens, our new girl, Marina, has a couple of friends looking for part-time jobs. They both live near the Open Air Theatre with their parents, so Dad might just be lucky. He's certainly not taking Marina with him, that's for sure. She's a star and I feel almost guilty coercing her here and away from the Crescent Gardens. Anyway, moving on.

Option four. Dad can't make up his mind what to do. If I was a betting man, or even a betting woman, I'd put a fiver on the last option. It seems to me that our Dad, lovely chap though he is, is easily led by the fairer sex. So, dear brother and sister, this is my plan.'

5.

'Dad, is it OK for me and Natalie to walk with the doggies down to the Ritson's for lunch. The weather's fair and the barometer in the Hall says it'll stay like that.'

'No, Lucy, it's almost a mile away and little AlfieBoy is still only a little puppy. We'll take him in the car with us but sure, you and Natalie can walk with Sebbie can't you?'

'Yes, OK, thanks Dad. We'll do that and we'll set off in good time so we arrive at the Ritson's at roughly the same time. We could feed the ducks in the Park on the way. I'll ask Jamie if there's some spare bread in the kitchen.'

'Actually, Lucy, I did read somewhere that bread isn't the best food to give them and …'

'I'll ask Mr Wilson at work. He'll know.'

'Well I can't imagine he gets many ducks brought into the surgery but sure, ask him anyway. It's a good idea to show Natalie a bit more of the local scenery too. So we'll see you there. After lunch I'll take a quick look around the Hotel Scarbados and make a list of the essential jobs to do before we move back in – well some of us anyway.'

Unknowingly, Peter had already fallen into the trap set by his offspring. They had decided that the more time Natalie spent with Lucy and the dogs, the more she would want to stay in Scarbados.

Putting on their anoraks and getting Sebbie's lead they set off for Peasholm Park armed with a little plastic bag full of bread crusts left over from breakfast. Crossing over the road and walking downhill past the indoor bowling centre, they soon arrived at the main entrance to the Park. There were lots and lots of people, mostly visitors but none of them seemed to be paying any attention to the wildfowl. It looked like they would have a monopoly of the ducks' affection as soon as they started chucking the crusts into the water. They walked to the edge of the jetty where canoes and pedalos were being prepared for the summer season ahead. Lucy threw the first crusts into the water and within seconds mallards, mandarin ducks, a coot and a moor-hen paddled furiously towards the edible flotsam. Natalie was thrilled.

'Can I do it now please? Oh please.'

'Sure you can. Here, you hang onto Sebbie's lead while I get some more bread out of the bag.'

In the three seconds it took to hand over the lead a large swan appeared and swam towards them. It's target was obviously the bag of crusts. It scared the heck out of the protective Sebbie who tugged the lead from Natalie's little hands and launched himself at the swan. In less than a second he was airborne and heading for the long neck of his imminent adversary. Fortunately he missed but landed two yards away in the murky green water. Naughty Sebbie!

Lucy regained her composure and stood on the end of the lead which fortunately was still on dry land. The swan skedaddled off at a rate of knots from whence it came and a soggy Sebbie scrambled back onto the jetty. The girls couldn't stop laughing.

'Gosh, I don't know what Dad's going to say. He'll be mad at me, for sure. If we hurry up we can get there before the others do. Mr Ritson will dry off Sebbie before Dad gets to notice with a bit of luck. Quick, let's get some photos on our mobiles before he's dried off. It's a little secret between us OK? We can look at the photos in the years ahead. We'll never forget today will we? Come on let's set off. The other Park exit is over there and then it's only a few hundred yards to the Ritson's place.'

'Lucy, is a yard the same as a metre? I get confused.'

'Well, er, I think a metre is a bit longer than a yard. And there are one thousand seven hundred and sixty yards in a mile.'

'That's a silly number isn't it? How did that happen?'

'I've no idea. Ask Dad, he'll tell you. Mind you he always talks in nautical miles which are longer than ordinary miles and …'

'You English people have crazy things.'

'Yes we do Sis, that's for sure. But if you go to school here, they'll teach you all that as soon as you know it.'

That was the first time that Lucy had called Natalie 'Sis' but it was quite deliberate and all part of Millie's plan. They quickened their step and took turns holding Sebbie's lead. That was all part of the plan too. Ten minutes later and they were knocking at the Ritson's front door. Fortunately the rest of the gang hadn't arrived yet. Shirley was first there.

'Oh my God, Lucy! What have you done to poor Sebbie? And this must be Natalie, your new little sister. Hello Natalie. Come in all of you.'

'Thanks Mrs Ritson. Yes, Sebbie had an altercation with a swan in the Park.'

'An altercation? What do you mean an altercation?'

'Well this swan tried to steal our bag of bread crusts and Sebbie … well he sort of decided to stop him and dived towards him, missed and landed in the water.'

'Well, I've heard that swans can be quite vicious and geese even more so. Especially those Canadian ones that were imported here. Lucy was about to correct her – they were known as Canada geese and hadn't been anywhere near the other side of the Atlantic – when Garry's voice cried out.

'I heard all that. Lucy, take Sebbie round the back straight away. I've got loads of doggie towels there. We'll dry him off before your Dad gets here. He won't be best pleased, I can tell you that.'

Lucy took Sebbie, still on his lead and looking very sorry for himself, down the short drive that separated the Ritson's house from their old haunt of Hotel Scarbados next door. Natalie followed a yard, or even a metre, behind.

'Natalie, look over to your left. That's where we used to live when we first moved here from Hull. And that's where we're moving back to soon. Well, not all of us maybe but me, Dad, Sebbie and AlfieBoy are.'

'Can I come with you too – please Sis, please.'

Lucy honestly didn't know what to say. Her immediate priority was the soggy Sebbie with what looked like a quantity of mossy green water discolouring his normally light brown fur. Garry met them at the back door with a bucket of soapy water and a selection of sponges and small towels.

'Goodness me, Lucy, your Dad will go bananas if he sees Sebbie looking like this. Crikey I can hear his car arriving and of course he's parking in the Hotel Scarbados's drive. It'll seem strange driving in there after a year or so won't it? Tell you what, why don't you take Natalie next door with you and show her where Sebbie's favourite tree is, or rather used to be. It'll give me another few minutes to get him spruced up and with a bit of luck your Dad won't notice anything untoward'

'Thanks, Mr Ritson, you're a star. Come on Natalie, follow me!'

Two minutes later and Lucy was showing her little sister the memorial stone that she had placed in honour of Duchy, the Aussie labrador, that the first owners had brought all the way from Melbourne, Australia. The grass had almost overgrown it and she made a mental note to clean it up as soon as they moved in. Her father, Peter, was in a similar frame of mind.

'I must say the garden looks a mess. It looks more of a meadow than a lawn. You'd have thought that the Home Office would have got a gardening contractor in wouldn't you? Now that contracts have been exchanged I suppose it's my responsibility.'

'Dad, if it's fine weather tomorrow why don't we all come down here for the day? We can mow the lawns and do some weeding at the same time.'

Five hundred yards away the miniature steam locomotive "Robin Hood" was just about to leave the Open Air Theatre for the fifteen minute trip to Scalby Mills and the shrill of its whistle gave Lucy an idea.

'Yeah, Dad, and I can take Natalie and both dogs on the train too. Please? OK?'

'Sure, I don't see why not. But where is Sebbie anyway?'

'Er, he's with Mr Ritson, probably getting an early lunch. You know how hungry he gets after a long walk.'

Peter's eyes suddenly had that glazed-over look in them. Sebbie didn't normally have his tea until around five-ish. Oh well. His thoughts were interrupted by the shriller voice of Shirley Ritson.

'Lunch is almost ready, you lot. Who'd like a sherry first?'

'And who'd like to carve? It's a small turkey. Seems to be quite the fashion at Easter these days – like a little Christmas. Don't worry, you young ladies, I've done a nut roast for you veggies. The lunch was superb, as always with Shirley's homely cooking. Trifle and coffee followed and then Garry disappeared for a minute but returned holding two small packages carefully wrapped in cellophane to show off the contents. They were two bundles of fine straw designed to resemble bird's nests and in the middle of each were a dozen small eggs, all painted to look real but that were in fact made of chocolate.

'These are a little gift, one each, for our two friends from Belgium. We can make chocolate here in England too, you know. Here you are Stephanie and here you are Natalie.'

Stephanie didn't quite know what to say in response to such acts of kindness. Here she was, replacing a lady who was Peter's first wife, being made welcome in the home of total strangers. Then she suddenly mentally corrected herself. First wife? Had she already adjusted herself to think that she might be his second wife? How presumptive was that? She decided to say a few words – all in English of course. For Natalie's benefit she threw in a few bits of Flemish as well.

'Thank you Garry and Shirley for a lovely lunch. Turkey is one of my favourites but we don't have it so much back home, er in Belgium. Do we Natalie? Next time it will be my pleasure to cook for you – I hope so. Natalie is already planning our next visit in the summer and ...'

She was interrupted by the dining room door being pushed open by the cold nose of a still damp labradoodle. It was Sebbie, closely followed by his son and heir AlfieBoy. Peter had the last word as they drained the last of the coffees.

'And Lucy, I'll just remind you that Sebbie is one hundred percent labradoodle. He is not a Portugese Water Dog. I'm not even going to try and guess what happened. Just take greater care next time you and Natalie are in the Park, that's all I can say.'

Stephanie did a bit more translating and Natalie beamed like a searchlight. So there was going to be a next time then!

Back at the Koala later that evening, Peter and Stephanie had a quiet few words together over a pre-bedtime hot chocolate.

'Stephanie, you and I need to talk, really talk. Do you agree? We simply can't let two young girls, not to mention two dogs, decide our futures. Can we?'

'You're right, Peter. What do you suggest?'

'OK look, I know a quiet little bistro in the Old Town. Most of the Easter visitors will be heading home tomorrow so how about I call them and book a table for tomorrow night? Just the two of us. What do you think?'

'Peter, that sounds like a lovely idea. But we have to agree to be honest with each other. Yes?'

'Agreed, I'll call them now.'

He kissed her on both cheeks, Continental style. Except that they were in Scarbados not Flanders.

6.

Just as Lucy had suggested, the next day was spent mostly in the back garden of the Hotel Scarbados. Peter tried calling the solicitors to ascertain a date for the completion of the purchase. He was out of luck – not even an answer-phone. Then he remembered that most solicitors, for reasons known only to themselves, always took the extra day off. He would have to wait.

Lawns were mowed and shrubs trimmed back, so woeful had the neglect been since the purchase by the two suspected money launderers who were still on Interpol's wanted list. The trail had gone cold and eventually the Home Office gave up and put the Hotel on the market.

Lucy and Natalie both helped with scooping up the mown grass and putting the excess shrubbery in the brown bins for gardening recycling. Natalie just loved it. She and her mother lived in a modest rented apartment in Bruges and had never enjoyed a garden of their own.

'Oh Lucy, I do hope we come back again soon. Will you have moved back here by the summer holidays? We finish school in mid-June for ten weeks. School doesn't re-start until the first week in September?'

Her mother, who was trimming a lawn edge only twenty yards away, indicated for her to "shush" in no uncertain manner. She reprimanded her in Flemish. Was she hiding something from the rest of them? Only time would tell. The sound of the "Scalby Mills Express" a few hundred yards away reminded Lucy of the other reason for coming here today.

'Dad, can me and Natalie go to the train now please? We've worked quite hard.'

Yes OK but make sure you're not too late. And before you ask the answer is no – you're not taking the dogs with you. In any case where the heck are they?'

'They're both asleep under Sebbie's eucalyptus tree look!'

'Right, off you go then. Straight there and back – no messing. And look after your little sister. Have you got some money for the train fares? I've no idea how much it'll be, do you?'

'No idea, Dad. Don't worry, I'll pay using my new iPhone.'

'You what?! Since when did you …'

'Millie fixed it for me. It's all on the Hotel Koala's new group contract apparently. Jamie's got one as well, he told me.'

Peter just shrugged his shoulders – kids these days. In his days he would have had to scrat around for a few shillings and, if he was lucky, a half-crown. Millie could have offered her father a new phone as part of the deal, surely? Then he remembered that he wasn't a shareholder any more. Soon he wouldn't even live there. The magnitude of the changes to come were only just dawning on him.

'Fancy a brew, Stephanie. I've got quite a thirst on now, have you? Then he realised that all the keys were either with the estate agents or the auctioneer. Only the tool shed with all the mowers and gardening implements was unlocked. Damn!'

I overheard you, Peter!

It was Shirley on the other side of the fence.

'Pop round here in five minutes and I'll have some tea and fresh fruit cake ready.'

'Peter, you are so lucky that you will have such nice neighbours when you move back here. When Lucy starts work full-time at the vet's you'll be thankful you have nice people to talk with – that is when you're not busy doing breakfasts and changing bedding in the guest rooms and …'

Peter didn't hear the rest. Was she playing mind-games with him already? She had a point though. In fact several points.

'The cake was my Mother's recipe, Stephanie. Its real name is a Simnel cake and it's traditionally made for Easter here in Yorkshire isn't it Peter? I said isn't it Peter!'

But Peter was miles away. He was envisioning trying to answer the hotel phone, washing up a ton of breakfast pots and taking two dogs out for "walkies." He was snapped out of his daydream.

'More cake, Peter?'

'Er, yes please. Thanks, Shirley.'

'And where did you say that you two were going tonight?'

'It's called Café Neptune and, as the name suggests, it specialises in seafood. It's fairly new I understand – got some good reviews on Trip Advisor though, I hear.'

'I don't suppose you get much seafood in Bruges do you, Stephanie. Isn't it all beef stew and horse meat burgers with chips? I'm only joking really. Me and Garry did a trip there a few years back, you know, before Covid. The mussels were beautiful, just beautiful. What time are you dining tonight? I hope you booked as the town is still surprisingly busy even if Easter has been and gone'

'The table is booked for seven o'clock and the taxi for six-forty five, to be on the safe side. In fact as soon as the girls are back from their train ride we'd best make a move. They should be back by now.'

Twenty minutes later they arrived back, both giggling and singing the "Locomotion" – a song made famous by Kylie Minogue.

'What on earth's got into you two?'

'We got talking to the chap in the ticket office and he told us that Kylie Minogue had done a concert here and the morning after had been on the train to Scalby Mills and made a video of it.'

'A likely tale and …'

'No, Dad, it's right. It's on YouTube, he said. Can we look on our big smart TV when we get home?'

'Yes, OK but right now we need to go back to the Koala. Get the dogs sorted. I hope Sebbie isn't still smelling of duck poo. If he is then you'll have to walk him home. Look sharp now!'

Seemingly, with every hour that went by, young Natalie was learning more and more colloquial English. This 'look sharp' was a new phrase and she mentally added it to 'hey-up' 'now then' and 'get a wiggle on'. She still had four days to go before the flight back to Belgium. How much more would she learn before then? Already she was dreading it.

The dogs went straight to their bowls almost as soon as they arrived back at the Hotel Koala. They were obviously hungry but seemed disappointed by the fare on offer. Perhaps they had been spoilt by the generosity of the chef at the Scalby Manor the previous day. The girls went straight into the lounge to hunt for Kylie on YouTube on the smart TV and almost ignored Millie who seemed busy on the Reception desk.

'Ah, there you are you lot. Hi Dad, hi Stephanie. How did the gardening go?'

'Just fine but I'm going to have to organise a 'Brown Bin' collection from the Council. Did we have brown bins before? I can't remember. I suppose we must have. Much happened here today?'

'Most of the guests just booked in for the Easter break package that we put together, so they've headed for home. Tell you what though, the online booking system seems to be working well already. There's quite a few advance bookings, I'm off duty soon so I hope you can take over, Dad.'

'Er, well no. Stephanie and I are going to that new Café Neptune for a bite to eat and a little tête a tête, if you know what I mean.'

'Oh heck, well hopefully Jamie can deal with anything that crops up. Actually, I'm going out for a couple of drinks with Marina, just to get to know her a bit better. And don't forget, Dad, best bib and tucker and steer clear of the oysters. You know what happened last time – only half of them worked!'

'Cheeky! Anyway, our taxi's coming at six-forty-five so if I don't see you before then you have a nice evening and we'll re-group in the morning.'

'You bet, Dad.'

Before checking off Millie had one more glance at the booking system. Six more reservations had been made in the last hour. None of the names were familiar to her. All the bookings coincided with the forthcoming formal opening of the Four Seasons Restaurant in a month's time. It had been well advertised on the website – yet another brilliant idea of Katya's. Not one of the new names were from folks who had stayed for Easter. There was a Mrs A. Armitage but no matching Mr Shanks. Another name that stood out was a Mr S. Fan. What a strange name. Oh well, time to get ready for her own little soirée with Marina. She was going to be so much fun to work with. Tomorrow they would have to start finalising plans for the Four Seasons Restaurant. Pamela

Hesketh had already hinted that she wanted to become involved as she had a few important visitors to invite. She seemed to have settled in very quickly at Sandpiper Heights and Millie was invited to go for coffee, now that the Easter rush at the Hotel Koala was over.

7.

The Nippy taxi was prompt and they arrived at Café Neptune just before the appointed booking time of seven o'clock. A middle-aged couple were just leaving and it was their table that was now vacant. They got more than a bit of a surprise. The departing couple were none other than Chloe's parents.

'Hey up, Fred. Ow are ya? And this lovely lady is...?"

'Er, Stephanie, I'd like you to meet Fred and Sarah – Jamie's girlfriend's parents.'

There were smiles and hands were shaken. Everyone was at ease. Peter spoke again.

'So, Fred, can you recommend this place? We've never been – it's our first time.'

'It's reet grand. You'll never guess who supplies a lot of the seafood.'

'I don't think I'll need three guesses, Fred!

Stephanie, Fred is a shellfish supplier and distributor. Needless to say Jamie will be using his services for the Four Seasons Restaurant – when it opens that is.'

'Have you got a date fixed yet then? We'll want to come to the opening, won't we, Sarah?'

'Of course we will. I can't wait! We thought we'd try this little spot as it's only a short walk from Quay Street. We just had a main course and a coffee, you know, to test it out.'

'And your verdict? What did you both have to eat anyway?'

'I had a Dover sole and Sarah had baked rolled plaice with a shrimp and fennel sauce. Both excellent. A bit pricey but you get what you pay for. That might be a mantra that Jamie could adopt but who am I to advise him? Any road, we'd best be off. Enjoy your supper and hopefully we'll see you again, Stephanie.'

'I hope so Fred, that is if Peter invites us back. My daughter, er our daughter, and I live in Belgium. We're just here for a few more days then a flight back to Brussels and …'

'Pull your socks up, Pete. A lovely lady like this. Of course he's going to invite you back. See you both soon.'

Back out in the fresh air Sarah was quick to reprimand Fred.

'You twit. That's Pete's ex-mistress from Bruges. Jamie did tell us she was coming over. Don't you remember? And she said *our* daughter because Pete is the father. Doh! You're getting older and dafter by the day, Fred Cammish.'

'Yes all right, all right. She's a smart lady though isn't she? A good fifteen years younger than Pete I reckon. Did you see some of those old family snaps that Jamie showed us? Mrs F looked a bit dowdy by comparison if you ask me. No wonder he was tempted when he was on foreign soil. Come on, let's pop into the Newcastle Packet for a snifter shall we?'

Back in the Café Neptune it was all smiles as Peter and Stephanie took their seats in a quiet corner. That was just fortunate as, not knowing the layout on their first visit, they had not booked a specific table. A smartly dressed waitress soon descended on them.

'Good evening, some menus for you. The specials are on the board over there. Now, can I get you some drinks?'

It was like a first date and immediately brought back memories of their very first evening together in Ostend. After a nice supper in a local bistro they spent the night together in the Burlington Hotel and from there it just blossomed. That was over a dozen years ago.

'Pete, this is just lovely but we do have to talk, really talk. Let's emulate Peter Sarstedt shall we?'

'Huh? What are you on about?'

'Surely you remember his famous song – *Tell me the thoughts that surround you, I want to look inside your head...* don't you?'

'Cheeky! I'm not that old! I was only a nipper when that came out.'

'Pete, I'm only pulling your leg. But you know what I mean. Just tell me, please. What is going on in that head of yours? I have to know, not just for me, but for Natalie's sake too. Please.'

Peter swallowed hard on the last of the Wolds Ale in his glass and signalled to the waitress for another one. He was 'on the spot' and didn't he know it. He reckoned he had ten to fifteen minutes before the food arrived – a Dover sole for himself and Whitby scampi for Stephanie.

'OK here goes, cards on the table. When I first met you at the Brasserie in Bruges, I just couldn't take my eyes off you. You were absolutely charming, spoke perfect English, and made me feel so good. You were really interested in my life on the ferries that sailed between Hull and Zeebrugge. I was flattered, really flattered. You were so different to my wife, Mandy, in every respect. You two could not have been more different – not better or worse, just different.'

'I think I can understand, but when you went home to Hull and the family, how did you feel? Did you feel guilty that you also had a lover on the other side of the North Sea?'

For Peter, this was the sixty-four thousand dollar question.

'Yes, I felt guilty when I slept with Mandy and I felt guilty when I slept with you.'

It was Stephanie's turn to take a long swig, in her case of a New Zealand Sauvignon Blanc. The ten second silence was an eternity to Peter.

'Then, Peter Fishburn, you are an honest man. Your turn.'

'Why didn't you tell me about Natalie? You essentially hid her from from me by sending her to live with your mother in Liege. Why?'

'What options did I have? You had a wife and family back in England. There is no way I could ever have asked you to choose. It was better to keep you in the dark … '

'I understand, at least I think I do. I will be honest and tell you that when I discovered we had a love child, my heart was ripped to shreds. It was a massive shock. I was delighted and devastated at the same time. I was very, very hurt at the time. But everything is different now isn't it? I am divorced and the past is the past. Mandy is history and is spending her money living the high life on the high seas. I guess the divorce was liberating for her too, in a different way.'

'So where do we go now, Pete? It's not just me, or even us. It's Natalie too. I have to tell you that she came into my room last night in her little pink PJs snuggled up under the duvet and balled her eyes out ..'

'What? What did she say?'

'She said she had never been so happy in her life. She is dreading going back to Belgium. It's partly due to losing her grandmother so recently too. They were very close as you might expect as she was an only grandchild. Only you and I can decide her future. We have to decide what to do. And I think we have to decide very soon. Agreed?'

'Yes, I do. It's almost as if she was born here. Her and Lucy are so alike in mannerisms as well as looks. Despite a six year age difference they are almost joined at the hip. They were even singing a duet together yesterday – some Kylie Minogue song apparently.'

'Yes, Millie told me. So how would you feel about you and Natalie moving to Scarborough? I mean permanently? You know that Lucy and I are intend to move back to the Hotel Scarbados, don't you? As soon as all the legal aspects have been tied up. But it's 'when not if' – a couple of months at the most.'

'No Peter, four of you are moving back.'

'No, Jamie and Millie are staying at the Hotel Koala – that's where their future lies.'

'Have you forgotten the dogs? They're the other two! And Natalie has fallen in love with both of them too. So, what are we going to do, Peter? Life is too short. Are we going to make a go of it?'

She laid her hand on top of his and squeezed it, offering up a silent prayer as she did so. What was going through his mind right now?

'Stephanie, we owe it to Natalie. Let's do it.'

He squeezed her hand back. He was just about to rise from his chair and embrace her when they were interrupted by the waitress.

'Sorry, I've forgotten, whose was the Dover sole?'

'That's mine, the scampi is for the lady. Oh yes, and I don't suppose you have a bottle of champagne do you?'

'We certainly do, Sir. Give me two minutes, please.'

Five minutes later and Natalie's iPhone pinged. It was a short message.

'We're coming back to live in Scarbados. Mama xx

8.

The atmosphere over breakfast the next morning was both animated and relaxed. Little Natalie had slept like a log in her own bed. There had been no need to seek solace from her mother, which was just as well. Had Peter chosen oysters instead of the Dover sole, then two of them would have worked. It was like going back in time. Jamie had already left for college and, with just a few short weeks of his Diploma studies to complete, it was important that he sprinted hard for the winning tape. Lucy had already caught the bus to the vet's but before she did, Natalie had already whispered the good news to her. She was 'over the moon' too but, being a little more aware, was mindful of the things that had to be done in the weeks ahead.

'Ask Dad about schools, Sis, don't forget.'

Thus, breakfast was a combination of coffee, cornflakes and twenty questions.

'Papa, where will I go to school?'

'Papa, when are you moving back to the Hotel Scarbados?'

'Papa, where can I learn some more English?'

'Papa, when can I …?'

'Natalie! For goodness sake. Let your father eat his breakfast.'

That first question, relating to school, hit Peter like a rocket. Good God, he hadn't even thought about that one. Over a decade had passed since he'd been concerned with schooling, when Lucy was five year's old. With being at sea himself, he had left most of that sort of stuff to wife Mandy. He didn't have a clue what to say.

'Yes, Natalie, of course we'll be looking for a nice school for you soon. When you and your Mum go back to Belgium I'll start to make enquiries. As for learning more English, well, I'll take advice from the teachers at your new school, whichever one we choose, OK?'

Stephanie nodded in agreement from across the table.

'It's one step at a time, Natalie, one step at a time. We have to pack up properly in Bruges when we get back. There is still a lot of your Grandma's stuff from Liege. Half of it is in Bruges but the rest is still in Liege. And then there's still some of my brother's affairs to sort out and …'

Suddenly she got a bit weepy. Two bereavements so close together had been almost too much to bear. Sensing her distress, Peter moved around the table and put his arm around her waist. Small tears ran down her cheeks and Natalie copied her father, snuggling her face into her mother's neck. All three of them were misty eyed by then. It was proof that, slowly but surely, they were bonding as a family. For the first time in a long time, Stephanie felt truly at peace with the world. Peter seized the initiative.

'Right, you two, I'll wash the breakfast pots up. Why don't you take Sebbie and AlfieBoy out for a little walk, the weather's fine? One dog each. Not too far though – don't forget that AlfieBoy is still only a few months old. Go on, coats on and off you go!'

Ten minutes later and Peter was on the phone to Garry Ritson – the font of all local knowledge.

'Hey-up, Peter, how's tricks? Has Sebbie stopped reeking of duck poo yet?'

Garry could sense that the episode with the swan in Peasholm Park was going to be a source of leg-pulling for a while yet. A shaggy dog story if ever there was one.

'Actually yes, he's fine, but I think that's scared him off swans for a lifetime. Anyway listen, a bit of local knowledge please if you have a minute?'

'Sure, fire away, mate. What is it this time? Don't tell me – you want to buy one of these little four by fours like I've got?'

'Er, well maybe, after we've moved yes. But listen, first of all, let me tell you that Stephanie and Natalie are going to leave Belgium and are coming to live here with …'

'Mate, I'm so pleased for all of you. Really chuffed. Wow! Wait till I tell Shirley.'

'Garry, main reason for the call, is that we need advice on schools. If Natalie was living at the Hotel Scarbados now, which school is in the catchment area? Any idea?'

'Gosh, you've got me there. How old is Natalie again?'

'She's ten, eleven on the …'

It suddenly dawned on Peter that he didn't even know his youngest daughter's date of birth. Garry half-rescued him.

'The thing is, Pete, if she's eleven before the end of August, I think, she'll need to go to a different school altogether. Then you'll have to choose either a State school or a fee-paying one, you know, a public school.'

For a few seconds, Peter froze. Fee-paying? Good grief! It simply hadn't even entered his head that it might cost him money, in fact quite a lot of money.

'You need to take advice, mate, seriously. You've got a few months though, to think about and to properly consider the options.'

'The other thing, Garry, is that Natalie will have to seriously work on her English. For a ten year old Belgian girl who's first language is Flemish, she is wonderful, but in the years ahead …'

'Yes, I see what you mean. Well if you don't want her to cultivate a reet Yorkshire accent then Scarborough College might prove your best option. Pricey though, I'm telling you, but probably worth it in this case.'

'Ow much per term?'

'I've no idea. Look, when the girls have gone back to Belgium, why don't you make an appointment to see the head teacher? There's no immediate rush is there?'

'I guess not. Do you have a name?'

'No way. It's over sixty years since I was there. The Head then was a Mr Denys Crews, but he's long gone now. Nice bloke he was. In fact, he interviewed me when I applied for a Scholarship or a Bursary.'

'A what? What on earth is one of those?'

'It's a sort of grant that is given to a handful of pupils every year, towards the cost of their fees. You'd have to ask for more details.'

'Thanks Garry, once again you've pointed me in the right direction. We're hoping to get a moving date soon, by the way. About a month we think.'

'That sounds positive. Before I forget, the Council have delivered you a new set of bins, including a brown one for garden waste. They came about an hour ago.'

'Wonderful, that's one less thing to worry about. I'll have to come round and scoop all that grass and hedge trimmings into it and …'

'Done it mate. But pop round for a coffee when you have more news on your move OK? You'll need a hand.'

Not for the first time, Peter thought about what wonderful neighbours that Garry and Shirley had proved to be, time and time again. Suddenly, he felt really excited about moving back, this time with a new family, in effect. After finishing his conversation with Garry he put in a call to the Solicitors handling the sale and purchase of the Hotel Scarbados. It was good news. Completion was set for just over three weeks, plenty of time to get properly organised. At least it was going to be a darned sight easier that the original move from Hull to Scarborough in the teeth of a snowstorm and only a few days before Christmas. He wanted it all done and dusted ready for whenever Stephanie and Natalie returned from Belgium. It would be summertime and not freezing cold.

He Googled Scarborough College and came up with the address and contact details. He needed some advice quickly.

'Good morning. My name is Peter Fishburn. May I speak to someone about the possibility of my daughter Natalie enrolling at the College later this year please?'

'Certainly, Mr Fishburn. Natalie, did you say? And her date of birth please.'

'I er, look, perhaps if you could give me the name of the right person to speak to, I could call back later?'

A half an hour later and mother, daughter and two dogs returned. AlfieBoy went straight to his basket for forty winks.

'Stephanie, darling, just jot down Natalie's date of birth please.'

'I've brought a copy of her Birth Certificate with me from Belgium. Give me two minutes and I'll pop up to my room for it.'

A short time later and Peter was perusing it for the only detail he really needed. He didn't have to don his reading glasses or be a qualified linguist to be aware of other details too. Stephanie van Gelder was listed as the mother, occupation Restaurateur. The father was listed as Peter Fishburn, occupation Sea Farer. Stephanie had never hidden the details of Natalie's father to the authorities. Only he had been kept in the dark. He felt immediately grateful. If he ever needed to demonstrate his parenthood then the Certificate would prove invaluable.

Armed with this new information, Peter put in another call to the secretary at Scarborough College.

'Hello again, it's Peter Fishburn. Sorry about that, I had another incoming call to take.' He fibbed.

'Yes, Natalie's birthday is 21st June 2014, so that makes her eleven next. Does that fit in with your admission criteria or is she too young?'

The secretary, a Miss Brown, was most helpful.

'No, that fits in perfectly as she'll be eleven by the start of the next academic year which starts in mid-September. As we speak, I'm just filling in a few details on the initial pro-forma. The more information we have before an initial interview, the better. Now, moving on, place of birth and nationality please, Mr Fishburn.'

'Er, well, the answers are Bruges and Belgian, I suppose.'

'You suppose? Is there some doubt?'

'I, er, well this is a little difficult. Natalie was born in Belgium to a Belgian mother. I'm her father but I am British, born and bred in Hull.'

'I see. Can I take it that Natalie is thus a foreign student, as it were?'

'I don't understand, sorry. Does it matter?'

Peter was starting to get a tad irritated with this line of questioning.

'We do take overseas students, in fact quite a lot of them, but they are mostly from the Far East. Let's start again. Is Natalie a British citizen?'

'Er, no, well not yet. Family circumstances dictated that Natalie had to spend her early years with her mother in Belgium. Look, would it help if I scanned Natalie's Belgian birth certificate and emailed it to you as an attachment?'

'Yes, that would be most helpful, Mr Fishburn. One of my colleagues will then set the ball rolling and hopefully come up with a mutually convenient time for the interview, possibly with Mr Merritt, the Head Teacher.'

'Thank you, but Natalie and her mother are returning to Belgium this coming Saturday and …'

'So she's not even resident in the UK then is she?'

'No, not yet, but she will be soon.'

'I see, at least I think I do. Please email me the birth certificate as soon as you can.'

'I will do and thanks for your help, Miss Brown.'

Three minutes later and the email, plus attachment, arrived in her inbox. She glanced through it perfunctorily and then she smiled and blurted out to a colleague:

'This Fishburn bloke's a bit of a character, I can tell you. His occupation is given as 'Seafarer.' What's the betting this Stephanie van Gelder was his "knock-off" at the other end of the ferry route to Zeebrugge? Anyway, I'll pop this on Merritt's desk with a post-it note and his phone number. Then it's up to him.'

9.

The incoming call from Guy Merritt, the Head Teacher at Scarborough College, caught Peter by surprise. Knowing that Stephanie and her daughter were returning to Belgium on Saturday, he suggested that they and Peter, came to the College for an informal chat, rather than a formal interview. Jamie had given them directions to get there as he travelled past it almost every day on his way to his own catering studies. You can't miss it, Dad, it's on the right on the main road to Brid about a mile south of the town centre.

They arrived ten minutes early before the appointed time of eleven-thirty. Punctuality was the trademark of many a seafarer. They waited in a comfy ante-room with the girls seated on a well-worn Chesterfield. Peter gazed approvingly through the window at sports fields and what looked like a hockey pitch with an artificial surface. Cricket nets looked neat and tidy but not in use. After all, the season hadn't started yet. In fact there were no students to be seen, just a few members of staff, probably admin folks. A heavy wooden door, with the Head's name, rank and letters on a brass plate, creaked open and a fortyish man emerged wearing a smart shirt and tie embossed with the College's motif.

'Good morning everyone, or is it afternoon? Please do come in and take a seat. I'm Guy Merritt, the Head Teacher. He smiled in turn at all of them, with a particularly lingering one for Natalie. He didn't want her to feel uncomfortable, quite the opposite. He deliberately spoke to Natalie first, which surprised her parents.

'Hello Natalie. Welcome to Scarborough College.'

He didn't get any further before he was interrupted – by Natalie! Stephanie was appalled.

'Mr Merritt, you are not from here are you?'

His ghast was flabbered but he felt compelled to give an honest answer.

'Er no, I'm not, but how did you know?'

'Because Canterbury is in Kent, not in Yorkshire. Isn't it?'

'I'm not from Kent. Actually I'm from Somerset. Why did you think I was from Kent?'

'It says so on your door: Mr Guy Merritt, MA Cantab. Canterbury is in Kent isn't it? I saw a sign for it when we came out of the Channel Tunnel.'

'How observant you are, young lady. But I must tell you that it means I went to Cambridge University, although there is an excellent University in Canterbury.' Stephanie intervened.

'She's a little minx, Mr Merritt, doesn't miss a trick I can tell you.'

'Well, I'm impressed. Natalie, your English is already excellent. You are streets ahead of most of the foreign students here, I can tell you. I don't think we've ever had a student from Belgium, not in my time here anyway.'

'Streets? I don't understand.'

'It's just an expression. Now, Natalie, at school which are your favourite subjects, apart from English?'

'I like Geography. I never knew my Grandfather in Belgium but my Grandma told me that he worked in Africa for years as a younger man. So I looked at a lot of old maps that he left in his possession. He was a pilot, wasn't he Mama?'

'Yes, he flew with SABENA the main Belgian airline at the time. Sadly it went bust a few years ago. Natalie, tell Mr Merritt what SABENA stood for, the joke name, not the real one.'

'Such a bad experience never again!'

Everyone laughed out loud, Mr Merritt the loudest. The rest of the so-called interview went like a dream. Peter and Stephanie hardly got a look-in. Merritt's parting words were quite reassuring.

'I'm sure that as soon as you have Natalie's residential status clarified by the Home Office, we can proceed with the necessary entrance formalities with a view to Natalie joining us in September.'

Peter had promised the girls a fish and chip lunch on the seafront before they flew back to Belgium so they took the main road back to town and headed for the car park on the West Pier. How different were his circumstances from the time they had first arrived and had a first peek at the Hotel Scarbados. What a lucky man he was.

They were out of luck with their first choice of venue – "The Lookout" – overlooking the inner harbour. The views of boats and the castle walls were unparalleled in the town.

'We're fully booked this lunchtime, Mr er..'

'Fishburn, Peter Fishburn. And your name is?'

'I'm Tiger. Oh yes, you must be Jamie's Dad, are you? Jamie comes in here quite a lot with his girlfriend, Chloe Cammish. He showed us the feature in the Scarborough News with lots of photos. Can you tell me something? How did you get permission for those huge neon koalas on the front of the hotel?

'Well, I er, got a prominent Councillor to formally perform the "switch-on" and we never heard another thing. Why do you ask?'

'We applied through the normal channels for a giant illuminated lobster to be displayed on the harbour side of the building. Guess what? We were turned down. Any advice?'

'Yes, actually I do. Get in touch with a guy in Teesside called Dave Gibson who runs a firm called 'We are Neon Ltd.' Get him to quote you for a massive illuminated tunny fish.'

'What? Why a tunny fish for goodness sake?'

'Because the tunny fishing lark was an important part of Scarborough's history and the "heritage nutters" will all go along with it. Trust me. Mention my name. He's a really good egg. If the price is reasonable, which it almost certainly will be, then get him to fix it up. Have a special evening, just after dusk, to formally switch it on and ask Councillor Elsie Thompson to perform the honours. She's the Head of Planning. You get my drift...?'

'Great stuff! Have you got his number?'

'Yes it's in the address book in my iPhone. Hang on a minute. I'm not much good with these things.'

'Papa, pass your phone to me. Is it listed under G for Gibson or N for Neon? It's OK I've found it. It's under D for Dave Gibson. You grown-up people are so slow with technology.'

Peter wasn't sure what to say but fate intervened when the telephone behind the counter started to ring. The tall, leggy blonde on duty with Tiger, answered it with a slight antipodean twang.'

'G'day, the Lookout, can I help you? Cancel, did you say? And it was booked for one o'clock? Sorry to hear that. I hope you get well soon. Thanks for calling. Did you hear that, Tiger? That booking for Table number 10 has just cancelled. Are these folks looking for a table? It's available now.'

'You're in luck, folks. Just think, if you hadn't stopped to chat about a new sign for this place then the phone would have rang after you'd gone. Table number 10 is the one over there in the corner. Actually, it affords the best view. Take your seats and Sky will come and take your orders in a couple of minutes.'

'Who? Sky? Is that her real name? And is your name really Tiger?'

'Well it's the only one I've got, so I guess it must be! And yes, she is called Sky. Quite why she came back here after working in the sunshine in Queensland, I'll never know!'

'Peter chose the house speciality, Seafood Chowder, and both girls the smaller portion of haddock and chips with mushy peas. Natalie proved to be her usual inquisitive self when the dishes were brought to the table.

'Sky, why did you leave Australia where it's nice and warm to come back here?'

'Well, you see Natalie, in Australia it's hot and sunny nearly every day. Here, it's different every day. Scarborough doesn't have a climate – it has weather. I love it here. I don't want to live anywhere else. You can't beat Scarborough.'

'Don't you mean Scarbados?'

Lunch was over all too quickly and as they still had a couple of hours left on the pre-paid parking ticket, they decided to show Natalie some of the glitzier amusements. Bingo was top of the list. They just had to have a go. Natalie was absolutely mesmerised.

'Kelly's Eye number one. Five and nine the Brighton Line. Two little ducks twenty-two.'

She screamed with delight when she got a "line" and won a large teddy bear called Yorkie.

'Papa, I'm not taking Yorkie back to Belgium. He's going to stay here in Scarbados. I want you to book him a room at the Hotel Scarbados as soon as you move back. OK?'

What could Peter say? At least Yorkie wouldn't have to be taken for walks.

'Come on you two. Let's go home and put the kettle on. Lucy will be home soon and you can introduce her to Yorkie.

Meanwhile, back at Scarborough College, Guy Merritt had dusted off a large ring binder labelled "Proposed School Trips." He had only given it minimal consideration since his arrival almost a year ago. Inside, split up by those colourful subject dividers, were details of previous school trips. They ranged from a day trip to Hadrian's Wall in Northumberland, to a three day trip to the Eden Project in Cornwall. The last suggested trip caught his eye. It was a four day trip to Belgium. He studied it closely.

PROPOSED FOUR DAY TRIP TO BELGIUM APRIL 2020

Day One: *Coach to Hull. Overnight ferry to Zeebrugge.*

Day Two: *Arrive in Zeebrugge. Coach to Bruges.*
                Check in to Hotel Karos in Bruges.
                Train journey to Ostend. Ride the Kostram to
                see Atlantic defences from 1944.
                Return to Bruges.

Day Three: *Train journey to Ypres to see the Menin Gate*
                memorial. Visit WWI trenches.
                Return to Bruges for dinner.

Day Four: *Morning: Canals tour. Visit to Bruges*
                Cathedral. Afternoon: Return to Zeebrugge to
                re-embark ferry for the overnight passage back
                to Hull.

TRIP CANCELLED DUE TO THE COVID EPIDEMIC.

He re-read it several times then removed the single page from the file. He photocopied it, folded the copy and placed it in his jacket pocket.

10.

The next morning, the day of Stephanie and Natalie's departure, they all made the effort to have a family breakfast together. The atmosphere was happy and optimistic. It being a Saturday, Lucy was not in a hurry to get the usual bus to work at the Vet's and it was not a "college day" for Jamie. They still had an hour to kill before Peter was due to take the girls to the railway station for the more than two hour journey to Manchester Airport. He had decided not to drive them all the way as extensive weekend roadworks on the M62 had been well publicised in advance. Both doggies were very quiet and attentive, standing almost to attention by the sides of Stephanie and Natalie. Last tit-bits of buttered toast were proffered to each of them. The two packed suitcases ready by the back door were perhaps a signal to both canines that changes and departures were afoot. Natalie was perhaps the most animated of all.

'Lucy, you won't forget to take "Yorkie" the bear back to the Hotel Scarbados, will you? He'll be sharing my room of course. Will my room be next to yours? I hope so. And you will WhatsApp me every day won't you? Promise!'

'Of course I will, Natalie. And you'll WhatsApp a selfie as soon as you get on the plane won't you? Don't forget.'

This was to be Natalie's first trip on an aeroplane, all her previous travels having been on coaches or trains. She was thrilled at the prospect. Jamie decided to add his "penn'orth" to the conversation. He was so pleased that his two younger sisters were bonding so well but he wanted to be a "big brother" too.

'And don't forget you have a brother too, Nattie.'

Alone in the family, Jamie had decided already to give Natalie a moniker that only he used. He hoped it would be something special and made him slightly different in her mind. It worked. And Nattie, don't forget as soon as we open the Four Seasons Restaurant full-time I want you to photograph some menus in cafés and bistros in Bruges and send them to me please. I'll need some ideas for "specials menus" and who knows, maybe even a "Belgian Night?"

He winked at Stephanie who had already suggested to him that he might like to consider the idea.

'That's cool, Jamie. Yes, I'll help you, of course I will.'

Peter glanced at the clock on the wall and decided it was time to start weaving.

'Right, you two. It's time to say our farewells and make our way to the station. Ever the organiser, Millie had just checked online that their train was leaving on time.

'Your train's on time and is leaving from Platform No. 3. You'll be back here in Scarbados before you know it. And don't forget to keep in touch with me and Jamie here at the Koala too!'

The farewells were deliberately brief but heartfelt nonetheless. It came as no surprise to anyone that Natalie's last hug was for AlfieBoy. After all, a week ago, hadn't Lucy offered that Natalie could be his mummy too?

The station forecourt was surprisingly clear with just a couple of taxis hovering for a fare. Peter lifted the two cases out of the boot onto the pavement. He hugged and kissed Stephanie first and whispered sweet nothings into her ear. Then he lifted Natalie two feet off the ground until their faces were level. The tears were his, not his daughter's.

'It's OK, Papa. We'll be back soon.'

And then they disappeared onto the platform and the waiting train. Fifteen minutes later and Peter was back at the Koala where his three eldest children were still seated around the breakfast table. They were all uncharacteristically quiet. On the table, in front of Millie, was another glossy postcard of a cruise liner.

'OK Dad, we kept this until Stephanie had gone. It's postmarked Lisbon, Portugal and the postmark is dated five days ago. It came yesterday. I'll read it to you.'

'I hope you're all settled in. See you soon. Mam xxx'

Peter, went white. Millie expanded on her thoughts.

'Assuming she's on, or was on, the liner on the postcard, the Aurora, then it's due to dock in Southampton this afternoon. I went onto the company's website to check.'

'That's all we need, Millie. Do you think she'll just turn up unannounced? And if she does, what's her game? Is she just teasing us, or what?"

Jamie decided it was time he contributed to the conversation.

'I've just had a thought … you don't think she's intending to attend the formal opening of the Four Seasons do you? How on earth would she know anyway? Her and Aunty Gwen have practically been around the world in eighty days since Christmas. Haven't they?'

It was Millie's turn to react again and she reached for her laptop.

'Oh heck, of course, look! Katya has announced the formal opening on the website. Look!'

Scarborough food lovers are eagerly awaiting the formal opening of the newest eatery in town. The Four Seasons Restaurant will open within the newly refurbished Hotel Koala on ….

Don't be disappointed. Book now online to avoid disappointment. And if you're travelling from afar, why not book a room too. Check now for availability.

Millie immediately checked the restaurant bookings against the room bookings. The mysterious Mr S. Fan and several other Oriental names were booked on the same table as Pamela Hesketh.

'Pamela did mention that she was bringing some 'high-powered' guests didn't she? They sound Chinese or maybe Thai to me – not that it matters. I can see that the Ms. A. Armitage, who has pre-booked a room for two nights, has also booked a table for two. That's a bit odd to me. Jamie, I make it there's only a few tables not booked yet. Have you booked in your own personal guests, like Samantha Lyon? And is she bringing a partner or what? You'll have to look sharp! And what about the restaurant and features editor from the Scarborough News? You'll need to get off to a good start with her. And make sure you ask her in advance if she has any special dietary requirements – you know, vegan, coeliac and all that lark. Jamie, are you listening to me or what?'

'Sorry, Sis, I was miles away. I'm just a bit worried that I haven't got my Diploma results yet. The course was officially over two days ago. I'm still waiting. I texted a few of the other guys on the course and they've already been notified if they made the grade or not. And what the heck do we do if I've dipped out? And Chloe will be absolutely furious with me ...'

From her coffee meetings and chats with Samantha Lyon, Millie already knew that Jamie was heading for a Distinction, a special commendation and possibly another award too. But she couldn't show her hand. Not just yet anyway. Jamie made a few additions to his guest list, jumped on his motorbike and headed for the Old Town to meet Chloe. She wasn't back at Uni yet so a walk along the seafront and their now customary hot chocolate at the Flamingo Bay was called for. They grabbed their default seats in the window and watched the world, and the seagulls, go by. Chloe sensed his disquiet. It wasn't like him at all.

'Jamie, look, I think you're worrying unnecessarily about the Diploma result. You've had good grades all the way through, haven't you? And as for your Mum, well she's unlikely to arrive without a booking is she? My thinking is that she's probably playing mind games with your Dad. Just put both issues out of your mind. Let's have another hot chocolate – it's my shout this time.'

He started to relax. The formal opening of the Four Seasons was possibly going to be the biggest event of his life. At least he was going to have Chloe by his side. He didn't know it yet but he was actually going to have two women by his side.

Back at the Hotel Koala, Millie and her father were chatting and trying to look ahead.

'Dad, after the restaurant opening, you are really going to have to knuckle down and see exactly what you have to do down at the Hotel Scarbados. Don't forget, it hasn't been occupied for many months now. It's not just a question of switching the heating on, you know.'

'Yes, I realise that, love. It's just that I've been so overwhelmed by the Stephanie and Natalie situation to think much about anything else. Lucy prodded me again yesterday about the kennels that I promised her she could have. And then of course there's the little matter of Natalie's schooling.'

'Not to mention the residential status of both of them. You'll need to contact the Home Office about permanent residency ...'

'Yes all right, all right. I know you're only trying to help. Let's have a brew shall we?'

A fresh cup of tea, or even several, had always proved beneficial in tricky moments. This was something he shared with Clive White, their Company Secretary and ad-hoc Chairman of Hotel Koala Ltd. He never made any major decisions without a "brew" as he always called it. But these dilemmas were family and personal, not business related.

'Maybe Mam's heading for Hull once she's back on dry land, Dad. Is Aunty Gwen still travelling with her?'

'How would any of us know? I just assume she is.'

'Well the words *see you soon* presumably mean just that. It's about as non-specific as you can get isn't it? I'm keeping an eye on the incoming online bookings just in case. In any event we'll be full soon. The sooner we get the remaining floors up and running the better. Pamela is going to talk to me about that in a few day's time. She called me the other day to confirm the six places at the Four Seasons opening.'

'OK, so we know that the Mr Fan is only one of them. Any ideas about the others?'

'No, none Dad. Oh and before I forget, and I know you won't thank me for it, I've drawn up another "to do" list for you in respect of the Hotel Scarbados. As you said, your mind has been on other things of late.'

Millie went to the hotel's main PC in Reception and clicked the mouse on a few targets. Within two seconds the familiar "clump" of the printer announced the imminent arrival of a single sheet of white paper in the collection tray,'

'Here it is, Dad. It's not too onerous this time but remember, this time the onus to complete it is solely on you.

I know Lucy is a willing horse but she has a lot on her plate now with veterinary studies.'

Pete gave it a cursory glance and groaned inwardly.

Double-check Hotel Scarbados security – alarms, fire extinguishers etc.
Order a main boiler service.
Check insurance cover. Remember, you are liable as soon as you exchange contracts.
Check the status of the website –
www.hotelscarbados.com
Issue a press release to advertise a new "re-opening" date
When Stephanie returns maybe consider a little opening Soirée?
Consider buying another vehicle with surplus funds.
Start thinking about the new kennels facility.

He poured some more tea and donned his reading glasses for a closer perusal. It was item number five that suddenly gave him a flash of inspiration – or more specifically the word 'new.' Mmm. He'd read somewhere that the word 'new' was the most-used in the world of advertising. To advertise that the hotel was under 'new' management was perhaps stretching the point a little but, after all, the introduction of Stephanie's expertise was a factor not to ignore. Then an idea hit him hard. Of course, why not add the word new, in neon, to the lettering on the front of the hotel. Yes! After all, it was only a short, three letter word. He would call up Dave Gibson shortly and mention it to him.

11.

Peter decided to take some air on his own with not even a dog for company. He donned a light anorak, exited the hotel, and walked south along the cliff top towards the castle. The solitude would do him good. It was a pleasant afternoon with just a light easterly wind and thus not much action for the "surfies" in the water who seemed to have claimed Scarbados for their chosen pastime in recent years. It wasn't exactly Waikiki Beach in Honolulu but, there again, Waikiki didn't have the backdrop of a splendid castle ruin. Peter walked slowly, just enjoying the chance to think. Along the way at regular intervals were green metallic seats provided by and maintained by the Council. Many of them bore small memorial plaques and one caught his eye. He read it out loud.

Rest a while and enjoy this wonderful view.
We did, every summer for fifty years.
You can't beat Scarborough for sea views.
In memory of
Dennis & Hilary Rispin & our dog Hetty.

The words really got to Peter and he took Dennis and Hilary's advice. He sat down, totally alone, and mulled over the events of the last two years. He'd lost a wife, gained a lover, lost a lover and been reunited with a former mistress. And now he was a proud father of four children. Where would he be without them now? Nowhere, that's where. He thanked his lucky stars.

Gazing seawards towards the eastern horizon, he spotted a Ro-Ro ferry, probably some ten miles distant, heading south. Its destination was almost certainly Zeebrugge, Belgium and for just a few seconds, which seemed like an eternity, he pondered on whether he would have preferred to have stayed at sea. He was snapped out of his daydream by his phone ringing in his jacket pocket. The caller ID told him it was Dave Gibson from *We Are Neon* in Teesside.

'Hi Peter, how are you? I got your voice mail message. Did I hear it right? You want another flippin' sign? What's going on now?'

'Yep, you heard right, Dave. Me and Lucy and the two dogs are moving back to the Hotel Scarbados soon and ...'

'What? You cannot be serious!'

Dave did his best to emulate the mercurial American tennis player of yesteryear, John McEnroe.

'Yes, in a few week's time. We haven't got a date yet. Actually, there'll be four of us plus the two dogs. I'll explain later when I see you. It's a long story. Anyway, bottom line, I need a new small sign, just one word, to go atop the illuminated Hotel Scarbados that's already in place.'

'Lemee guess, that one word is NEW?'

'Heck, you're right! What made you think that?'

'Pete, lots of places have given themselves a re-brand or a minor makeover since Covid. You'd be amazed. In fact I've pre-made quite a few in anticipation of further orders in a variety of sizes and colours. From memory the main existing sign is in green isn't it? So we want the NEW to stand out, in a different colour and at a jaunty angle. It's got to be eye-catching. Let's give it some thought and I'll get back to you OK?'

'Yeah, that's fine Dave.'

'Oh yes and I nearly forgot – we tried to book online for the opening night of the Four Seasons but according to the website it's fully booked. It can't be can it?'

'Actually, Pete, it probably is but don't worry I'll speak to Jamie when I get home. Just plan on coming. I can't promise accommodation though, but again, leave that one with me. I'll sort something.'

'Cheers, Pete, and start thinking about that colour.'

In the short time he was out the wind had freshened and maybe it was time to head for home and a brew. He took a lingering look at the plaque on the seat. Nice words, nice people.

Marina was on duty on Reception for the afternoon shift.

'Ah, there you are, Mr Fishburn! A Mr Gibson called a short while ago, the lighting man I think he said? I gave him your mobile but he said he already had it and would call you directly.'

'Yes, he did, thank you, Marina. Any other news or messages?'

'Actually, yes, two things. A chap called from the RNLI wanting to book a table for four people for the Four Seasons opening night. He said that "her indoors" had tried to book it online but failed. Hang on, I took his name and number.'

'You said two things.'

'Oh yes, it looks like the suggestion box has received its first input too. I'll read it to you.'

We thoroughly enjoyed our two night stay at the Hotel Koala. Unfortunately we had to leave our family dog back home in Sheffield – a three year old Bedlington terrier called Max. We noticed several outbuildings near the car park which we thought might be suitable

for conversion to overnight kennels. Just a thought.
Thanks again. Julie Arkwright.

'Right, tell you what. Send them a nice reply by email if you can. Thank them for their suggestion and tell them that our plans for kennels will hopefully be completed soon. And don't mention any of this to Lucy, or I'll never hear the end of it.'

'I'll do that but I didn't know you had plans for kennels here and …'

'We don't, not here any way. I need to speak to Jamie. Any idea where he is?'

'I think he's gone to meet Chloe. Is she his girlfriend?'

'I suppose she is. He's worried about his Diploma result so he's probably looking for a sympathetic ear. I wonder where they've gone. Any idea?'

'Yes, into town, I think.'

'Town? That's unusual. They usually meet at that Pelican place on the seafront.'

'I think you mean Flamingo …'

'Whatever, it's a bird anyway. I'll call him on his mobile.'

There was no answer, only the voicemail message.

'Oh sorry, actually there were two suggestions in the box. It wasn't signed so I took a mental note of it and chucked it in the waste paper bin. The suggestion was that we should offer a few complimentary newspapers for guests to read. That is actually a very helpful idea, I think.'

'Really, why? It's only more waste to chuck out, surely.'

'I don't agree. I've got a copy of this week's Scarborough News in my bag to read later. Hang on a mo. Look, here's a story about which star acts are coming to the OAT – the Open Air Theatre – this summer. So just imagine a guest might glance at it over his or her breakfast, see that one of their favourite bands is performing here later in the year, and book a room and a ticket at the same time. On a sad note, there's another story here reporting that the Brunswick Centre is closing imminently to make way for the development of a multi-screen cinema.'

'Sad? Why is that sad? That's going to be a major boost to the town centre isn't it?'

'Yes sure, in the long term. But meanwhile the existing shops are having to close, one by one. That nice coffee shop is closing next week and the News Kiosk won't be far behind. Such a shame.'

A mile away, as the herring gull flies, Chloe and Jamie were sat drinking their last Cappuccino and Mocha from Esquires coffee shop.

'We had our fist little date here didn't we Chloe? It was during your lunch break from the Perfume Shop. Remember?

''Of course I do. It was a holiday job and you came in to buy some "Odour Toilet" for your father's lady friend.'

'And now she's out of the frame and been replaced by a Belgian lady who has presented Dad with a ten year old daughter and me with a half-sister. What a crazy, crazy world eh?'

Yes, it might be, but its fate Jamie, just fate. Just like you and me. Come on, let's have another one for the road and say cheerio to the lovely staff. They'll be redundant very soon. Just awful.

12.

Jamie got back to the Hotel to find his father sat down at a table with his "to do" list, a pen, a calculator and the inevitable mug of tea.

'Ah, there you are, Jamie. Grab some tea, there's plenty in the pot, and come and join me. Got a couple of things to update you with.'

'Gosh, Dad, you look terribly organised. OK give me two minutes and I'll get some tea too.'

Peter ticked off one item on his "to-do" list – the "new" added neon sign for the Hotel Scarbados and waited for Jamie's return from the kitchen.

'OK, fire away, Dad. What's on your mind?'

'Jamie, I know its not really any of my concern any more, but the opening night of the Four Seasons is worrying me. How on earth are you going to fit in all the folks that want to come? Dave Gibson and his wife are hoping to come and I didn't see their names on the list. I'm also told that two guys from the Scarborough Lifeboat and their wives, also tried to book online and failed and …'

'Dad, I'm sorting it. My head's been up my bum for days now. It's those Diploma results, or lack of them.'

Less than twenty feet away and just within earshot, Millie had just relieved Marina on Reception duty. She didn't like to see her "little brother" suffer any more. She texted Samantha Lyon within seconds.

'Sam, Jamie is having kittens – not got his Diploma results yet. What's the problem? Millie.'

The reply came within thirty seconds.

'Sorry, a problem at the printers. Special font and inks needed. I'll call him now. Sam.'

A minute later and Jamie's iPhone buzzed in his pocket. The caller ID told him it was Samantha Lyon. Instantly his heart jumped into his mouth.

'Hello, Sam. This is an unexpected pleasure. Is there something I've forgotten?'

'Jamie, are you on your own and sitting down?' Jamie froze.

'Er, yes and no – er, I mean no and yes. I'm sitting drinking tea with my Dad and going through a few things concerning next Saturday night and …'

'Jamie, just relax and switch your phone to speaker mode please.'

'If it's bad news I'd rather be on my own and …'

'Just do it please. Done it?'

'Hi Mr Fishburn, can you hear me?'

'Loud and clear. What's up?'

'Nothing's up as you say. Jamie, I am delighted to tell you that you have passed your Chef's Diploma with Distinction. Congratulations. I'll just let that sink in.'

'Oh wow. I don't know what to say Samantha. Thank you, thank you, thank you!'

'You have a very talented son, Mr Fishburn. You must be very proud of him.'

'Of course I am. And so will his mother be too when she eventually gets the news. She's at sea somewhere.'

'She will too, I'm sure. If you remember, I was there at the Hotel Scarbados when she presented him with that set of French chef's knives and wished him luck in his chosen career.'

'Oh yes, of course, it seems a long time ago.'

'I'll explain later why your Certificate is later than anyone else's. Now, are you still sitting down? I hope so because I have another piece of news. You have been awarded, by a totally neutral panel, the Duncan Lyon Trophy for the most promising Chef of the Year at the College.'

'What? I've never heard of it?'

'No, you won't have. Since the year 1993 it was presented at an annual dinner every year, in fact right up until Covid. It is only being resurrected this year. Well, say something!'

'I honestly don't know what to say. Er thank you, again. Duncan who?'

Lyon, Duncan Lyon. He was Head of this Department for many years up until he passed away suddenly in 1992.'

'Is there any connection, with the names I mean? Did you know him?'

There were several seconds of silence and the faintest emotional intake of breath that was audible to both Jamie and Peter.

'Yes, on both counts. He was my loving father.'

No sooner had the conversation ended than Millie stepped into the dining room and gave her brother a massive bear hug. She had known for several days about the results and the trophy but had kept shtum.

'Now, your mind is clear you can concentrate a hundred percent on next Saturday night. Listen we've had more enquiries and provisional bookings than anyone would believe. Too many! So we took the liberty, after a while, of asking if they wanted the first or second sitting …'

'What? Two sittings?'

'Jamie, I'm sorry to have done this without your say-so but well, to be honest, you've been a pain in the neck for weeks now and incapable of thinking straight. We've split bookings into early, at seven o'clock and late, at nine o'clock. There are forty places per sitting.'

'We'll never cope, we'll never cope. Just with staffing alone we'll be .'

'We will cope, Jamie, we will. Marina has recruited a couple of extras to help on the night. It'll be tight but ..'

Suddenly Jamie had a flash all of his own. He Googled Esquires Coffee Shop, found the website with the phone number and pressed the speed-dial button. Within ten seconds he was speaking to John the "team leader."

'Hi John, it's me, Jamie Fishburn.'

'Oh hi, Chloe's boyfriend? Yeah, how can I help? You need some temporary staff for your new restaurant, you say? Hang on, let me speak to the girls.'

Within two minutes, John, Lydia, Gemma and Sarah had been recruited. Perhaps it was a new start for them too.

'Jamie, just tell me how you managed to do that?'

'Dad, how many times have you told me in the past? It's who you know not what you know.'

Perhaps Jamie was a chip off the old block after all.

Within a couple of hours Jamie morphed into Master Chef mode. He double-checked the menus for the Saturday evening. Taking Samantha Lyon's advice to keep it as simple as possible, diners would have a choice from just three starters, three mains and three desserts. There would be something for everybody and vegetarians, vegans and Neanderthals would all be accommodated – just! He needed to double check his sources of supply. Nothing would be more embarrassing than, say, running out of beef if the majority of guests favoured the Aberdeen Angus over the baked cod â la Portugese and the aubergine Wellington. He called the beef supplier, Radfords of Sleights, to guarantee a more than adequate supply of their finest sirloin. Needless to say that Chloe's father, Fred, would be supplying the lobsters and languistines for the starters. That reminded him to call or text Chloe with his Diploma news. Unusually his call was diverted to voicemail so he left a short message giving her the news. Should he call or WhatsApp his mother? Sure, why not. She might be leading a new 'life on the ocean wave' these days but she was entitled to hear the good news, for sure. It was time to talk to Millie.

'Sis, it's the staffing bit now that concerns me. If forty people are sitting down to eat, roughly at the same time, how many waiting staff do you think I'll need? Four? Six? Eight?'

'Bro, you should have thought this through days ago. You'll need one 'front of house' to show people to their tables. Two more to serve drinks from the Bar and do you have one who could act as a Sommelier? You can't do that. You'll be too busy shaking hands and schnoozing up to VIPs.'

'What VIPs? Do you know something I don't, Sis?'

'Well, for a start, there's the mob from Best Eastern Hotels including that guy called Fan – a Hong Kong Chinese billionaire, if Pamela is to be believed. And you can almost guarantee that one diner will be there undercover from a newspaper, probably the Yorkshire Post and ..'

'Sis, you're beginning to get me worried. What if anything goes wrong?'

'Plan properly and it won't. Now, back to staffing matters. Ideally, on a night like this, you should have one waiter or waitress per table but when you have one table with six diners and several with only two, you'll have to compromise a bit. These extra people from Esquires – how well do you know them? Serving Cappuccinos and milk shakes to daytime shoppers in a mall isn't the same as silver service in a restaurant is it?'

'No, I take your point.'

'Look, how about inviting them all down for a dummy run on Friday evening? None of them will have found new jobs yet. You'll have to pay them of course, say for two hour's of their time. Can you get hold of John, the Team Leader, and see what the score is?'

'Good thinking, I'll do it now. I've got his mobile number. Give me five.'

Millie just smiled and shook her head as soon as Jamie's back was turned. There were loads of things she was sure Jamie hadn't even considered but fortunately she, Pamela and Samantha had them all covered. Jamie soon returned to Reception with a broad smile.

'Yeah, the Esquires gang are all coming. One of the girls, Lydia, is a Cockney, from Ponders End, so let's hope she's understood – you know, "apples and pears", "old pot and pan" etc.'

'Well, just make sure that neither apples nor pears aren't on the menu then, to avoid confusion.'

'John says the four of them are all coming here for the rehearsal at seven o'clock on Friday night. They're all coming in one taxi so we'll pick up the tab for that – and the taxi home later.'

'You do realise that they'll all have their eyes on working here in the future, don't you?'

The next few days positively whizzed by. With the brilliant news of his Diploma success, not to mention the added bonus of the surprise extra trophy, Jamie started to really relax and concentrated on the main job in hand – the menus for the big night. Changing his mind umpteen times and after numerous chats with Samantha Lyon, he finally settled on his three starters, three mains and three desserts.

STARTERS

Traditional Atlantic prawn cocktail
A Trio of Yorkshire puddings with
caramelised red onion gravy
A Waldorf salad with your choice of dressing

MAINS

Roast sirloin of beef with home-grown horseradish sauce
Baked rolled local plaice with a shrimp and caper sauce
Mixed bean chilli with pilau rice OR vermicelli

DESSERTS

Hotel Scarbados gateaux
Rhubarb crumble with a vanilla custard sauce
Fresh fruit salad

A selection of teas and coffees.

Millie took a long perusal of the menu and had only one question.

'Brill Jamie, just brill. Simple but mouth watering. But how much are we going to charge for this? Twenty-five pounds a head? Thirty?'

'Nothing, it's all complimentary, the food is anyway. It was Sam's idea. It's a promotional evening and according to Sam the last thing you want in the opening days is some smart-arsed reviewer giving you one or two stars in the "Value for money" category. Drinks and wines can be ordered and paid for separately. So what do you think, Sis?'

Millie wasn't quite sure what she thought and if she did, then, just for once, she kept her thoughts to herself.

13.

The great day, the formal opening of the Four Seasons restaurant, finally arrived. It was going to be the biggest day of Jamie's life – so far anyway. Nothing, absolutely nothing, was going to spoil it for him. The planning had been meticulous, well almost anyway. Nothing had been left to chance. The food, all fresh produce, had been delivered and if necessary, refrigerated. The "dummy run" with the former members of staff of Esquires coffee lounge had gone well and they all looked immaculate in the new waistcoats embossed with the Koala logo in grey and green on the lapels, Their first names also appeared on the brass badges that Samantha Lyon had provided at the last minute – yet another thing that Jamie had totally forgotten about.

By lunchtime, all the table settings in the main dining room had been double-checked with the table numbers matched to the seating plan on display as diners walked in. Only one table remained something of a mystery – the reservation in the name of a Ms A. Armitage who was also booked in for a single night's accommodation. Thus a "table for two" didn't really make sense. Perhaps it would all come out in the wash?

A table for Mr Stephen Fan and his entourage had been requested with the best window view in the room. Who was Jamie to argue? My mid-afternoon many of the guests started to arrive in dribs and drabs – mostly by car. The hotel's car park could accommodate getting on for thirty vehicles so in-house parking wasn't a problem. A silver-grey Bentley Continental Coupé with the registration SF888 was parked nearest to the rear door of the hotel. Like all his Hong Kong compatriots, Stephen Fan was superstitious. He had inherited the plate from his late father who had already invested in real estate in the United Kingdom, mostly in Sussex to facilitate his interests in horse-racing in general and in "Glorious Goodwood" in particular. Thus far, Fan Junior had not expressed interest in the Sport of Kings, not in England anyway.

Just after four o'clock, a white Station Taxi pulled into the forecourt of the hotel and keen for a generous tip, the driver opened the passenger door and removed a single posh-looking suitcase from the boot of the Ford Mondeo. She was smartly, but not ostentatiously, dressed.

'Thanks, love, but I can my carry my own case inside. Have a drink on me.'

She waived a twenty pound note in the air which caught the driver by surprise. He'd read in the Scarborough News that the new restaurant was being formally opened tonight but was for 'invited guests' only. He glanced sideways at the parked Bentley with the private plate. There must be some 'big nobs' coming tonight he thought. As he was closing the boot lid two more expensive cars arrived as if in convoy – BEH1 and BEH2 read the plates. Who the heck was driving these? They looked Oriental to him, as did the female passengers alongside both drivers. By 'eck there was some brass involved here, he thought. He was right. Meanwhile his female fare, probably in her late fifties, had strolled into the lobby and walked into reception. Marina was on duty.

'Good afternoon, madam. Do you have a reservation?'

'Afternoon to you too. Did you honestly think I would turn up without one? Anyway, the name's Armitage,

Amanda Armitage. I have a room booked for one and a dining table booked for two for the first sitting for dinner. What's my room number? It's quite smart here I must say. Now I can see why it's a hundred and twenty-five quid a night.'

Marina didn't quite know what to say.

'Thank you. Let's see – you're in Room 101 on the first floor and …'

'Well, I'd guessed that by the number. I would have preferred a room on the top floor to be honest, for the better sea views and ..'

'Yes, of course, madam, but it's early days since the reopening and only the ground floors and the first floors are functioning at the moment. Perhaps next time if you told us in advance we could …'

'Next time? What makes you think there'll be a next time young lady? Is this my key, this big brass thing? It's high time you invested in those plastic electronic keys, if I may say so?'

'Perhaps, madam could put a written suggestion along those lines into the suggestion box over there before you check out? Now, if you'll excuse me, I'll attend to these other guests who have just arrived.'

Ms Armitage walked the short distance to the nearest lift, taking her modestly sized suitcase with her. The wheels on her case left twin tram tracks in the new pale green shag pile so recently laid by Home Office sponsored contractors. The electronic 'ping' announced her arrival on the First Floor and unsurprisingly her room, 101, was almost adjacent to the lift. The immediate inspection of her room proved satisfactory and the imprint of a koala in the small complimentary bar of scented pale-green soap in the bathroom made her smile. By 'eck, they must be doing well.

She filled and switched on the small low-ampage kettle to make a quick brew with the tea bags provided – Yorkshire Tea of course, she was pleased to note. None of your cheap catering pack tea to be seen here! With her shoes kicked off it was time for a little lie down with Britain's favourite beverage. It was also time to send a quick text to someone she had never even set eyes on.

'Hi, I've arrived at the Koala Hotel.
It's lovely, just as you said.
See you in the Bar at say six forty-five?
Time for a little sherry before we eat.
Looking forward to meeting you.
M'

Downstairs in the lobby and Reception, things were hotting up and getting busy. Millie was taking over Reception duties from Marina for an hour to enable her to get a quick break before events really got under way.

'How's everything going? Have nearly all the overnighters checked in now, as far as we know?'

'Yes, I think so, Millie. Clive and Betty White arrived about twenty minutes ago. They're in Room 102, next door to the mysterious Ms. Armitage who also checked in about ten minutes ago. She wanted to know why we still used old-fashioned brass keys. A bit of a "moo" she was, I thought. Who is she and why is she on the guest list? '

'She booked online via the website before we were really organised. That's why we needed to organise two sittings. We need to be very cautious. A couple of years back a troublesome anonymous guest proved to be the Editor in Chief of a major magazine travelling incognito and …'

'Oh my God. Maybe she's from one of those posh restaurant guides where they say nice things to your face and then rip you into shreds a few weeks later?'

'I think I'd better tip Jamie off although, to be honest, he's probably worried enough already. Where is he right now?'

'Well, presumably in the kitchen doing last minute preparation. He's got three soux chefs tonight thanks to Samantha Lyon. It won't always be like this though, will it? What's it going to be like when he's a one man band running the whole show?'

Actually, Jamie wasn't in the kitchen. He was outside sitting on one of those green benches overlooking the North Bay. He glanced nervously at his watch. It was just after five o'clock. She was only fractionally late.

'Jamie! Jamie! I'm just coming, love.'

She crossed the road to the cliff top and threw her arms around him.

'Mam, Mam, I'm so pleased to see you.'

'You didn't really think I was going to miss out on the biggest day of my only son's life did you?! I booked via the website, once we could get a good wi-fi signal on't ship. That was a brilliant idea of yours to book in under my maiden name – Amanda Armitage. Do you think anybody has rumbled me yet?'

'No, I'm sure they haven't.'

'Now, son, I'm meeting that young lady of yours, Chloe, for a sherry in the Bar at six forty-five. You seem determined that I meet her. Are you smitten, lad?'

'Yes, Mam, I am, I really am.'

She gave Jamie an even bigger hug and a little tear ran down her cheek.

14.

Jamie did not wish to embarrass folks more than necessary. Accordingly, he arranged a little private reunion for his mother and both his two sisters before the evening's events got truly under-way. Millie wasn't totally surprised and despite still harbouring minor grievances against her mother, was as daughterly as she could be.

'Well, Mam, I have to say you're looking good. A life on the ocean wave obviously suits you. I'd guessed from those postcards that it wouldn't be long before we saw you.'

'Thanks Millie, you're looking good too. Now, where is your father anyway? I've not seen hide nor hair of him since I arrived over two hours ago.'

'Oh, he's popped down to the old place, Hotel Scarbados. Said there was something he wanted to bring here especially for tonight. I take it you heard that he and Lucy are moving back there soon with both dogs and …'

'Both dogs? What do you mean both dogs?'

Lucy interrupted her mother quite sharply, in fact very sharply.'

'Mam, you've never been one to keep in touch since you opted for a grander life with Aunty Gwen. Sebbie and the Ritson's dog, Candy, got together and we now have one of the pups – a little dog called AlfieBoy. In a few week's time we'll be back at the Hotel Scarbados. Dad has bought it and as soon as arrangements allow then we're moving back there and we're going to build proper kennels in the back garden and ...'

Millie was suddenly frightened that Lucy might accidentally spill the beans about Stephanie and Natalie. Now wasn't the right time or place, so she steered the conversation into calmer waters.

'Dad and Lucy can make a fresh start unencumbered by the demands of a busy hotel and it will be a lot nicer atmosphere for Lucy to continue her veterinary studies. The New Hotel Scarbados, as he refers to it, will be a sort of dog-friendly AirBnB.' Lucy looked downcast.

'Mam, you haven't even asked about my studies yet, nor even enquired about Sebbie. You just live in in a world of your own now, well don't you? Don't you?'

Suitably chided, Mandy backed off and changed the subject.

'Well good luck to you both.That's all I can say. As it happens I've met someone too – an American gentleman, a widower from Long Island, New York. He's invited me over to spend the summer in his condo.'

'That's great, Mam. Don't forget to send us a postcard.'

Millie smiled inwardly and was so pleased that her little sister was more than capable of showing a little steel of her own.

'Look everyone, let's all start to get ready shall we? The guests will start to arrive soon and gather in the lounge for pre-dinner cocktails. Mam, when Dad gets here do you want me to tell him you're here?'

'No! Don't you dare. I want to surprise him. Just ask him to pop into the Bar about six forty-five OK?'

Millie nodded in agreement. There was no point in causing any further fuss. The evening had all the hallmarks of being quite eventful enough. Peter and the two dogs arrived via the rear entrance. He was clutching what looked suspiciously like the top half of a drum on a small length of rope. What on earth was he up to?

'Dad, where the hell have you been? It's almost zero hour! You're supposed to be "front of house" this evening, glad-handing folks and looking the part of a Maitre D. For God's sake get upstairs and get ready. And what the heck is that object you're holding?'

'Don't you remember it? It's the old dinner gong from the Hotel Scarbados. We accidentally left it behind when we moved. I've found it! I'm going to surprise Jamie by using it to announce "Ladies and Gentlemen, dinner is served."'

'Dad, just leave it here for goodness sake and get ready.'

Peter took one of the lifts to the top floor and the owner's accommodation. As it rose past the first floor he heard the clunk of the other lift door closing as its sole occupant stepped inside and pressed the '0' button. She was dressed to the nines. In his wildest dreams Peter would never have guessed that the occupant was his ex-wife, Mandy.

With a ping her lift arrived at "ground zero" and Mandy stepped into the lobby within sight of Reception and her eldest daughter, Millie.

'Jee-zuzz, Mam, that dress must have cost a bomb! Is it Armani? And aren't those Jimmy Choos shoes? They must have set you back a grand I reckon. You've come a long way since M & S in Hull, haven't you?'

'Less of your cheek, young lady. I want to look at my best for Jamie's big night. Now, where can I find his girlfriend, Chloe?'

'She's just gone into the Bar two minutes ago. She's wearing a black trouser suit with her hair tied back. Probably ninety-nine quid from Next – you should ask her for some shopping advice.'

'I just said, don't be cheeky. I'm not in competition with her, it's not a fashion parade.'

'Well, if I didn't know better I'd have guessed that you were on the pull!'

If only Millie knew that she'd hit the nail on the head. Her mother's original target had been Peter who must still have some serious wonga to his name. Her own savings had been hard-hit by an extravagant and ungrateful sister in the last twelve or more months almost continuously at sea. Her lie about meeting a rich American had been partly true, except that it was her sister Gwen who'd had luck on her side. As she walked into the Bar she paused briefly to look at the table plan. There seemed to be more than a few single and unaccompanied men even if she couldn't pronounce their names. Then she spotted Pamela Hesketh's name on the same table as most of them. Like a submerged submarine commander looking through a periscope, it was time to change targets. She would bide her time but meanwhile it was time to meet Chloe. She spotted her immediately from the brief description that Millie had given her. It looked like she was sipping a "mocktail" of some sort judging by the unfurled umbrella, a glaced cherry speared by a cocktail stick and a lime wedge skewered on the rim of the high-ball glass.

'Hi, you must be Chloe. I'm Mandy, Jamie's mam. Pleased to meet you, Chloe.'

'Er, you too Mrs Fishburn. I love your dress by the way is it from Next or Monsoon?'

Chloe knew darned well that it was an Armani but was determined that the lady from Hull wasn't going to talk down to her.'

'No, I bought it from one of the on-board boutiques on my last cruise. And these "Choos" too – the lot for under two grand. A bargain, if you ask me. Now, where's the waiter with the champagne?'

Two swift glasses of L'Anson Black label and the former Mrs Fishburn's eyes were darting all over the room. Suddenly, she spotted Peter hovering at the doorway clutching the gong that she remembered from the old Wendover Hotel, now the Hotel Scarbados. He looked like a Caucasian version of the Oriental chap who banged a huge drum at the beginning of every Rank Organisation film. She wanted a quick chat first before he banged the gong. She walked slowly but purposefully towards him.

'Don't speak then, Peter.'

It took Peter several seconds to recognise his ex-wife. Gone was the frumpy housewife from Hull. She had obviously had a Gok Wan type of makeover. Her hair was shorter with highlights but the reddish tints still betrayed her Viking ancestry. She had lost at least a stone in weight and was probably cruising at an altitude of three inches on what what looked like a grand's worth of footwear. She gave him port and starboard air kisses which were more perfunctory than heartfelt.

'Pete, tonight is Jamie's night. Any differences to discuss can be left until later, or even tomorrow. Agreed?'

'Absolutely, Mandy. Let's stay friends. Gosh you're looking good I must say. For just a few seconds he realised why he had fallen for her all those years ago. His male hormones started to stir and if the events across the North Sea in recent months hadn't happened he might be sorely tempted. He tried to banish naughty thoughts from his mind. He only partially succeeded.

'OK, look let's chat after dinner. I'm on "gong duty" right now.'

She planted two smackers, one on each cheek, and left the classic red lips like emojis. Pete strode to the dining room door and struck the gong three times as firmly as he could.

'Ladies and Gentlemen, dinner is about to be served. Please take your seats in the Four Seasons dining room in accordance with the seating plan on display just here and ...'

He was almost bowled over by the rush. Miles Carter from the Cricket Club led the stampede closely followed by at least eight Oriental gentlemen and four women, Pamela Hesketh being the sole Caucasian. Mandy soon spotted Pamela who had been her love rival a year or two ago. She smiled in her direction and received a reluctant long distance wave back. Mandy would keep her powder dry. If her charm offensive against Peter fell short then she would take a leaf out of Pamela's book. She had long learnt to "follow the money" and was obviously turning a science into an art. No longer rivals, she could perhaps learn a few tricks from her. In the meantime she would get to know Chloe a little better and enjoy the dinner.

The temporary waiters and waitresses seconded from the former Esquires Café were hard pressed to keep up. It was fortunate that Samantha Lyon had brought in extra staff at the last minute. Had she not done so, there would have been serious delays in folks getting fed – exactly what you don't want on a formal opening night. For weeks now Samantha had harboured fears that, in the long term, Jamie would not be able to cope. She had kept her thoughts to herself but deep down she knew that in the not too distant future she would have to broach an idea to him. Glancing around the sea of diners she sensed a lull of a kind between the "starters" and the "mains" courses being served. It was a timely moment to present Jamie with his Diploma Certificate and the special trophy. She signalled to Peter who banged the same gong repeatedly until silence reigned.

'Ladies and Gentlemen, It gives me great pleasure this evening to present Mr Jamie Fishburn with his Certificate and ... where is he?'

A sheepish and slightly embarrassed Jamie emerged from the kitchens in his Chef's whites and the black and white check trousers that were the hallmark of his profession. His mother and Chloe started clapping closely followed by everyone else. Despite being on her fifth glass of champagne, Mandy managed to maintain a standard of decorum that travelling First Class had taught her in the last year. She wasn't in Hull now and she knew it. Samantha Lyon continued her task.

'Ladies and Gentlemen, I can also tell you that for the first time in quite a few years we are awarding the Duncan Lyon Memorial Trophy to the College's most promising student.'

Tears filled her eyes and she could barely get the words out.

'Only a handful of you here this evening will know that Duncan, my late father, headed up the Department at the TEC for years before his early retirement. Sadly he passed away shortly after that but a small part of his estate was bequeathed to provide for this special trophy that is now displayed on that side table over there.' She pointed to it.

'Yes, you're right, it's a large wooden spoon except it is cast in solid 999 silver. You can see that it's mounted on a silver plinth and is detachable. Like the Claret Jug golf trophy the names of the recipients are engraved on the plinth. It has to be returned after one year for the next winner to receive it.'

Samantha retrieved the heavy glittering spoon from the table and presented it to Jamie who was genuinely stumped for words. The silence was short-lived as someone at the back nearest the Bar stared singing "for he's a jolly good fellow" and much to Jamie's relief that marked the end of the presentation. He dived back into the relative refuge of the kitchen to a cacophony of cries from all directions:

'Chef, we're running low on prawns. Nearly everyone has ordered the prawn cocktail.'

'Chef, only one person has ordered the Yorkshire puddings, there's tons of mix left.'

'Chef, every single person on the "China table"except the English woman, has ordered the plaice. What's going to happen if the same goes for the second sitting? We only have four servings left.'

'Chef, nobody's ordered the salad yet. Shall we put it on one side?'

'Chef, some smart-arse has asked if the shellfish is locally sourced – they'd read about an environmental issue.'

'Chef, one of the Chinese guys has asked if he can have sole instead of plaice.'

Quickly, in fact far too quickly, it was dawning on Jamie that running a restaurant was very different in practice than in theory.

Back at the "China Table" the discussions, all in rapid Cantonese, were getting a little animated.

Herbert Wong, the owner and driver of BEH 1 was in deep chatter with Stephen Fan.

'Did you say we've got fifty percent of the shares of this outfit? This young "Cookie Boy" is never going to be able to cope is he? Let's be realistic. You say he actually owns twenty-five percent of the business? Dew lay lo mo! Let's buy the little Gweilo out and get some top, experienced people from London in here. What do the rest of your think? Pamela didn't say anything. The two Chinese ladies were getting bored and left the table to head for the Bar. Were they wives or concubines? They weren't expecting business matters to be discussed over the far more important matter of food. Spotting the gaps in the table places, Mandy decided to make a move and with a champagne flute in her left hand walked towards the "China Table" and spoke to Pamela.

'Pamela, nice to see you again. At Jamie's eighteenth wasn't it?'

'Er yes, I think so.'

'And these gentlemen are?'

'Sorry, yes this is Herbert Wong and his brother Albert, both major shareholders and directors on the board of Best Eastern Hotels.'

Mandy shook hands gently with them both in turn. Neither were wearing wedding rings she noticed and the display of a gold Rolex on one, and a Patek Phillipe, on the other betrayed their obvious wealth. Both were in their early fifties and obviously looked after themselves. The customary "Asian handshakes" of offering their business cards soon followed. Pamela added some grist to the mill.

'You might not have realised, gentlemen, that Mandy was one of the original shareholders and we bought her out only recently. She and her ex-husband, who we also bought out, are here to see their son Jamie tonight. Mandy lives mostly on cruise ships these days, don't you Mandy?'

Mandy ignored the touch of sarcasm in Pamela's voice.

'I suppose you could say that, but you never know do you? I'm always open to new adventures in life.'

The normally inscrutable Albert Wong smiled and looked up from his dinner and carefully mouthed "call me later" without anyone else at the table noticing.

'Well, it's been nice to meet you but I must get back to my table now. Jamie's girlfriend looks a bit annoyed that I left her alone. Bye.'

'Mrs Fishburn, who on earth are those people you were talking with?'

'Oh they're just Chinese businessmen. They get everywhere these days don't they?'

The second dinner sitting did not pass without incident. They ran out of beef and plaice and several people had to have the vegetarian chilli whether they were veggies or not. It was just as well that the food was on the house and nobody appeared to be a critic in disguise. Shortly after eleven o'clock Chloe ordered a taxi to take her home and Jamie, still in his chef's garb escorted her to the car waiting in the car park. She gave him the most intimate of kisses on the lips.

'Jamie, I'm so proud of you but … well I don't quite know how to say this but …'

'Chloe, just say it, we know each other well enough by now. Don't we?'

'Jamie, I think your Mum's up to no good. You didn't see any of it but she was definitely flirting with at least one of those Chinese guys from Best Eastern Hotels. They both gave her a business card. The last I saw of her she was at Reception talking with Marina is it? She's just extended her stay by two more nights. I thought I should tell you. Just be careful, love, OK. Taxi's here, I'll call you tomorrow. Nite nite, love you.'

Back in the Bar only two people were left – Mandy and Peter.

'Let's have a nightcap shall we, for old time's sake? Your usual? A double Remy Martin on the rocks?'

'That wasn't the type of nightcap I had in mind, Pete – but it'll do for starters.'

15.

The "morning after the night before" consisted mainly of a three hour clean-up. Most of the overnighters, still full of beef, Yorkshire puddings and gateaux, had settled for simply tea or coffee and toast. Mandy was one of the last to make an appearance and looked very jaded indeed. She hadn't had the extra "nightcap" that she had made available and was disappointed that her ex-husband hadn't taken the bait, as it were. Still, with another two days added to her itinerary, there was time a plenty to try again. What had she to lose? Before turning her bedside light out she had sent Albert Wong a text. Why not?

> *'So nice to meet you Albert. If you're still in the area this evening perhaps we could have dinner together? I love meeting Oriental gentlemen. Call or text me later. Mandy x'*

She had hesitated before pressing the "send" button and she had wondered if the "x" at the end of the message, so perfunctory and almost meaningless in European eyes, would cause offence. It was almost eight o'clock in the morning before Albert was awake enough to read the message. He prodded his partner awake and came up with a suggestion.

'Listen babes, how about you take the train to Leeds today, check into the Marriott for a couple of days and do some shopping. There's a Harvey Nichols in Leeds too – you and Herbert's friend could have a fun time. You've got a BEH credit card. Herbert and I have a few loose ends to tie up.'

'Yah, OK, honey. Great idea.'

Albert knew that the Harvey Nicks hook would be too juicy not to swallow. He waited until she was in the shower before sending a reply to Mandy.

> *That would be lovely Mandy. Shall we meet in the Bar at say seven o'clock? I'll book a table for two at La Lanterna restaurant and arrange for a car to pick us up. A'*

Mandy's mobile had pinged twice just as she was on her second cup of coffee. She sent a quick reply in the affirmative and popped her mobile back into her day-bag just seconds before Millie entered the dining room.

'Oh there you are, Mam. Sleep well did you? You had enough cognac from where I was looking …'

'You're getting too big for your boots, young lady. Who do you think you are – Miss Trust House Forte? Just remember that it was my inheritance that got us all here in the first place and …'

'Mam, you left us all in the lurch at the old place. Remember? Lucy was still a young schoolgirl. No wonder she spent so much time with animals. She got more affection from Sebbie than her own mother. And you must think I'm stupid if you think I couldn't see what you were up to last night. I saw you cozying up to those two Chinese guys. Run out of brass have you?'

'How dare you speak to me like that?!'

'And don't play with Dad's emotions. I think you're jealous that he's finally found happiness again ...'

Millie faltered but it was too late.

'What do you mean again? Don't tell me he's found another trollop from another glossy magazine?'

'Mam, I'll just remind you that 'that trollop' is the only reason you could sell your shares in this hotel. Pamela has also been most helpful with Jamie's endeavours. What did you do to help your only son? You just bought him a set of chef's knives and then naffed off to the sunshine. Well didn't you? Why don't you just finish your coffee and then go out for a long walk?'

'That's a good idea. It'll give me some peace and quiet. I might even take Sebbie with me.'

You can't! He's already out with Lucy and AlfieBoy. In any case he's probably forgotten who the heck you are. You didn't even greet him with a little treat when you arrived. Lucy was most upset, I can tell you.'

With a huff, a puff and a glare like a laser, Mandy left the dining room. What had Millie meant when she said her father had found happiness again? She would find out, for sure.

A half an hour later and Millie, her father Peter and brother Jamie were in the lounge with a pot of Yorkshire Tea and some ginger biscuits. They had asked Clive White to join them too for an informal inquest or post mortem on the previous night's events. Had it been the total success they had all worked for or were there lessons to be learnt? With mugs full and biscuits grabbed, Millie asked Clive if he would pour forth with his thoughts first. Millie took notes. As always, she was the only one that did.

'Clive, your thoughts, please?

As a creature of habit he took a long swig of his tea followed by a small bite of a GingerNob.

'Well, OK here goes, warts and all.

Firstly, Jamie, the food was nice, in fact very nice. I have to say though that I think some of your creations down at the old "Hotel Scarbados" were more adventurous and a bit more, shall we say, up-market.'

Jamie immediately looked crestfallen and inadequate.

'You mustn't take it to heart, Jamie. I'm sure everyone enjoyed it but, well, the basic problem was that there were too many mouths to feed. Two sittings was always going to be one sitting too many. A single sitting of, say forty people, would have been much more manageable.'

Millie decided to rescue her brother from his solace.

'You're right, Clive. We invited too many people but only because we didn't want some folks to be upset that they weren't invited. We had a few "thank yous" to make. Like Dave Gibson and his wife, the owner of *We are Neon*. We couldn't even offer them accommodation. Fortunately Nadine from the Crescent Gardens Hotel helped us out. It prompted her to make a suggestion that we have an informal arrangement to recommend each other's hotel when one of us is full.'

'That's wonderful. You could even take that a stage further in the fullness of time.'

'How do you mean, Clive? In what way?'

'Well, what if a visitor to Scarbados, perhaps a first time visitor, wanted to sample the North and South Bays within the same holiday? A "four nights in one, three nights in the other" type of arrangement perhaps? A sort of package to your mutual benefit. It's worth looking into.'

Millie was scribbling furiously. That's what she liked about Clive. He was always thinking outside the box.

'Anyway, to continue. The Chinese and other Orientals seemed to be quite demanding all night, egged on I have to say, by Ms Hesketh! Why on earth one of them tried to insist on swapping his plaice for Dover sole I just don't know for the life of me! Also, I have to say that although all the staff were most attentive, they just had too many people to keep happy. At least one of them, John I think his name was, seemed to have had some training in the world of wine. He was very impressive indeed. He seemed to know his Muscadet from his Merlot and his Pinot Noir from his Pinotage. Perhaps the girls could be similarly trained if you're going to employ them again?'

Jamie brightened up a tad. At least Clive's criticisms were constructive.

'So, looking ahead, I would say this – manage your restaurant bookings with more care. Concentrate on the profit margins per meal and sell as much wine and spirits as you can. I'm sure you'll agree with that, Peter? You know what the margins were like on the Pride of Bruges. In fact how much wine did you sell last night?'

Jamie looked sheepish and was almost reluctant to reply.

'Er, well actually I left that side of things to Dad. He stocked us up weeks ago in anticipation of ...'

'Jamie, that's not good enough. Your Dad won't be here much longer. He'll be back down at the New Hotel Scarbados with his mind on other things. It'll be be just you, Millie and spreadsheets in the not too distant future. Crickey is that the time? Betty and I had best be off soon. I hope my remarks are useful and of course you know where I am.'

'Thanks, Clive, as always.'

But, like Colombo, he had just one more question.

'Peter, did you recognise two of those Chinese guys?'

'No, I can't say I did, why?'

'I'm absolutely certain they were the two guys bidding against you to buy Hotel Scarbados at the auction. You know, they had a bit of a row between themselves when we made the final bid and the auctioneer's hammer came down. They were livid but as you know the auctioneer, Arthur Price, was on our side.'

'Good grief. I think you might be right. And if that's the case were they bidding privately or on behalf of Best Eastern Hotels?'

'Who knows, it's yours now anyway. The old maxim of "inscrutable Orientals" still holds true. Anyway, we've got to hit the road. Keep in touch.'

With the Whites waved out of the car park, Millie motioned for her Dad to pop into her little office.

'Dad, while we're alone, did you agree with Clive's observations, you know, about the menu and the restaurant in general? Be honest with me.'

'Millie, I think Clive was right. There is no way that Jamie will be able to run this restaurant on his own. It's just too much. Having a fancy certificate, distinctions and a trophy are one thing and might prepare you well for Master Chef, but not how to manage a busy restaurant. Where is Jamie now anyway?'

'I just heard him leave on his motorbike. I'll bet you he's gone to the Old Town to see Chloe. She's going back to Uni in York tomorrow.'

'And where's your mother? Did I hear you having words earlier?'

'I think she thinks you've met another "trollop" but I wouldn't be surprised if she doesn't go back to Hull permanently soon. It sounds like Aunty Gwen has bled her dry over the last couple of years.'

'Well, if that's the case, I feel a bit sorry for her to be honest.'

'Dad, don't! She only cares about herself now. Gone is the warm, friendly housewife from Holderness Road, Hull. She's now Eric the Red's great, great granddaughter – minus the horns!'

They both laughed and it took the tension out of the conversation. Suddenly, out of the blue, Peter's mobile rang.

He checked the caller ID. It was Stephanie, calling from Bruges. As if by magic he was transformed into a different world and persona.

'Peter, I haven't heard from you! How did the restaurant opening go last night? You promised to call me this morning ... Natalie, please be quiet .... sorry Peter ... oh all right you can speak first... your daughter wants to speak to you.'

'Hello, Papa.'

In seconds, all Peter's thoughts on Mandy, the Hotel Koala and the Four Seasons Restaurant, dissolved into the ether. He knew that from this day onwards, he must concentrate on the New Hotel Scarbados. He must leave Millie, Jamie and Best Eastern Hotels behind.

16.

Shortly before six o'clock, a smart white Mercedes, complete with a driver, pulled into the Hotel Koala's car park. The driver was obviously waiting for somebody. He had to wait somewhat longer than he had anticipated. Inside the Bar of the hotel, Albert Wong was already in animated conversation with Eric the Red's descendant. Like most Chinese, he drank little alcohol but his escort for the evening had already availed herself of a miniature bottle of Remy Martin from her room's mini-bar and was now on her second glass of Prosecco. At least she hadn't mixed the grape and the grain – not yet anyway. Once again Mandy was dressed to the nines, this time in an emerald green that gripped her like cling film. A year ago she would not have been able to squeeze into it but the onboard yoga, pilates and zumba classes had performed their tricks and she looked fit and 'up for it' as the saying goes.

Albert Wong looked at his Patek Phillipe watch and decided there was time for another drink, for her anyway. In reality the table wasn't booked until seven o'clock. He just wanted a bit more time to lubricate Mandy's brain before he started to broach the real reason for the date. Hopefully she would be receptive to a business idea as well as a little bit of something else.

The car took them on the scenic route to the Lanterna via the Marine Drive. It was still early evening and hundreds of visitors thronged the foreshore licking ice creams, munching waffles and generally enjoying themselves. The drinks were having a warming effect on Mandy and she didn't baulk when Albert slipped a hand on her thigh. In fact she was flattered. She'd never got this from Pete and she felt like the Queen of Sheeba. She could get used to this. She was snapped out of her daydream by the loud voice of the driver who was obviously a local.

'Lanterna, Sir. Will you need collecting later, Sir?'

'Well, yes of course. Ten 'o'clock please.'

'Yes Sir, of course Sir.'

Albert cursed silently under his breath. Did this Gweilo clown honestly think they'd be going back to the hotel on a No. 21 bus? Still, both the car and driver were only on a month by month contract. It was useful while they were still scouting the area for new business possibilities and a chauffeur driven car was always useful for impressing people. The maître d was on the ball.

'Your table for two, Mr Wong. Nice to see you again, Sir.'

Had Mandy been a little less oiled she might have picked up on the 'again' but that was not to be. Their table was in a discreet corner which made it difficult to be overheard by anybody. A waiter arrived with two food menus and a separate one for drinks and wines.

'A drink while you're waiting to peruse the main menu, Madam … and you Sir?'

Albert, like a lot of Hong Kong Chinese, was a lover of cognac. In colonial days it had had the highest per capita consumption of proper cognac – none of your cheaper "knockoffs" from Cyprus or South Africa. Most if not all the items on both menus were in Italian and, not unnaturally, the products of that country proliferated. Mandy was well versed in this respect, the Italian cruise liners in the Mediterranean being her favourites.

'Grazzi, I'll have a glass of your best Prosecco, por favore. To eat I'll start with a little anti-pasti – some pitted olives perhaps.'

'Certainly, senora, and for your main course? Perhaps some beef ravioli? It's made fresh daily, our own pasta?'

'Grazzi, and some aqua minerale frizzente, por favore.'

'Certainly, and for you, Sir?'

Albert tried to pretend that he was un-fazed by Mandy's apparent knowledge. The lady from Hull was maybe not as uneducated as he had come to believe. If he wasn't careful then this evening's task could prove to be a darn sight more expensive than he had previously thought. Simple wonga might not be enough. He might have to perform! He was reluctant to order anything involving pasta. How many Europeans knew that pasta had originated in China and that but for the adventurous and entrepreneurial talents of Marco Polo in the thirteenth century, Italians would probably still be eating bread, olives and rotten tomatoes? He kept his thoughts to himself.

'Thank you. I'll have the minestrone soup please followed by the Tuscan pork loin Rotolini with some zuccini, calabrese and asparagus please. I take it it's fresh as it's in season?'

'Yes of course, Sir, and to drink?'

Realising that the odds he might have to perform were shortening by the minute, Albert decided to be cautious.

'Just a small Campari with lots of soda please.'

They made small talk about the décor and the wall-mounted prints and paintings until the drinks arrived.

'Have you been to Italy, Albert? The paintings and prints on the walls here are all classic Italian vistas. That bridge behind you is the Bridge of Sighs in Venice and the one over there is the Ponte Vecchio in Florence. Both are stunningly beautiful. In their day they were every bit as important as the Humber Bridge is today.'

Albert took his cue from the first bridge and was about to say "how interesting" when the drinks waiter arrived. They clinked glasses – cheers and Yam Sing, Mandy.'

'Yam Sing? What does that mean?'

'It literally means "bottoms up" in your colloquial English, I believe. Now, Mandy, I want to be perfectly honest with you and, in turn, would you please be honest with me?'

'Yes of course, Albert. You're starting to sound serious. I thought this going to be a purely social evening.'

Mandy pouted her lips and rounded her vowels as she spoke the word social. She wanted more than a nice dinner – if she could get it. Just as Albert was about to reply another waiter arrived with their starters. The classic Italian minestrone looked and smelt perfect, as only Italians can make it.

'Parmesan, Sir?'

'No thank you, definitely not.'

'It's the normal accompaniment, Albert, I do assure you.'

'We Chinese are not generally big fans of dairy products, to be honest. Most cheeses are anathema to us. And as for custard, don't get me going on that one.'

'OK, Albert. So far it's a chauffeur driven car, a posh restaurant, by Scarborough standards anyway, and as much drink as you can tempt me with. Now, what's the real reason we're here?'

This lady was not going to be the soft touch he had anticipated. She had obviously learnt a lot since leaving her previous life as a Hull housewife behind. Fraternising with moneyed men on cruise liners had left its mark.

'You just called this restaurant 'posh by Scarborough standards.' Why did you say that?'

'Well this is Scarborough, not San Francisco. It's mostly fish, chips and mushy peas and …'

'So do you think that the Four Seasons Restaurant will do well if it aims for an up-market clientèle?'

'Well, yes, we all hope so. As Jamie's mother, of course I'm very proud of him. Last night was the biggest event in his life. As soon as the Hotel Koala is firing on all cylinders, or should I say all three floors, then the restaurant will be full most nights, I'm sure. Don't you think so, Albert?'

'No, we don't think so, to be brutally honest. Jamie will not be able to cope, not even with extra assistance brought in from other establishments.'

'What do you mean *we* don't think so? Who is *we*?'

The presence of some many members of the board of Best Eastern Hotels last night was no coincidence. We were there to suss out the potential of the hotel as whole, including the restaurant. I understand the word "suss" is commonly used in Yorkshire. Yes?'

'Yes, your command of everyday English is amazing, Albert.'

'Thank you, but let me continue please. The overall potential for the Hotel Koala is huge. But there is no way that potential is going to be realised under the current set-up. It needs lots and lots of money pumped into it. BEH Ltd. only owns half of the company's shares – fifty percent, no more no less. The board is not prepared to invest further funds unless, or until, we own at least seventy-five percent of the company.'

'Meaning what exactly?'

'We wish to buy your son's shares entirely. Last night's problems and delays were not entirely accidental. We deliberately caused some of them to make Jamie realise, sooner rather than later, that the whole project will be beyond his capacity to deliver. For example, my brother asked for his fish to be changed from plaice to Dover sole. Of course we just knew that he wouldn't be able to do that. It might seem cruel, Mandy, but that's business.'

'Oh I get it, you make Jamie feel so inadequate that he wants "out" then you guys move in with a low price to …'

'No, Mandy, a high price. He must leave on good terms. It's vital. His sister, Millie, would remain as a shareholder. She's a rising star. Pamela tells us that her organisational skills are amazing and that without her both the Hotel Scarbados and the Hotel Koala would have failed long ago. Is she right?'

'Well of course I can't speak for the Koala but yes, in the early days that's correct.'

'We have it in mind to appoint her to the Board by the end of the year. But back to Jamie …'

'He'll never sell, I can tell you. He's so happy where he is.'

'Happiness is a state of mind, not a state of reality. He will sell at the right price, trust me. We have adequate funds in place, excuse the pun, to make it happen. The figure we have in mind is three hundred and fifty thousand pounds. In addition a further six figure sum is available as an "agent's fee" to the third party who makes the deal happen.'

'Really, and who the heck might that be?'

'I'm having dinner with her right now.'

Mandy was almost speechless. The remains of her anti-pasti were removed and replaced by her main course of Ravioli. Albert's Tuscan pork arrived seconds later and he smiled approvingly.

'You see, Mandy, these people here are highly trained and experienced. Everything is co-ordinated. The other night some of our party were finishing their main courses just as others were receiving theirs. No, once the deal is done, we'll put in some of our own experienced staff on a temporary basis until locals are fully trained.'

In her and her son's interests, Mandy decided to play hard-ball. Why not?

'What if I don't succeed in persuading him to sell? What happens then?'

'Then the hotel and its fancy new restaurant will wither on the vine and never really take off. It will be something of a white elephant, to put it mildly. On the other hand with over a third of a million in his "sky rocket" he'll be free to go it alone and possibly buy a smaller, more manageable establishment that he owns outright.'

Mandy ordered two large Remy Martins from the waiter and smiled.

'OK, Mr Wong, I'll do my best. Leave it with me. But in the immediate future there is something you can do for me.'

'Go ahead.'

'In all my travels I have never "entertained" an Oriental gentleman.'

'Meaning?'

'I'm in Room 101.'

17.

To Mandy's huge disappointment, Albert Wong declined the invitation to extend her social circles. She did not sleep well and perhaps she should have known that fine cognac stimulates the mind and can prevent sleep, rather than enhance it. She lay awake most of the night being awoken far too early by the screech of seagulls soon after first light. Mandy made some tea and gazed out of the east-facing window. The clunking of the lift adjacent to her room and the opening and closing of the doors, surprised her at this early hour. Minutes later the noise of two biggish cars departing the Hotel's car park caused her to look out again. It was the two Jaguars BEH1 and BEH2 leaving the premises. Perhaps that was reason her advances had been rejected – Albert knew he was rising early. Oh well. She had some thinking to do, and if all went well, some money to make. Without a substantial capital input, would the hotel 'wither on the vine' as Albert had so succinctly put it? She might have fallen out with her eldest daughter, Millie, but there was no way she would see her only son suffer if she could possibly avoid it. It was time for some considerable thought, not to mention, a motherly chat with Jamie. She dressed and went downstairs for some breakfast shortly after eight-thirty. There was no way she could avoid walking past reception and Millie barely glanced up from the computer screen she was fixated on.

'Ah there you are, Mam. I'm surprised you're up. Enjoy your Chinese takeaway last night, did you?'

'What on earth do you mean? Albert and I went to the Italian *La Lanterna* if you must know.'

'You know what I mean. You practically dragged Mr Wong into the lift at a very late hour. How's your Cantonese coming along? What's "rumpy-pumpy" in Chinese?'

'How dare you?! I might not be a shareholder and director any more but I'm still your mother! Now, after I've had some breakfast, where can I find Jamie please?'

'I think he might have stayed over at Chloe's last night. He seemed a bit quiet and downbeat to be honest. A couple of negative reviews on Trip Advisor have unsettled him. Have you seen them?'

'How the hell do you think I could have managed that?'

Millie punched a few buttons on her keyboard and rotated the monitor's screen to face the front of the desk.

'Here, look for yourself.'

First time visitor.
Two stars.
Went to the grand opening – not so grand. Slow service. Food more like a seafront café. Staff polite but inexperienced. I won't visit again in a hurry.

New visitor.
Two and a half stars
Food acceptable but bland and unexciting.
Will visit again when it's under new management.

Mandy smelt a rat as soon as she read that last line. Whoever wrote it can only be one of the Board members who is in the know. Could it even have been Albert? She was not "best pleased" as they say in Yorkshire. These reviews were designed to put pressure on poor Jamie already. She decided to text him.

Jamie, I'm still at the Hotel. I'm leaving on the 11:58 train to Hull. Please meet for a coffee at the station around eleven. It's urgent. Mam x'

'OK Mam. See you there. Jamie xx'

The ordered Nippy taxi was punctual and delivered Mandy and her suitcase to the railway station just before eleven o'clock. She spotted Jamie through the huge glass windows that gave a great view of the Stephen Joseph Theatre in the Round, one of the town's most loved attractions. He looked totally dejected and even a peck on each cheek and the offer of a hot chocolate initially failed to stir him from his melancholy. She felt really sorry for him.

'Cheer up. Love. I take it those two reviews on Trip Advisor have hurt?'

'Yes, and after the very first night too. How can people be so cruel?'

'Let's get some drinks and grab that table over there in the corner. It looks nice and quiet. A hot chocolate for you and a flat white for me. I'll get them. Take my case with you.'

There didn't seem to be any trains departing before the Hull train and it was fairly quiet.

'Now look, Jamie, I'm sure I can throw some light on this for you. Are you ready for this?'

'Mam, you're sounding very serious. What's up?'

'Jamie, to cut a long story short, certain people on the Board of Best Eastern Hotels seem determined to buy you out, leaving Millie as the sole remaining Fishburn as a shareholder. They're trying to squeeze you out by making you feel uncomfortable, even inadequate. They will soon be making you a financial offer for your shares.'

'What?! How do you know this? Are you sure?'

Mandy was too embarrassed to reveal the full story and was careful to keep the personal incentive totally hidden.

'I had dinner last night with Mr Albert Wong, and let's just say that he let his guard down and spilled the beans. It wouldn't surprise me if you get a written offer within a few days.'

'No! I'm happy where I am with Millie. And what on earth would I tell Chloe? Did you like her by the way? I do hope so.'

'Jamie, she's just lovely. You seem a perfect match to me. I'm so pleased for you.'

'So what do I do if and when the offer arrives? I'm a chef, not a businessman.'

'And I'm your mother, first and foremost, not a contestant on The Apprentice.'

'So, what do I do in practice then. Help!'

'I think you should speak to that nice Mr Clive White. He's always been there for us hasn't he? '

'You're right Mam, but I don't have his number.'

'Then call your sister straight away and get it. Do it now, then call him immediately.'

Two minutes later and Jamie was speaking direct with Clive White in Beverley.

'Hello, young Jamie, this is a surprise. What can I do for you?'

It took Jamie three painful minutes to get out what he wanted to say. It hurt.

'Oh heck. I did wonder when they might make a play, to be honest. They're getting very acquisitive according to a lot of people in the City I speak to. What's that noise in the background? It sounds like a railway station public address system.'

'That's exactly what it is, Mr White. I'm just seeing my Mam off on her way back to Hull.'

'Right, look sharp, and get a day return ticket to Beverley. We can have a proper chat here over coffee and sandwiches. OK?'

'You bet, Mr White and thank you. The train will get into Beverley about one o'clock I see from the departure board.'

'I'll meet you at the station. By the way I think you should tell your Mam, everything. And I do mean everything. Your family is dysfunctional enough as it is and I think some clarity and honesty is called for.'

'Do you really mean everything?'

'Yes, Belgium, Stephanie, Natalie – the lot! Go for it. See you soon.'

'Right, Mam, I'm coming on your train – as far as Beverley anyway. I'll just pop over to the ticket counter and get a day return. Wait there, I won't be long.'

The three carriage train from Northern Rail was on Platform No.4 and was almost devoid of passengers. Jamie lifted his mother's case onto the train and into the luggage compartment adjacent to the door. The train left on time – next stop Seamer and all points south. Jamie decided to grab the mettle and do what Clive White had advised. By the time the train reached the County Town of East Yorkshire, Mandy knew everything. They embraced tightly before Jamie got off the train.

'Thank you, Jamie for telling me. I would sooner have heard all this from you than anyone else.'

Clive White was waiting in his car on the station concourse, as promised.

'Hi Jamie, hop in. It's only five minutes to my place. You

don't really know Beverley that well do you? Not like your Dad, anyway.'

'No, not really. Where is it you live?'

'We live in North Bar Without ...'

'Without what? That's an odd name.'

I suppose it is, to a stranger anyway. I guess that means outwith the old walls. When I worked at the Bank the last Branch I worked in was just down the road. I could walk to work. When I retired we decided to stay in Beverley. It's a really nice place.'

'So who's the Manager now then? Do you keep in touch?'

'Jamie, where have you been for last two years? There's no Branch any more, with or without a Manager! In the good old days a small business owner could just pop into his local Branch for a bit of advice. Not any longer. I think that's one of the reasons that so many small businesses struggle today. You can hardly take advice from somebody in a call centre can you?'

'True. Particularly if it's in Bangalore and not Beverley!'

'Hey up, we're nearly there. Betty's laid on some ham and cheese sandwiches. Hungry?'

'Famished. Got lots of questions to ask you as well.'

Ten minutes later and they were sitting in the lovely front room overlooking the broad, tree-lined avenue that was North Bar Without. Betty brought the tea, coffee and enough sandwiches to feed the proverbial five thousand. The trolley left tram tracks in the deep patterned Axminster.

'I love that trolley, Mrs White.'

'I've told you before. It's Betty. We feel almost like an Uncle and Aunt to you and Millie, not forgetting Lucy of course. How is she anyway?'

'She's fine, studying her vet stuff hard and of course looking forward to moving back to the Hotel Scarbados soon. She can't wait.'

'I'll bet she can't, and as for the trolley it belonged to my great-grandmother. It's solid oak and the only place you can see anything like it is on the Antiques Road Show. You won't see one in Browns! Anyway, I'll leave you two in peace. Just shout if you need any more coffee, Jamie.'

'OK, Jamie, fire one. Something to do with these Chinese guys, you said on the phone?'

'Yes, Clive, it's all very unnerving to be honest. It's like this …'

Five minutes later and Clive was totally in the picture vis a vis the adverse Trip Advisor reviews and the almost hostile bid for Jamie's shares. He poured himself some more tea, as he always did, before deliberating.

'Jamie, in the grand scheme of things, I thought this would have happened one day but certainly not for a year, or even two. One thing I can absolutely guarantee you is the Chinese guys are trying it on. How much did they offer you?'

'Mam said three hundred and forty-five thousand.'

'Ha! Cheeky sod. Look when the written offer comes in. indeed if it comes in, just totally ignore it. Don't even be tempted to send a sarcastic reply OK? Just scan it and get Millie to email it to me OK?'

'Sure, OK, but then what?'

'Carry on as you intended with you and Millie working closely together to make the Hotel Koala the very profitable business it deserves to be. Go back to first principles with the Four Seasons Restaurant. Think back to those gourmet meals you served up at the Hotel Scarbados. I think that with all that's been going on in recent months you've been too close to the woods to see the trees. It happens. The opening night was more akin to mass catering, not what you're good at. Pause a while and step back. I'll speak to

Millie soon. In fact no, we'll do better than that. Betty and I will come through for a couple of nights soon. The evenings are lengthening and you can't beat Scarborough on light, early summer evenings. Now, what time's your train back?'

'Not sure, Clive, but I think I'll walk. I want to call in at the Olde Pork Shop – if I can find it.'

'You can't miss it, Jamie. You have to walk straight past it.'

18.

Jamie's train left Beverley on time and he was quite pleased with himself. He'd received some sound personal advice from a family friend he could trust, updated his Mam in accordance with that advice and, just as importantly, had acquired several kilos of the late John Hillman's special recipe sausages, including a goodly number for Lucy of the vegetarian variety. Both dogs should be pleased too. He sat back, relaxed and was just taking in the lovely East Riding agricultural vista when his phone rang in his back pocket. Had he accidentally left something at Clive's? No, it was his sister Millie's ID.

'Hi Sis, what's up? I've had a great chat with Clive …'

'Never mind that for the moment. Do you have any plans for tomorrow night? I've checked the hotel's diary and I can't see anything that would …'

'Sis, what on earth are you talking about? A game of darts at the Albert pub after the guests have been fed dinner might be on the cards, but apart from that nothing. Why?'

'OK, listen up. I've just had a distressed Nadine on the phone from the Crescent Gardens Hotel. They have a massive problem and she wants to know if we can help them out. She knows it's short notice and she'll quite understand if we can't but ..'

'For God's sake, spit it out. What are you on about?'

'Well, did you know that the Scarborough Branch of the Yorkshire Guild of Sommeliers regularly holds its meetings and tastings there?'

'No, how would I?'

'Well anyway, they do, and it's their monthly tasting and supper evening tomorrow night.'

'Let me guess, we're invited, right?'

'No. Let me finish. They have a major electrical problem with much of their kitchen equipment and ..'

'They want us to cook the food and take it round there?'

'No. They want to switch the venue to the Hotel Koala, just for tomorrow's function, you understand, not permanently.'

'Wow! Can we do it? How many people for supper?'

'Forty-four according to Nadine. That includes Members, Guests and two visiting speakers from some fancy vinters in Bristol. Those last two will need overnight accommodation as well.'

'Forty-four? No way. Look how hard it was on the opening night.'

'Just let me finish, will you?'

'Go on then.'

'It's a fixed menu – one main course followed by a cheeseboard at the end of the evening. The main dish is pan-fried breast of chicken with vegetables in season. Two members have requested a fish option and two a vegetarian option. One of Nadine's staff will bring the food to us late morning, uncooked of course. Then the rest is up to us. What do you reckon?'

'I say let's do it, Sis. What about the brass? How do we get paid?'

'Nadine already has the money. The Club Treasurer, Patti somebody, has already done the hard work. Nadine can transfer it to our account at the Blackbird Bank as soon as we give her the nod.'

'I can't see any downside can you? Tell her we'll do it.

I'll be back in Scarbados within the hour we can chat then. What about the wines?'

'Apparently we just supply a bottle or two for "supper wines" on the table. The wines to be presented will arrive in the afternoon with plenty of time to chill the whites. The members do all the pouring. Nadine said she'll also bring along a couple of members of her staff to help out – Rachel and Ashleigh I think she said their names were. They'll arrive after six-thirty and the members like to get proceedings under way, so that folks are eating, by seven-thirty,'

'Sis, ring Nadine now. I think we're going to enjoy this!'

For the first time in days, Jamie had a spring in his step. If all went well the resulting publicity would be marvellous. He had already donned his "marketing hat" and started to think ahead. He would also offer the diners and tasters some of those white wines left over from the Four Seasons' opening night. It would be a way of getting rid of some "bin ends" and hopefully create a good impression at the same time. Soon he would have to consider replenishing his wine stocks and now that his father had his head firmly on the move back to the Hotel Scarbados, it would all be down to him. Who knows, he might even make a contact or two at the tasting tomorrow night.

Jamie got the bus opposite the railway station almost all the way home.

'Hiya, Sis. I'm back. Anything else cropped up? I'm really quite excited about tomorrow. We've got twenty-four hours to make a perfect job of it. I've mulled over a few ideas on the train home.'

Millie smiled inwardly to herself. Whatever Clive had said to him had obviously done him the power of good. She hadn't seen him so enthused for a long time. She was so pleased and they still had the main chat with Clive to come in a few day's time. He'd called her while Jamie was on the train and Clive and Betty would arrive on Friday afternoon and stay until the Sunday. It was something to look forward to for all concerned.

'Right, Jamie, before I forget. Did you bother to look in the Suggestion Box that you spent so many hours fashioning from what Sebbie dug up?'

'Er no, why? To be honest I completely forgot.'

'Well here it is – only one suggestion from someone anonymous. I'll read it out.'

'Hi, we enjoyed the meal tonight – good food even if the service was a little slow.

Just one thing – try to remember to switch on the Four Seasons Restaurant light outside next time!
It can't have been cheap – use it!

'Oh my God! I can't believe that I forgot to switch it on. How stupid! I wonder if anyone else noticed? Or maybe they did but were just too polite to point it out. I wonder who the writer is?'

'Jamie, use your loaf. Read it again, especially that last line.'

The penny soon dropped with a thud.

'Of course, it must be Dave Gibson from We Are Neon Ltd. He knew what it cost to the penny. I'll call him and thank him.'

'I already have done. It was embarrassing that we couldn't accommodate them here that night but we were genuinely full. He and his wife are coming for a long weekend next month. It might be business and pleasure combined as he's going to fix the "NEW" sign up for Dad down at the Hotel Scarbados.'

'Are you sure we'll be able to accommodate them even next month I thought ..'

'That's another development during your temporary absence today. Just after lunch an email came in from BEH Head Office to say that funds were being made available to completely open the second floor of the hotel. That's twenty more letting rooms. All we have to do now is fill them with guests! Right, I'll pop the kettle on for a brew then we'll have a run through about what's to do for tomorrow night, OK?'

'Not another one of your famous "to do" lists, Sis? You used to drive me and Dad bonkers with those, you do know that don't you? Where is Dad anyway?'

'He's down at the New Hotel Scarbados – with a new "to do " list I gave him!'

The Yorkshire Tea was brewed, stewed and poured.

'Right Jamie, tomorrow. Firstly there are only six guests staying in for dinner tomorrow so we'll feed them in the small dining room first, say six-ish? I asked Nadine for a seating plan of sorts for the forty-four attendees but she says they never, ever have one. Apparently members just turn up and bag a seat next to a close friend. She says it often causes friction say when a bloke can't get a seat next to his wife or guest or whatever.'

'Mmmm, well it's not our job to be social engineers is it? If it was our permanent task I would suggest an online booking system, like a theatre. You'd be able to see what seats are already taken and then reserve yours accordingly. With only forty odd attending it would be a doddle wouldn't it?'

'Are you thinking what I'm thinking?'

'You mean like we could do our own wine tastings?'

'Wine not?! Let's see how tomorrow night goes first, Bro. Now, next on the list …'

19.

Peter returned from the New Hotel Scarbados just after five o'clock with No. 2 daughter Lucy and both dogs. Immediately on her return from the Vet's she had changed, grabbed both dogs' leads and walked straight down through Peasholm Park to the smaller hotel that would soon be her home once again. She simply couldn't wait and from the second of her arrival had bombarded her father with questions.

'Dad, when are we moving back in?

Dad, when are Stephanie and Natalie coming back to England?

Dad, am I going to have the same room as last time?

Dad, can Natalie have the room next to mine?

Dad, will Sebbie and AlfieBoy be allowed to sleep upstairs now?'

Peter was mentally drained. It was like Twenty Questions, an old radio programme, not that Lucy was old enough to remember it. Peter had an equally important question for his son when they entered from the car park.

'Hi Jamie, what's for tea? I'm starving!'

'Well it's good news on that front everyone. I made an impromptu trip to Beverley today and guess what I brought back – three guesses everyone? Don't all shout at once then.'

Lucy was the first to cotton on.

'Don't tell me! You went to Ye Olde Pork Shop. You didn't did you? Really?'

'Yes, and I remembered to get you some of those special veggie ones – tomatoes, fennel, chives and the rest. I'm going to have to use some of them for two guests tomorrow at a wine tasting evening we're hosting but there'll still be tons for you today and some to pop in the freezer too.'

'And what about Sebbie and AlfieBoy?'

'It's on their supper menu tonight too with creamy garlic mash and tinned tomatoes.'

'They won't like garlic!'

'Well they sure didn't complain last time they had it.'

'What? You never told me, that's not fair.'

'I thought you would approve – garlic's a vegetable after all, isn't it? Anyway, I'll serve our suppers at around six-thirty. Now, who's going to volunteer to help me peel the spuds for the mash?'

There were no volunteers – that's gratitude for you. Supper went down well, to put it mildly! Sebbie and AlfieBoy even hung around in the hope of "seconds" – some hope. It was perhaps a good thing that they didn't know that they were moving back to the old place soon and that a 24/7 friendly kitchen just a few sniffs away would be a thing of the past. After coffees Peter had a liitle announcement to make.

'Right, listen up everyone. This is important and affects us all.'

He sounded almost too serious so he decided to add a touch of humour and looked directly at the two dogs.

'Even you two, so pay attention. I've heard from Stephanie within the last twenty four hours that she and Natalie will be arriving quite a few weeks sooner than anticipated and ..'

'Horray, hooray. Oh that's great news. Dad. Did you hear that AlfieBoy? Natalie's coming home. Isn't that just wonderful news?'

Right on cue AlfieBoy barked out loud. Just the mere mention of Natalie's name, absent for many weeks, had initiated a sharp canine response. No matter that the word "sausage" might have had the same effect.

'When, Dad, when, when?'

'Be patient, Lucy, for goodness sake. I'm just working out the options.'

Everybody looked puzzled. Options? What options?

'OK it's like this. Consultations with Natalie's school in Bruges and with Scarborough College have brought about a change of plan. The original intention had been for Natalie to see out the summer term in Bruges and then she and her mother would come here some time in the summer, and Natalie would start her new school here in late September. However, it's been suggested by Scarborough College that it would be better all round if she could attend here for the last few weeks of the summer term, get familiar with her new school and surroundings before the summer holidays, and then in September it would be a seamless start to her new school life. Any comments?'

Millie felt only partly involved in all of this despite developing warm relations with Stephanie as best she could.

'In theory that sounds great Dad. But in practice how do they actually get here? Belgium has always been their home. They must have simply oodles of stuff, personal possessions, pieces of furniture even. That doesn't all get here on a magic carpet does it?'

'You're right of course, Millie. And there's the rub. With no direct Zeebrugge to Hull ferry any more it's going to take some thinking through. I've asked Stephanie to draw up some sort of manifest of what she wants to bring here. Cast your mind back to the awful hassle we had when we left Hull. We had great advice from that removal chap from Brid, what was his name again?'

'Clayton James! Dad, that's it! Ask Clayton if he'd be interested in doing the job. He can only say no thank you, can't he?'

'D'ya know what, you might have a point there. How far is it from Europort to Bruges, by road. Hang on, I'll Google it. Let's see – one hundred and seventy-five kilometres and about two and a half hours travel time. It's doable, you know that. Let's look into it in more detail before we contact Clayton, you know, ferry sailing times, costs etc. Let's do the research before we ask him OK?'

Everybody slept well that night, particularly Lucy who couldn't wait to see her half-sister again.

Millie was the first to rise next morning, or at least she thought she was. It was not yet seven o'clock but already the sun was streaming across the North Bay making the Sea Life Centre look like a white and gleaming Great Pyramid of Giza. She made herself some coffee and settled in front of her laptop. She wanted Clayton James to give this matter his fullest attention as soon as possible.

'Dear Clayton

I hope you remember us? It's the Fishburns here from the Hotel Koala in Scarborough. Remember you moved us a long while back from Kingswood in Hull to the Wendover Hotel near Peasholm Park?

We have another job for you to consider please. We have to move family effects from Bruges in Belgium to the same spot – now renamed the Hotel Scarbados. I have made provisional enquiries only from the ferry company that now operates the Hull to Europort sector. Arriving in Europort at approximately eight in the morning, it returns to Hull around six in the evening – in other words it has a ten hour turnaround time. Allowing two and a half hours drive each way to Bruges that gives you several hours to load up and drive back to Europort.

Please let me know if you think this is feasible?

If you decline I will of course quite understand. After all it is a bit unusual. Please call me me on my mobile number below if you would like a chat.

Regards.

Millie Fishburn'

Twenty miles to the south in an also sunny Bridlington, Clayton was just polishing off his last slice of toast when his wife came into the kitchen.

'Hey, Clayton. Remember that crazy lot you moved from Hull to Scarborough a long time back?'

'How could I forget! It was during the Covid pandemic and we got them moved during a snowstorm just in the nick of time. Why, what is it?'

'They want you to move some stuff to Scarborough again but this time from Bruges in Belgium.'

'You must be joking. Are they mad? Bloody Belgium?!'

'I'll read you the whole email word for word. Listen up.'

'Well, that's a new one, I must say. I think I'll call Millie now. Read out the number love and I'll dial it.'

'Gosh, hello Mr James. That was quick. I thought you might have a think over the weekend first. You do remember us then?'

'How could I forget? How many boxes of clothes did you and your sister initially want to bring? And all those sodding palm trees in the van too. How are you all anyway? How's your Dad, Peter isn't it? And that flippin' brother of yours forgot to empty his motorbike's petrol tank – that I do remember. What's with Belgium?'

'Mr James, let's just say that Dad left part of his family behind in Bruges and they're moving to Scarborough soon. There are no people involved as far as you're concerned – just stuff. It's unusual I'll give you that but do you think it's feasible?'

Millie, yes it's feasible all right. I have done a similar run before quite a few years ago. An antique dealer in Beverley successfully bid for all sorts of small pieces of furniture at an auction in a place called Sluis not far from Bruges. He got carried away, bought too much to bring back in his Volvo estate and he asked me to go and get it. That was when the ferry ran direct from Hull to Zeebrugge so it was a bit of a doddle really. Me and the lad even had time for a bit of sightseeing in Bruges. Remember that film a few years back called *In Bruges?* It was a bit quirky. Some bloke fell off that big tower into the square below. Anyway the lad wanted to climb up it to see for himself. It was quite an adventure. Now, thinking on my feet, there are several things to consider. How much stuff needs bringing back for starters? Will it all be pre-packed in those cubic metre boxes like you used? If so how many? And what about other stuff like items of furniture? How big are they and how many of them? Once you've given me the answers only then can I progress matters.'

'How accurate does this have to be?'

'Fairly accurate because only then can I make the decision as to which of my three vans to take. Then I can get a price from P & O Ferries and work out a quote. Then there's the little matter of HM Customs as we're no longer in the EU. Are you taking notes, Millie?'

'Yes, I am. I'll be onto Dad straight after breakfast to tell him to contact his 'friend' in Bruges as a matter of urgency.'

'I'll need measurements of any bits of furniture mind. Maybe then they can take photos and send them to you on WhatsUp or whatever it's called?'

'I'll see that's done over the weekend. Anything else you need to know?'

'Yes, dates. Give me some alternative dates as soon as you can. It's two overnight cabins, there and back, don't forget. It won't be cheap, I'll tell you now. I must go now, got a big job on today. My best to your Dad. Bye.'

Millie sighed and went to the kitchen for a coffee refill. Passing the main dining room door she was amazed to see Jamie already setting the tables for the meeting tonight of the Yorkshire Guild of Sommeliers. She kept silent for a few minutes as she watched him do his stuff. He had what looked like a wooden ruler in his hand as he moved from place setting to place setting. He was measuring the distance between wine glasses to the nearest millimetre. He looked like one of those Royal butlers before a formal banquet at Buckingham Palace. Millie decided to break the silence.

'Morning Bro. Coffee?'

20.

By late afternoon the main dining room looked absolutely splendid. There were six tasting glasses at every place setting, each one gleaming like Waterford crystal. Forty portions of chicken breast were almost ready for the pan, having been marinated in white wine and truffle oil for the last few hours. The supper wines the Hotel were providing were in the chiller, and Jamie rehearsed the few words he wanted to say about each one. He had selected a Chablis from France, a Frascati from Italy, a Riesling from Germany and a real rabbit out of the hat, a Chardonnay from Gozo, Malta's sister island. He stood back and took a final look at the tables before going back to the kitchen and re-donning his whites. Without him even knowing it, Millie took several photos of the room from several different angles. That might just come in useful later, she thought. She thought right.

Just before six-thirty a taxi pulled up in the car park. It was Nadine and her two staff members from the Crescent Gardens Hotel. Millie welcomed them all and showed them into the Bar for a little "snifter" before procedures got under way. They all settled for a dry Martini cocktail on the rocks and Peter obliged them in his own inimitable way. He had resurrected his old Steward's waistcoat and looked every inch the part.

'Ladies, I do hope you enjoy your evening with us – even if you are working. If you don't mind we'd prefer the Members to wait and assemble in the Bar first before I sound the gong for dinner. Is that all right with you?

Nadine gulped and smiled.

'A gong?! They don't get that at the Crescent Gardens I can tell you. I'll be interested to see how it goes. It's usually a mad rush for seats as soon as the more enthusiastic members start to arrive. And it can be a bit rowdy sometimes and the Chairman often has to intervene.'

Peter was appalled. They wouldn't have stood for any nonsense in the good old days of P & O First Class. He was suddenly interrupted by a smart middle-aged lady brandishing a posh leather briefcase.'

'Good evening, I'm Tilly Thompson, the Sommeliers Secretary. I take it you're the hotel porter are you?'

'The what? Well actually I don't really know what I am at the moment. Can I help you?'

'There's been a slight delay following a misunderstanding with the venue. All the tasting wines have been delivered to the normal venue, the Crescent Gardens, and not to here as I specifically requested. Gosh, this is so annoying. We've organised two taxis to solve the problem but as it's a Monday night and usually quiet, they only have one driver currently available.'

Peter thought quickly on his feet, something he'd had to do a thousand times at sea which was often in a choppy state.

'Can I suggest that the white wines are sent here first just in case they need extra chilling prior to being served, followed by the reds in the second taxi?'

'Good thinking. I'll call them now.'

Peter dashed into the kitchen to find Jamie about to perform his magic but took him to one side just in time.

'Jamie, looks like there's going to be slight delay …'

Back in the Bar, Tilly Thompson was about to have her first litter of kittens that evening. She was on the phone and becoming more agitated by the second.

'You are kidding me! I don't believe this. What do you mean only the red wines have arrived? And you're telling me that you have no idea where the whites are? I don't believe this is happening, I really don't. I'll wake up in a minute. I need a drink.'

Nadine did her best to calm things down.

'Look, this did actually happen once before a few years ago. A couple of Committee Members raced out to Morrisons to buy what wines they could at short notice. But you might not have to. Why don't you just ask Jamie Fishburn what he's got in his cellar here? In fact, even from where I'm standing I can see numerous bottles of whites in those posh champagne bowls. Let's go and take a wee look shall we? Any chance of a "top up" Peter? Thanks awfully.'

Jamie came out of the kitchen and into the Bar to talk with Tilly Thompson.

'Hi, I'm Jamie. Look, I hear you've got a problem with your white wines not arriving on time, is that right?'

'Yes, you heard right. It's an awful situation.'

'Listen, I can solve this for you, no problem.'

'You can? How?

Jamie led Tilly into the dining room and the champagne bowls containing the four bottles of white wine he had selected.

'See these whites here? I selected them especially as supper wines to get rid of them to be honest. I know a little bit about each one – enough to give a two minute speel, if you know what I mean.'

'Well that's very good of you but one bottle of each won't go very far will it? We've got a full house of forty-four folks tonight and …'

'Tilly, I have loads in the cellar. I've got at least six bottles of each in store. Let's act quickly and I'll get them shifted into the proper chillers. In fact your members can drink as much as they like within reason, to be honest. OK?'

'Jamie, that is not the sort of comment that I would like some of our members to hear, if you don't mind. Let's just say that a few of them are rather too "fond of the grape" so we'll just pretend that it's a normal night shall we? I'll tell our nominated pourers to be on the safe side. I'll pass the word around that due to a logistical problem there'll be a half an hour's delay and members can wait in the Bar and just generally have a nose around. Is that OK?'

'That's absolutely fine, Tilly. Right, I'd better get weaving.'

Jamie smiled to himself. His plans did not exactly overlap with Tilly's. If he was going to get the Sommeliers Club out of a hole then, by God, he and the Four Seasons Restaurant were going to take full credit and advantage for it.

A few cars started to arrive in the car park from members who were obviously intent on leaving them there overnight. Millie let Sebbie and Alfie Boy out for a wee before they started to get really busy and she couldn't help but see the nice shiny red Ferrari parked in a vacant slot nearest to the hotel's rear door. The owner had phoned an hour earlier to ask if it was OK to leave it there overnight, at his own risk of course. There were also a few Audis and Mercedes similarly parked. This lot must have a few bob, Millie thought to herself. They must be encouraged to come back to the Four Seasons and spend money on future occasions. She suddenly had a brilliant idea and when both dogs had finished their ablutions, she dashed back to her PC and desktop publishing feature. She had a job to do, and quickly too.

By just after seven-thirty the Bar was heaving with members, eager to commence the evening's proceedings.

The Branch Chairman, John Randerson, had a job making himself heard above the cacophony of the members' voices, accentuated not unsurprisingly by the consumption of more white wine than was normal. In fact quite a lot more. It all seemed to be on the house too, which to Yorkshire folk made it all the more enjoyable. A little earlier, Jamie had had a quiet word with both Rachel and Ashleigh.

'Just keep pouring it until the cows come home. If anybody asks just tell them these are foretastes of what's to come later. There are another four bottles of each opened in the champagne bowls and lots more in the fridges in the kitchen. I want them all well-oiled before they start to sit down. Jamie was not going to be disappointed. By the time his father Peter arrived with the gong to announce that dinner was about to be served the average consumption was slightly in excess of three glasses per capita.

'Bong-bong! Ladies, gentlemen, members and guests, please take your seats in the dining room. Please sit where you please. There are none reserved for Branch officers, Committee members – just one for Mary Onedin, a Director of Onedin Wines and a direct descendant of the founder in the late eighteen hundreds. She will also be talking us through the reds when the time comes.'

There were a few minor scuffles as the more inebriated members tussled over the seats with the best view over the North Bay and the Castle in the distance. Eventually Chairman Randerson managed to establish some sort of order over the masses but the tapping of a fork on the side of a tasting glass was almost totally inaudible over the collective din.

'Good evening everyone and thank you everybody for coming to the Hotel Koala and the Four Seasons Restaurant. Without further ado I would like to thank the Fishburn family for kindly providing us with this splendid alternative venue following the unforeseen difficulties over at the Crescent Gardens.

I'm delighted to welcome our guest speaker this month, Mary Onedin, who Mr Peter Fishburn has already mentioned to you. As you have probably gathered, Sod's Law has somehow diverted the intended selection of white wines to another destination, So, as you have already seen, these have been replaced by the Hotel's stock and I'm pleased to tell you that immediately after we have eaten supper Jamie Fishburn himself will give us all a little talk on each of the white wines that all of you have already been sampling – some more than others I'm guessing by the general lack of decorum amongst many of you, I'm sorry to say and ...'

He didn't finish as a sudden explosion of laughter emanated from the end table of eight members, where someone had just recounted a rude anecdote.

'Thank you. If you don't mind, you lot at the end there on the "Flaming Ferraris" table, I'd just like to finish the Parish notices. Thank you. Mary will then talk to us about the six red wines that her company has kindly supplied tonight which as is our custom will be in parallel with the serving of our cheeseboard tonight and ...'

Another rude joke had obviously just been told by another member on the same table of recalcitrants as before. Randerson decided to give up at this point.

'Anyway, I see the waitresses are coming in so enjoy your chicken suppers, or seafood alternatives, and I'll speak to you again later.'

Two hours later and the last of the members were leaving, all without exception in pre-booked taxis. Millie and Jamie were just chilling in the outside fresh air for ten minutes before turning in.

Crikey, Bro, what a night. What a rum lot eh? I wouldn't like to do that every month would you?'

'No, but you know what, if only half of them come back for a meal or two at some time in the future it will have been worth it. I mean, in reality, what did it cost us? A few broken glasses and a couple of dozen bottles of wine – at cost. And what were those cards I saw you printing and leaving at every place setting?'

'I didn't think you'd have time to read it so I've got one here. Let me read it to you.'

Dear member of the Yorkshire Guild of Sommeliers.

The management and staff of the Hotel Koala and the Four Seasons Restaurant are delighted to welcome you as our guests this evening. We appreciate the unique circumstances of the occasion and we have done our very best to accommodate you all.

As you know we are a newly-opened business and recommendations are highly prized. Can we thus please ask you to kindly take a few minutes to place a favourable Review on Trip Advisor? It would be very much appreciated.

I hope we can look forward to seeing you all again at some time in the future.

Wishing you all a safe journey home.

The Fishburn Family

'Wow, Sis, that's just brilliant. Come here and give your little brother a hug.

21.

After breakfast the following morning Millie and Jamie got their heads together – alone. Their father, Peter, had already disappeared down to the New Hotel Scarbados and taken both dogs with him, armed with his latest up to date "to do" list. Lucy had gone off to the Vet's as per normal.

'So Bro, lessons to be learnt from last night, as I see it anyway. Firstly, you can manage forty plus diners at a time. You proved that last night beyond a shadow of a doubt. We were undoubtedly helped by the "fixed menu" nature of the evening but, compared to the opening night, it went like a dream. We've already had an email in from Nadine thanking us helping them out last night. The members of the Sommeliers certainly seemed to enjoy themselves.'

'You can say that again, Sis. That bloke with the red Ferrari was quite a hoot wasn't he? His car's still outside by the way, I just checked. No doubt he'll be coming later to pick it up and then drive home – wherever home is.'

'I think he's fairly local. I don't think he commutes from Modena, do you?'

'Mod what? Where are you talking about?'

'Modena in Italy, where they make Ferraris.'

'And what did the Secretary mean about the Flaming Ferraris table? What did she mean?'

'I Googled it 'cos I didn't know either. Apparently in the City of London a couple of decades ago it was a slang term for a bunch of very successful wheelers and dealers who made squillions on the stock market, FOREX dealing and the like. It was said that they all bought Ferraris with their huge profits, drank champagne by the bucketful and smoked expensive cigars. – hence the moniker the Flaming Ferraris. That was way before our time. That couldn't happen in Scarbados of course. But there again, if I had to nominate a local industry that will profit more than any other over the next twenty years, then I would have to nominate the hotel and hospitality sector.'

'Crikey, Sis, do you really believe that or is it just wishful thinking? Be honest.'

'Jamie, the sky's the limit with what we can do here. Trust me. Don't forget that Clive's coming on Friday for an internal review of where we are. By the way, this will be a nice surprise for you, look at the screen here. I've just got Trip Advisor up on our page. You will see that the first two postings were those adverse ones after the opening night. Now feast your eyes on the next half a dozen. Go on!'

SOMMELIERS MEMBER

Five Star
Wonderful experience at the Four Seasons Restaurant last night. The food was cooked to perfection and splendidly served by attentive staff. Booking soon for our silver anniversary dinner.

LITTLE OLE WINE DRINKER ME

Five Star
The Four Seasons was our unexpected host last night for our monthly tasting. What a fab night. Great food, nice staff and copious volumes of wine. The Gozitan Chardonnay was my favourite. I must ask them where they source it. We'll come again.

Jamie was almost in tears. He was so happy.

'Right Bro, now just shift your eyes down to the last entry.'

A FLAMING FERRARI

Five Stars

What a great night at the Four Seasons. Apologies if I was a little raucous and out of order. But you know what they say – 'In Vino Veritas' – in wine there is truth! I'm going to contact the North of England Ferrari Owners Club secretary to see if we can organise our summer rally in Scarbados later this year, with the Hotel Koala as the Rally HQ. The back-drop of Scarborough Castle is just too good to miss for photo opportunities. I'll be in touch again soon. Thanks again.

Jamie's jaw almost fell to the floor. They were interrupted by a ring of the front doorbell and a shout from the postman.

'Postie here! Something to sign for please.'

'What? What is it?' exclaimed Millie. 'We never have anything to sign for.'

She used an electronic pencil on a screen about two inches square and by the time the thing had slid to all four corners of the two inch square her signature looked more like "Mashburn" that Miss M. Fishburn. No matter, the postman obviously didn't care if it was signed by a human being, an alien or a spider. He'd delivered it and that was that.

'What is it? Sis. It looks very official.'

'Well for a start, it's addressed to you not me so you'd better open it. Here's a sharp knife. It's sealed up like a haddock's bum.'

Jamie examined it at close quarters. He wasn't used to this.

'It's postmarked London WC1. Isn't that where Best Eastern's Registered Office is?'

'Jamie, just get on with it. Stop dithering. You're just like our father at times. So what is it?'

Jamie carefully unfolded the letter which was printed on high quality vellum. He was right, it was from Best Eastern's offices. It was only two paragraphs long and signed by Mr Albert Wong above his own personal "chop" in Chinese characters.

'Basically, Sis, it's a written offer of £340,000 for my shares in Hotel Koala Ltd.'

So, what are you going to do?'

'I'm not going to do anything, Sis. You are going to scan it, email it to Clive in Beverley and then shred it! Now please.'

Millie had never seen her brother act so positively in his entire life. It was an Epiphany moment. From this moment onwards they would never look back.

Tell you what, Bro. Let's go into town for a celebratory brunch. We'll go to that fairly new place called Café Seven in York Place. I saw on Trip Advisor that they do a mean Breakfast Bagel Stack. Neither of us had time for brekky so let's go for it. My treat OK?'

'You're on, Sis, you're on. Let's walk shall we, it's a fine day?'

They didn't just have a spring in their step – they had a summer and an autumn as well.

Café Seven was busy, very busy indeed. The proprietress, a young lady called Izzy in her early twenties, found them a table for two right at the rear in a sort of semi-conservatory area.

'Hi there, what can I get you?'

Millie spoke for both of them.

'Two Bagel Breakfast Stacks please, one Americano with cold milk and one hot chocolate please.'

'Sure, no problem. We can just about do that for you. Since somebody mentioned those Stacks on Trip Advisor we've had a run on them. I think we've done ten just this morning. We're going to move it from the Breakfast section on the menu to the All Day section. Are you two visitors here, by the way? Not seen you before, that's all.'

'Not exactly no. We run the Hotel Koala on the North Side, near the cricket ground.'

'Oh right, that's nice. I always like to meet other folks in the hospitality industry. We've all got to help each other, I say. Just excuse me a second.

'I'm sorry Sir. We do allow dogs but can you keep it in the front half of the café please? Thank you!'

'Sorry, where was I? I'd be happy to display a few of your Hotel's flyers for you. I don't suppose yours is a dog-friendly hotel is it? We're always getting asked by visitors.'

'To be honest, not really, no. But we have a sister establishment opening soon which will be dog-friendly in the extreme.'

'Brill, look pop in another time soon OK. Nice to meet you. A waitress will bring your orders soon.'

'You see, Bro. Trip Advisor is a tool to be used, not feared.'

By the time they got back to the Hotel Koala two hours later, there were four more favourable postings to read. Jamie's instructions to Ashleigh and Rachel had worked to perfection.

'Get them well-oiled before they even start.'

Marina was on Reception duty, waiting to be relieved by Millie.

'Oh. There you are. It's all been happening while you've been out to lunch. Where did you go anyway, anywhere nice?'

'Yes, we tried that newish place Café Seven in York Place. Their Breakfast Bagel was mega. I could only just finish it. So what's been happening then?'

'Well, firstly, that chap from the Cricket Club , Miles somebody, dropped this in for you. He said he was sorry he missed you and he'll call you later about an Australian cricketer who's arriving tomorrow.'

'He's got to be joking! Did he mean arriving in England or arriving in Scarborough?'

'He didn't know exactly.'

'What? He must know!'

'Apparently not. He said the Club had received an email late this morning from the chap saying he's arriving tomorrow. But is that his tomorrow or our tomorrow? He tried emailing him back but got no response. I Googled the time difference. Apparently Perth is seven hours ahead of British Summer Time.'

'Well I'm guessing then, that the chap's already in the air and is now un-contactable. We'll just have to play it by ear. We'd better have a room ready for him.'

'Done it, sorted. I've allocated him one of the newly opened rooms with a large window right alongside the 'Koala' on the front of the hotel. That should make him feel at home anyway.'

'Do they have Koalas in Western Australia? I've heard it's mostly desert with nice beaches! So what else did you say Miles brought with him?'

'I opened the envelope – it's the Club's fixture list for the forthcoming season. Here take a look.'

'Mmm, I see the first really big match here in Scarbados is Yorkshire vs Surrey from the 22nd to the 25th July. We must make sure that all the floors are fully open by then. With luck we'll fill all sixty plus rooms that week.'

'You can say that again Millie. On paper we're full already.'

'We can't possibly be.'

'Oh yes we can. Look at all these bookings that have come in by email this morning. Apparently the fixture list went live on the Club's website last night and as you know there is a link to our own website.'

'Oh my goodness. Can you please quickly check to see if a Mr & Mrs Fred Coates are included in those bookings?'

'Half a tick. Yes, here we are, their email was one of the first in this morning. Do you know them?'

'Indeed we do. They were amongst our first guests when we opened the Hotel Scarbados. Lovely old folks from Skipton way. They're absolutely cricket mad. I hope Fred remembers to bring his hearing aids. Any other news?'

'Yes, that lady from Bristol who spoke at the Sommeliers wine tasting, Mary Onedin I think, she says she's got an idea to put to you and she'll call you at the weekend. And so now you're bang up to date. I'm going off duty now, into town for a bit of shopping then home for some tea and put my feet up.'

Millie smiled the widest smile of her life.

'I told you, Bro. You and I are gonna make this place sing. No disrespect to Dad, but the sooner he, Lucy and the dogs move back into the Hotel Scarbados the better off we'll all be. Hey-up what's this other email Marina's printed out? She must have forgotten to mention it in the excitement of everything else. Oh look, it's from Clayton James, the removals guy. It looks like his quote for moving Stephanie's stuff from Belgium to here. I'd best give it to Dad as soon as he gets back here. Let's hope he's made some progress on his "To Do" list that I printed out for him.'

Some hope. He was next door at the Ritsons supping tea and munching on Shirley's famous fruit cake. Never mind, time was on his side. If only he'd seen Clayton's quote and the proposed dates of the move. If all went according to schedule, his former mistress and love-child would be back in Scarbados in less than two week's time.

22.

'Hello, is that you, Mr Carter?'

'Please, it's Miles after all this time. I'm sorry we missed each other late this morning.'

'No problem. Jamie and I were in town just having a quiet couple of hours to ourselves over a bit of brunch. Now then, thanks for the fixture timetable, we're onto it. In fact we're already fully booked for the first four-day match against Surrey.'

'What, already? You can't be surely?'

'Yep, already. Such is the influence of the internet and links between websites. So, Miles, our part of the deal was to act as host for your two overseas players. You told Marina that "Aussie Boy" is arriving tomorrow. Does that mean in England or Scarborough?'

'To be honest, we're not sure either. Maybe he's here in the UK already and doing a bit of sightseeing. As far as I know he's never been to England before. I'm sorry, I don't think we ever gave you his name did we? It's Graeme – Graeme Patterson. We did a video WhatsApp with him a long while ago. He had just come off the playing field and was smothered in sun block. You know how paranoid the Aussies are about too much sun. He's quite tall, six feet plus with blonde hair but the Western Australian sunshine is probably responsible for that.'

'Ha ha, he sounds like another Shane Warne from your description, bless him. Anyway we'll give him a warm welcome whenever he arrives. While I'm on, do you have any update on the young chap from Barbados, Courtney Morgan. When do you expect him to arrive?'

'Well jolly soon, we all hope. Our original No. 3 batsman announced yesterday that he's getting married next month and his intended is apparently unhappy with him committing himself to playing for the rest of the season. Leave it with me, Millie. Digressing, how's your Dad, Peter?'

'Oh, he's OK thanks. He's down at the Hotel Scarbados which he's about to rename by putting the word "New" in front of it.'

'You what? What's going on? You're kidding me! I thought that was all in the past.'

'Miles, I'll let Dad tell you when you see him. Let's just say he had a secret life in Belgium that the rest of us have only recently known about. To cut a long story short, he had a mistress called Stephanie and a love child called Natalie who is now aged ten. He and Lucy, Stephanie and Natalie are all going to live at the old place.'

'Crikey, the old snake! I'll pull his leg something rotten when I see him. Who'd have thought it, eh? Nod's as good as a wink and all that lark.'

'Well just go easy on him with the humour please. Obviously he knew about Stephanie but the love-child bit was hidden from him. So Jamie, Lucy and myself now have a new half-sister too. I'm sure it'll all work out in the end – it just takes a bit of getting used to that's all. While I'm on, is there anything at all you can tell us about this Graeme Patterson? You must know a bit more about him, surely?'

'Not a lot really. He's mid-twenties and his family own and manage some sort of motel near a place called Hillarys Boat Harbour. Actually, the wife and I have been there about ten years ago. We were visiting some of her cousins just to get a bit of winter sun but to be honest it was too darned hot for us. We didn't get any further than WA – that's short for Western Australia by the way. The Aussies either abbreviate or shorten everything. It's simply infuriating. Everybody was so laid-back it wasn't true. Nothing happens quickly out there and the joke is that WA really stands for Wait Awhile but never mind I'm sure you'll all get on well. He's here until the end of the playing season, about mid-September. I'll sign off now, Millie, and let me know when Graeme arrives safely please. My best to your Dad and tell him I'll catch up with him soon.'

'I will, Miles, and thanks for the heads-up.'

Five minutes later and Peter's car pulled into the hotel's car park. Within seconds the two dogs were running into the kitchen looking for an early tea.

'Hi Dad. You've just missed Miles Carter on the phone. The young Australian chap is called Graeme Patterson and he should be here by tomorrow. Oh yes, and here's an email for you from Clayton James. I've printed it off for you. It's quite long and I must admit I only took a cursory glance at it. Take it into the lounge and I'll bring you a cuppa. Then we'll talk about your "To do" list for the New Scarb ....'

'Millie, give it a rest, love. Now where's my reading glasses?'

'Exactly where you left them this morning – on the table when you were reading the Yorkshire Post and Yorkshire's fixture list.'

'You're beginning to sound more like your mother every day. OK, thanks, I'll be in the small lounge.'

Five minutes later and Millie took her Dad a mug of steaming Yorkshire Tea.

'So, what are the two bottom lines then?'

'Two? What do you mean two?'

'Well, let's be right, the only two things that matter are the cost quoted and the available dates.'

'Yes OK you're right, as always. The price is reasonable I think at £2,995 but it's not good news on the dates. The only days he can do it are either the weekend after next or the one after that.'

'Well, what's wrong with that?'

'I can't see Stephanie being ready to pack up and move in that short time frame? Can you?'

'Why on earth not? Look, Dad, I'm thinking out loud here but how's this for a idea? Why don't you fly over there and help her pack up, then fly back to England, all three of you together. I'm sure Natalie would love that. Why not?'

'Do you know what, that might not be such a bad idea. Yes, in fact the more I think about it the more I ...'

Peter didn't get to finish the sentence. Unbeknown to them both Lucy had just come back from the Vet's and was already looking for both dogs' leads.

'I heard all that. Brill idea, Millie. Just one thing though. I want to come too. Like Natalie, I've never been on a plane either.'

'And what about the dogs. Who's going to look after Sebbie and AlfieBoy? It could be two or three days. Millie and Jamie will be far too busy running this hotel. It's really hotting up.'

'We'll ask the Ritsons of course. It'll be like going home for AlfieBoy.'

Peter very quickly realised he was on a loser and relented.

'Oh all right then. I'll speak with Stephanie tonight then we'll fix the dates with Clayton. Let's go for the option two weekends away. It gives us a bit more time to plan.'

'Yes, Dad, and just how far down that "To Do" list have you got? Not very far I suspect. How was Shirley's fruit cake by the way?'

'What do you mean?'

'There's a sultana and at least two currants attached to your shirt – you must have plonked your elbow onto a plate or something.'

After supper Peter put in a long call to Stephanie in Bruges. She was delighted with the progress being made and the offer to come across and help in the last two or three days was especially welcome.

'Peter, Natalie will be over the moon when I tell her that Lucy is coming with you too. There's just a little problem that perhaps I should mention now. When the removal man Mr James asked for the list of everything to take, I forgot about the stuff in the garage plus two items but they're quite heavy.'

Peter's heart sank. Here we go again. It would be just like the nightmare of moving from Hull to Scarbados more than two years ago. Hadn't Clayton warned them that nearly everyone forgets what's in the garage and the attic.

'So what are they exactly? Heavy you say?'

'There's a small writing desk cum-bureau and a sort of sea chest except it's never been on a ship as far as I know. They both came from Africa and were brought back by my grandfather during the days of working for Sabena.'

'Heavy you say? How heavy?'

'Very. Both made from Rhodesian teak. Made from recycled railway sleepers I believe. When I moved them here from Antwerp the removal man said he would send me the bill from his osteopath. I never knew whether he was joking or not to be honest.'

'Well look, apart from the weight issue, just get me the overall measurements will you in centimetres. At least Clayton has gone metric. And have you worked out how many of those cubic metre boxes you'll be using? Are you sure you'll only need ten between you? Millie and Lucy started off by needing ten each at first. Then we almost forgot about Jamie's motor bike and ..'

'Oh yes, that reminds me, the bikes. We each have an electric bike, Natalie's is a junior one of course. We travel kilometres, or even miles, on them at weekends. They were gifts from my mother so they are special to us. We must bring them.'

Peter's worst fears were starting to unfold. Two years ago it was petrol in Jamie's motor bike that was an issue and a possible insurance problem to Clayton. Now it was electric bikes. He felt duty-bound to tell him. He'd read all sorts of horror stories about exploding batteries whist they were being charged up. He made a mental note to call Clayton later. Still, at least the dates were now fixed. He'd better start looking at online airline tickets to Belgium and back. Then another thing suddenly hit him. Did Lucy even have a passport? Glancing at the calendar on the kitchen wall he saw that he had sixteen days to sort everything. Now, where was that "To Do" list again? He pulled it out from his shirt pocket and as he did so another sultana fell out onto the floor. AlfieBoy didn't miss a trick and within two seconds it became just another doggy treat.

23.

The Trans Pennine Express train from Manchester, via York, glided almost silently past the world's longest platform seat and came to a halt at the buffers at the very end of Platform Number 1. Had it arrived an hour earlier it would have had to arrive at either Platform 2 or Platform 3 as the longest platform had been occupied by a "Scarborough Flyer" steam train on a special day excursion. It was the first one of the season and the attraction this time had been a locomotive called the Evening Star – the very last steam loco built for the old British Rail. It was normally in residence at the National Railway Museum in York but during the summer it was loaned for special occasions. It was a breeze-less day and the air still had a niff of steam and smoke from the proud old loco of yesteryear. At the very end of the train a suntanned young man in his twenties emerged onto the platform and gently lifted down two items of luggage – a large suitcase on wheels and what looked suspiciously like a long sports kit bag. Both bags sported a QANTAS Airways sticker and a LHR luggage label denoting Heathrow as the destination airport.

The man took his bearings as he glanced round three hundred and sixty degrees, taking in various views. He recognised the spire of the War memorial from the little research he had done online about the seaside town that was to become his home for at least the next four months, possibly longer. 'That must be that Oliver bloke' he muttered to himself – the highest point around here. It was a particularly long train – six carriages in all and it was few minutes before he found himself exiting the station concourse towards where he hoped he would find a taxi rank. There were at least six parties waiting for a taxi, all in the queue before him as he'd had the furthest to walk from the end carriage. Oh well, he would just have to wait. He felt distinctly cool and noticed the early signs of goose pimples on his forearms. Five minutes later and a white diesel Ford Mondeo pulled up almost under his nose. The driver jumped out to help his fare with his luggage, the boot lid having already been opened by the internal lever.

'Here, let me help you. Crikey, this is heavy. Are you telling me the airline allowed this? It's even got a "HEAVY" sticker on it.'

'Yih, I had to pay quite a large excess baggage charge – eighty-five bucks.'

'Bucks, what do you mean bucks? Been on holiday to Florida have we, Sir? You look nicely tanned I must say.'

'No mate. Never been to the States. I've just landed a few hours ago. I'm from Western Australia, not far from Perth.'

'And if you don't mind my asking, what's in the kit bag? It rattles a bit doesn't it?'

'Bats, mate, bats.'

The driver looked even more puzzled. He'd taken Goths to Whitby holding stuffed black bats.

'What kind of bats?'

'Cricket bats. What did you think I meant? Vampire bats?'

'Oh I see, right. Jump in my friend. Where to?'

'Hang on mate, I've got it written down. Here we are – the Hotel Koala, off North Marina Road.'

I think you mean North Marine Road. It's past the cricket ground then turn right. It faces the sea. Are you staying a week or two, may I ask?'

'Well unless they sack me and send me back home early I'll be staying about four months. I'm contracted to play for Scarborough Cricket Club for the whole of the summer season. Not much of a summer though is it? I'm frozen. I hope it warms up a bit. Do you mind if I sit in the front? I'd heard that most of you lot like to sit in the back of a taxi – you know like Royalty. Mind you, since poor old Betty passed away there won't be so much of that now will there? I'm Graeme, by the way. Graeme Patterson.'

'Charlie, Charlie Wagstaff. Welcome to Scarborough, or should I say Scarbados. Tell you what, as you're a new arrival I'll take you via the scenic route and the seaside. No extra charge and in any case I knock off shift soon. You're my last fare before I go home for some scran. I hope her indoors has knocked up summat nice. I think it might be some nice sausages and mash.'

We call them snags, mate. And who the heck is her indoors? Do you have a servant or something?'

'No, of course not! It's Yorkshire slang for a wife. Have you got one?'

'No way mate. I wouldn't like it if she told me I couldn't play cricket at the weekend because she wanted to go shopping in the City, say. No way! Is that a marina on the right?'

'Yes it is and Scarborough Yacht Club is based there. Why, do you sail?'

'Yih, in our summer I do. I borrow a mate's boat and sail out to "Rotto" for a picnic every now and again.'

'What is "Rotto?" That's a rum name.'

It's WA slang for Rottnest Island about twenty clicks west. Usually it's invisible in the heat haze.'

'Ha! Well you won't see any of that here. Mind you, we get something we call a 'sea fret' like a thick cold fog. It happens when cold air off the North Sea meets with warmer air off the land. Quite common, even in summer.'

'Well if this is summer I dread to think what your winters are like. No wonder you blokes go out to Oz for the winters. Perth's like a Pommy ghetto over Christmas time I can tell you. Heck, what's that big old building with no roof up there on the hill to the left, mate?'

'That's Scarborough Castle. Built in the eleven hundreds I think. Not sure, history isn't my strong point, to be honest.'

'No, mate, mine neither. In Australia you're lucky to find anything at all over a hundred years old. And in Perth anything over fifty years old – except people of course. I read somewhere that people in Oz live an average over twenty years longer than here in the Old Country. No wonder WA is full of you Poms who called it a day here and moved over. My great grandparents were Scottish and emigrated to Australia just over a hundred years ago. Ironically, they came from Perth in Scotland. He was in the Army in the Black Watch Regiment, so I understand anyway. Is that far from here, Charlie?'

'Well yes, it's probably about two hundred and fifty miles north, I'd say.'

'Mmmm, well that's only about five hundred clicks isn't it. That's just up the road as far as most Aussies are concerned. I'll borrow a 'ute and drive up there when there's no matches on. Crickey, what are those, the white pyramids I can see in the distance? Looks like a mini-Egypt!'

''That's Scarborough's Sea Life Centre. It's got quite a name. They rescue injured seals and porpoises, not to mention the odd turtle. It's worth a visit, I can tell you. We're not far from the Hotel Koala now. We turn left past those swanky apartments then up the hill to the left. There look! You can see it now. Two minutes and we'll be there.'

Charlie pulled his white taxi into the car park of the Hotel Koala, finding a slot not too far from the rear door.

''This is it, Graeme. Take a look at that sea view. It's a very clear horizon today.'

'Isn't it just. I can see lots of surfers in the water so it must be quite warm, is it?'

'Er no, quite the opposite. If you were down there at sea level you'd see that they're all wearing wet suits. Although it's a fine sunny day the sea temperature is only about ten Celsius. So be warned. Don't have any ideas about swimming to Denmark – that's the next stop over the horizon by the way.'

'How far is it?'

'About four hundred nautical miles I think.'

'Oh, no problem mate. That's just "up the road." They both laughed.

'How much do I owe you for the fare, Charlie?'

'Nothing mate, it's on me. And you buggers don't tip in Australia anyway. So I've heard.'

'You heard right. But listen, give me your card and I'll meet you for a couple of schooners one night. Do you live far away?'

'Not really. I live in Castle Road – that's up near that old building with no roof as you put it!'

'Cheers, Charlie. I'll be in touch after I've settled in.'

Graeme carried his two bags into Reception and approached the only human being in sight – a pretty redhead in her early twenties.

'Hello, can I help you?

'G'day, I'm Shane Warne.'

'Yeah right, and I'm Liz Hurley! You must be Graeme Patterson and my real name's Millie Fishburn.'

'Hi Millie, can I call you Bluey? Is that OK?'

'Bluey? Why on earth do you want to call me Bluey?'

'Oh well it's a common nickname Down Under for anyone who's got red hair, male or female. I guess it's just Aussie humour, you know.'

'No, I don't know and if you ever call me Bluey I'll call you Bruce, OK?'

They both laughed like drains. They smiled and shook hands politely. There was no ice to break. The attraction was mutual and instantaneous.

'So, Millie, that's a deal – no more Blueys and no more Bruces. Are you just working here for the summer season, Millie? I take it you're from Scotland with lovely hair that colour?'

'No I'm not! Not all redheads are Scots or Irish you know. Both my parents are originally from Hull and the reddish hair almost certainly comes from Viking genes – so you'd better look out! And no, I work here permanently. I'm just one of two family members who stayed on as working shareholders following a partial buyout by Best Eastern Hotels. The other one's my brother Jamie and he's also Head Chef.'

'Crikey, so you're one of the bosses. I'd better watch out what I say. Heck, I'm suddenly starting to feel really tired. It was a long flight.'

'Jet lag! I've never travelled far enough to get it. How long was the flight anyway?'

'Let's see – maybe twenty hours. If I was still it'd be … er I think about midnight. No wonder I'm starting to nod off.'

'Take a look at all those clocks over there … over there!'

'Graeme strode a dozen paces to his right and stared at the one the farthest to the right.'

'It says two o'clock in the morning! Oh hang on, that's Melbourne time. Taking two hours off to make it WA time and it's midnight. So I was right! What have you got six clocks for anyway?'

'Well if you take a look at the little brass tags beneath each clock you'll notice that they're all great cricketing centres aren't they? Well aren't they?'

'Well I think that as a matter of courtesy to your new guest you should replace Melbourne with Perth don't you? You wouldn't know this but the "east coast mob" as we call them, look down on folks from WA, they even call us "sand gropers" can you believe that?'

'Why do they do that? That's not very nice is it?'

'Well, to be honest, there is a lot of sand in WA and as a result the soil's not very good. But as a result we do have fab beaches. We even have one called Scarborough Beach.'

'Wow! Is it as big as our beach here?'

'If it's the one the cabbie just drove me past, then I'd say that ours is about ten times as long, maybe more. Listen, if you don't mind, I really need some shut eye. If you tell me what room I'm in I'll make my own way …'

They were interrupted by the sound of Peter's voice and the entry into Reception of the two dogs who immediately made a bee line for the newcomer on the off chance of a treat from a stranger.

'Graeme, you'd better meet Sebbie and his son AlfieBoy. Oh yes, and this is my Dad, Peter Fishburn. Dad, this is Graeme Patterson, our cricketing guest from Western Australia.'

'Hello, Graeme, and welcome to Yorkshire – God's own county. I see you've been chatting up the staff already!'

'Hi, Peter, er Mr Fishburn. You have a charming daughter.'

'Thank you. Well I've got two more in reserve if this one isn't suitable.'

He winked at Graeme who winked back. In the years ahead Peter would look back on this conversation and ponder whether he had chosen the right words.

24.

With his body clock in ruins and his brain still set on Western Australian Time, Graeme awoke at first light just after 6AM. It took him more than a few seconds to realise where he was. Immediately absent was the hum of the twin General Electric turbofans that had powered the Dreamliner all the way from the Antipodes to the Old Country. It was eerily silent until a passing herring gull screeched past his window en route to the harbour and perhaps a tit-bit of shellfish cast from a fishing boat. He filled the kettle provided to make some tea and then stepped into the en-suite bathroom for a shave and a shower. Unlike most of his sporting contemporaries, who seemed to prefer three days growth of stubble on their chins, Graeme liked a clean-cut appearance. In any case, sun block didn't look good atop the human equivalent of a long-haired possum. He opened the curtains and was stunned by the vista in front of him. The sun had risen and was just starting to climb above a clear horizon. The distant Sea Life Centre, recently clad in solar panels to appease the eco mob, reflected beams of sunlight in numerous directions. He would take the cabbie's advice and take a walk there soon. But first he wanted to visit somewhere on his own. He finished his cup of tea, got dressed in appropriate clothing and crept down stairs. Guessing correctly that no staff would be on duty yet he unexpectedly found the main door unlocked and stepped outside. He had looked on Google Maps and knew that the cricket ground was left and left again along North Marine Road. The sun was rising quite rapidly now on his left and was gaining altitude to the right. This floored Graeme completely until he realised that, of course, he was now in the northern hemisphere and that at noon, the sun would be in the south, and not the north. He walked past the little cinema called Hollywood Plaza and crossed over the road. He knew he wasn't far from his destination when he spotted a small hotel called, appropriately, the Boundary Hotel. There could only be one reason why it had that name and Graeme quickened his pace in hopeful expectation of finding what he was looking for. He almost walked straight past the main entrance to Scarborough Cricket Club without realising it. It was only the familiar sound of a large mounted grass cutter that caused him to look to his right. He strode up to some tall iron gates and was mesmerised by what he saw in front of him. Having seen photographs on the Club's website he knew roughly what to expect but this was beyond his wildest expectations. Seeing that the gates were unchained and partially ajar, he pushed one side open. They parted without the slightest creak. Somebody had had the oil can out. He walked twenty odd metres to some plain wooden bench seating, sat on the top row, and just admired the view. The grass was the greenest green he had ever seen. Suddenly the noise from the mower ceased and the driver dismounted and started to walk in Graeme's direction. Was he trespassing? After all he hadn't really checked in at the Club yet had he? The driver was almost at the white boundary rope when he stopped and cupped his two hands together to fashion an impromptu loud hailer.

'Morning! I don't suppose you've got a light have you, Pal?'

'Sorry mate, I don't smoke. Maybe you could rub two Boy Scouts together?'

By now the two men were only a few metres apart and something suddenly dawned on the driver of the mower.

'Don't tell me you're the new chappie from Australia are you? With a tan like that and an accent like that it must be. Graham somebody?'

'That's me, mate. Graeme Patterson. I just arrived last night. Apart from the cab driver and a handful of staff at the Hotel Koala, you're the first person I've met. 'Ower yer going mate? Pleased to meet you.'

Graeme's handshake was like an iron vice.

'Blimey, I hope you can grip a bat like that. I'm Steve Dodds, head groundsman. Does the Club actually know that you've arrived yet?'

'Dunno, mate. I got my Mum to send an email to the Treasurer, Miles somebody.'

'That'll be Miles Carter. He's the font of all knowledge around here. There's a Committee of course but he's the head honcho, if you know what I mean? He controls all the brass so effectively he runs the whole show. So how come you're up so early anyway?'

'Jet lag mate. Listen, do you fancy a cuppa? I noticed a café just opening down the road opposite the cinema.'

'Good idea. I'll pinch a light there too although I'll have to smoke my roll-up outside. It's hard to believe that twenty years ago tobacco companies were major sponsors of cricket tournaments. Now they're treated like pariahs.'

'Yih, same back home mate. Breweries used to be our Club's main backers but now it's Banks and "Muesli-munchers" as I call them – you know health bar manufacturers.'

''You mean concrete oats stuck together with mortar?! Talking of summat to eat, let's get a bacon butty with our teas shall we?'

Less than five minutes later and they were in the Viking Café with two steaming mugs of tea and two bacon sandwiches were on the way.

'I take it that a butty is a sandwich then Steve?'

'You've got it, Graeme. It'll take you a while to pick up the local chatter. By the time you've learnt most of it you'll be on your way back Down Under. Unless you decide to stay on, that is.'

'Well, I've got a visa that's no problem as I'm under thirty and qualify as a "young person" under the new Rules. I'm contracted to play for the Club until mid-September. I think my first match is a week on Saturday at a place called Driffield. How far away is that?'

'It's about twenty miles south of here. It's a market town with a very strong team. They were league champions last year. And by the way, I did hear a rumour that your first match might be this coming Saturday. One of our all-rounders has pulled a muscle and it's highly unlikely he'll be fit in time.'

'Crikey, well I'm not sure I'll be ready. This jet-lag can last for days apparently. And apart from that I'm a bit rusty. Not swung a bat or bowled a ball for two weeks. And by the way, what on earth are you doing mowing the wicket at the crack of dawn anyway? We only do that back home to avoid the heat of the day. That can hardly be the reason here, now can it? I've got permanent goose pimples and it's early summer. I think I'll need to wear at least one jumper when I'm out in the field. When the heck does it warm up here?'

''We have a saying in Yorkshire – nay cast a clout until May is out.'

'What the heck does that mean?'

'Opinion is split on that one. Some say it means wear a jumper until the end of May – others say wear a jumper until the Mayflower is out in the hedgerows.'

'So which is it?'

'Dunno, Graeme. Hey-up the butties are here. Now, tell me, what do reckon to your first taste of Yorkshire bacon eh?'

'Bonza! Absolutely bonza!'

Steve looked puzzled and said nowt else until they both finished eating.

'Any road, what did you make to your first views of the ground this morning? Did you like it?'

'Mate, it's mega impressive. It's very much bigger than my Club's ground I can tell you. How many people can you get in?'

'When Yorkshire are playing one of their four day County games here we can get about eight thousand. But that's only a couple of times a year. And a lot of the folks are on holiday here at the same time so if the weather's good it's a full house. Years ago, before my time, I understand that the side touring England that summer, whether it was Australia, the West Indies or whoever, would always play their last match here at Scarborough before flying home. In the Pavilion there are some wonderful pictures of those teams on display. There's one in particular that would interest you I'm sure, Graeme.'

'Yih, which one?'

'It's of the 1961 Australia Touring Team taken right here. Guess who the Captain was?'

'No idea mate.'

'Richie Benaud. He loved Scarborough and for many years after he stopped playing he came back here for the annual Scarborough Cricket Festival.'

'No way. Wow! Thanks for telling me. I had no idea that Scarborough Cricket Club was held in such high esteem. When I accepted the offer to play here for a summer it was to give me the chance to travel and gain a few life experiences. I'm absolutely gob-smacked, mate. Isn't that a phrase you use here? Am I right?'

'Yes, you're picking up the local lingo nicely. Heck, look at the time! I'd best be off and finish that mowing. There's light rain forecast for this afternoon and it'll do it no end of good – if I get it finished. Cheers then Graeme. I'll see around the Club soon I'm sure. The tea and butties are on me, I've paid the bill. Welcome to Scarbados my new Aussie friend.'

Graeme crossed the road and walked back to the Hotel Koala. With luck the early staff would be on duty by now and he wanted to ask Millie a few things like where he could change some Aussie dollars into sterling. Then it dawned on him that he had almost no English money bar a few one pound coins. It was just as well the taxi ride and the early breakfast had been paid for by generous locals.

He strode through the main door and was happy to see the flash of red hair from behind the Reception desk.

'Morning Millie, or should I say G'day in my lingo … oh sorry I thought it was Millie.'

'Good morning, no I'm Marina. It's Millie's day off today. I think she took an early train to York to meet Chloe, that's her brother Jamie's girlfriend. If I know Millie it'll be coffee, shopping, lunch and then more shopping before the train home. Can I help you? It's Graeme isn't it? From Australia – you're a cricketer. Actually, Millie did leave you a note. I was under strict instructions not to wake you up as you're still recovering from the long flight. Here it is – it's her phone number and just a few scribbled words. Anything else I can do for you Mr er, Graeme?'

'Er well yes there is. Where can I change some Australian dollars into sterling? Where's the nearest bank or Bureau de Change?'

'Ha ha! This is Scarborough not Sydney! You'll need to get to a bank in town. By the way breakfast is available now in the main dining room. You're certainly up with the larks aren't you?'

'Well I've already had a good chat and a bacon butty with the head groundsman. The early bird catches the worm. Isn't that what they say?'

Marina wasn't sure if he was pulling her leg or not. She'd heard that Australians had a laconic sense of humour. It was only just after seven o'clock. How could he possibly have done that?

Graeme took the lift up to the top floor and read the note from Millie as it ascended.

'Hi Graeme, I hope you slept well. I'm not on duty this evening so if your body clock is up to it how about a little walk and a drink in a local hostelry. This is my mobile number – if you've got a UK sim-card in your phone. If you haven't then get one!

Millie.'

25.

It proved to be quite an eventful morning for Peter. The information as to the amount of furniture and boxes required had come in by email from Stephanie in Bruges. It transpired that there wouldn't be a problem with electric bikes as long as the batteries in them were run down to zero. The weights of the "sea chest" and the desk were still unknown but it probably didn't matter as long as the dimensions were accurate. It looked as if ten one cubic metre packing boxes would suffice and Stephanie would have to acquire those locally and have them packed and "good to go" as the turnaround time in Bruges would be limited. Clayton had estimated that his three ton van would be adequate for the job and confirmed the booking with the ferry company for a week the following Friday. Sailing early evening, they would arrive in Europort around eight in the morning and be in Bruges for eleven. With an allowed turnaround time of three hours maximum, it should be a doddle to get back to Europort for the seven o'clock sailing back to Hull. In theory anyway. But Clayton's wife, who did all the paperwork, still wasn't too happy with the still unknown weight of the two pieces of furniture. Something was nagging in her head and then she suddenly remembered. They had moved some furniture on a previous occasion made out of reclaimed Rhodesian Railway sleepers and they'd had problems. So she decided to thumb through some old invoices to try and jog her memory. Her immaculate alphabetic record keeping of former clients had soon enabled her to check who the client had been and where he hopefully still was today. They had assisted a Mr Stuart Abbott when he and his family had moved back to England after a long stint of living in South Africa. The manifest had included a dining room suite of a two and a half metre table, eight standard dining chairs and two carvers. Plonked on the end of the manifest was something called a settle – a sort of indoor park bench that could seat two to three people. Maybe that would be about the same weight as the bureau? She decided to check and phoned Mr Abbott.

'Hello, Mr Abbott? It's Clayton James' wife here. We moved a lot of your African furniture from Hull docks to Scarborough for you a couple of years back.'

'Oh yes I do recall. How is Clayton? I hope he got his vertebrae sorted out …. only joking!'

'Mr Abbott, that's why I'm calling actually. We're helping a new client move some furniture from Bruges in Belgium, back here to Scarborough via the ferry from Europort to Hull. The lady in question has two items of furniture she says are made from Rhodesian teak, reclaimed railway sleepers and …'

'Gosh, do I remember that or what?! It's the heaviest wood in Africa, if not the world. It's not a dining suite is it?'

'No, its a bureau or desk of some kind – over a metre long. Oh yes, and what the lady describes as a sea chest. Apparently both items came from the Belgian Congo over sixty years ago and have been in Belgium ever since. The original owner, the lady's grandfather was apparently a pilot with SABENA, and based there for years in the Congo right up until Independence in 1960.'

'Mmm, well it was well-dodgy place in those days. He probably got out in a hurry and the bits of furniture will have been shipped out, probably to Antwerp. So how can I help you exactly?'

'It's the weight we're worried about and which van to use for the job.'

'Well from your description that bureau could easily weigh a few hundred kilos with the sea chest a bit lighter. Do you know if they're empty? That would make a big difference too? Anyway, as I recall you used one of those trucks that has an electrically powered lifting platforms at the rear. Do you still have it in service?'

'We certainly do. It's not used often but we keep it in our fleet just for jobs like this. We probably won't use anything like its capacity but the powered lift might prove invaluable. Thanks for your help, Mr Abbott.'

'You're welcome and my best to Clayton please.'

Mrs James made a call to the ferry company to slightly alter the booking arrangements to allow for the longer and heavier truck. They would have to increase the Invoice estimate too, in line with the ferry company's bill. She emailed the new information to Peter at the Koala within a few hours although he was actually down at the Hotel Scarbados at the time, struggling with amendments to his "To-do" list that his eldest daughter Millie had printed out for him prior to her departure on a shopping trip to York with Chloe. Even though he was checking items off as he progressed with the various jobs, every time he gave it to Millie it seemed to be longer whenever she handed it back. The latest amended list was headed up TEN DAYS TO GO meaning that was his departure date for the flight to Brussels for himself and Lucy. They'd had to make a special application for Lucy's passport to be issued as an emergency – and pay an extra fee of course. Didn't all Government departments seem to rip you off at every available opportunity?

Glancing down at the "To Do" list for the umpteenth time that morning he decided to try and prioritise the items that were essential and his eyes fell first on matters concerning the boiler system. Was it still in full working order? Although it was early summer and heating unnecessary, there would be hell to pay from the three females if there was no hot water. It was only just beginning to dawn on Peter what it would be like. He would only have Sebbie and AlfieBoy for male company most of the time. Jamie would be fully occupied at the Koala, particularly as it got busier with the summer build-up. Peter had never lived without his son at his side, that is when he wasn't at sea. They would only be a mile apart, or less as the seagulls fly, and he hoped they could make time to be be together. Realistically though, he was coming to realise that Jamie's relationship with Chloe was slowly taking on more significance. Not for nothing had Jamie gone out of his way to ensure that his mother had not only attended the opening of the Four Seasons restaurant but that she had been introduced to Chloe. If the relationship was to progress beyond the boyfriend/girlfriend level then Jamie would want his mother's approval.

The boiler fired up at the first touch of the correct button and both heating and domestic hot water were tested for half an hour. Another 'tick' on the flippin' list. Next on the list was to switch on the freezers and fridges, not they would be required until all four of them arrived back in Scarborough. Bedrooms and bedding were next on the List so he started to make his way upstairs to the owners' accommodation. He was just halfway up the first flight of stairs when he was interrupted by the front doorbell and the sound of the main door opening followed by a familiar voice. It was Garry Ritson.

'Hey up, Pete! I thought I heard your car arriving in the drive. Your exhaust sounds like it needs a bit of attention by the way.'

'Morning, Garry. Yes, I know. It's got more than a few dints in it too. When it's all settled down I might follow your lead and get a small 4x4. Not sure at the moment what cash will be available.'

'Does Stephanie drive?'

'Do you know what, Garry, I'm not sure. It hadn't even occurred to me! And even if she does she'll be driving on the wrong side of the road for months, now won't she?'

They both laughed and conjured up images of Stephanie driving on the right hand side of Scarborough's highways.

''Well look, keep the old car you've got now and let her use it. Get a new one just for you and the dogs! And has Lucy been badgering you yet about learning to drive? '

'Oh God, you've got me thinking now. Oh heck. I think I need a coffee.'

'That's the main reason I've popped round, Pete. Shirley's just made a big fresh pot. Come on mate, put that flippin' List down. You need to "take five" or even a bit longer.'

Two minutes later and they were all in the Ritson's comfortable front room.

'Thanks, Shirley, but I'd best pass on the fruitcake. Apparently I took some of it back home on my shirt sleeve last time and Millie spotted it. She doesn't miss a trick. This "To-do" list is really getting me down. Look.'

'The bedding is the main problem, love. Listen, when we've finished coffees I'll pop round with you to see what needs to be done. I can look at it with a fresh pair of eyes. The last thing you need is stale bedding. It probably hasn't been looked at for months, you know, when the Hotel was unoccupied and under the control of the Home Office wasn't it?'

'I'm not sure, Shirley. What a carry on it was. It's only nine more days before we're moving back in. And all the other items on the List are never ending.'

'Peter, it's one step at a time. Come on, supp up and show me the rooms you want to occupy first. Will it be three or four rooms?'

'She smiled and winked at Garry.'

'Er, well three I think!'

'Come on. There's no time to lose. Within a couple of days those rooms will be fit for a Queen and two Princesses. We'll drive out to Dun Elm this afternoon. Fold down the back seats on your estate car and bring a debit card. It'd be the thick end of a grand by the time we've finished.'

Peter swallowed a gulp.

'A grand? On a few sheets and pillows?'

'You men just have no idea do you? Pick me up at two o'clock sharp. But first I want all the beds stripped to the mattresses and all the windows wide open. Everything needs to be aired. And them windows all need cleaning too. Garry, get onto that new Polish chap will you – you know the one who uses his own water from a van and has all those long poles like giant fishing rods. All the windows need doing badly. The seagulls have had a field day while it's been empty for the last few months. You can get your own back on Millie by telling her she missed "windows" off her supposedly accurate list. And she's also missed carpet cleaners off the list too. They'll all need to be done. Garry, where's that number for that firm we used last time …?'

By the time Peter drove back to the Koala for a snack and a check on any emails, he was in a much better frame of mind.

Marina, on duty at Reception, passed him the slightly amended and increased estimated invoice from Clayton James. He was still happy and it was best to be play safe with the bigger truck which also boasted the lift.

'Oh yes, and the travel agent in town called you about the flight tickets to Brussels. She thinks you made a mistake in only wanting two outward tickets but four return tickets. I put her right, don't worry. Also, she wanted to know if young Natalie was travelling with her own passport or on her mother's. I didn't know, so I said you'd call her back. Is that OK?'

Peter didn't know either. Oh heck. He immediately sent a WhatsApp message to Stephanie and awaited a reply with trepidation. He didn't have long to wait.

'No problem Pete, honey. She travels on my Belgian passport.'

Phew, one less thing to worry about. Or so he thought.

26.

After walking into town from the Koala, Graeme started to get his bearings in the seaside town that was to be his temporary home for the next four months. He soon found a branch of the Dogger Bank plc in the same street as the Town Hall and changed a thousand Australian dollars into pounds sterling. He was pleased with the rate of exchange and walked out with just over five hundred pounds – enough to last him a while and until the first fee payments came in from the Club. Then it suddenly dawned on him that he didn't have a UK bank account. He turned round at the end of the street and walked back to the bank to speak with a member of staff in the banking hall. Her badge revealed her name as Vikki and she was very helpful but couldn't help him in the immediate term. Opening a bank account for a foreign national was not as simple as it used to be what with money laundering regulations and all the associated red tape that seemed to go with everything connected with money and banking these days. Nonetheless, she went through the motions of taking his name, UK address, mobile phone number and other details and promised to get back to him within twenty four hours. Then he remembered that Millie had told him to get a UK compatible sim-card for his phone.

'Thanks er, Vikki, but I don't think my Aussie phone number will work here! Any ideas?'

'Try Vodafone. Go out of the bank, turn left and left again and it's on your left about two hundred yards up the road – that's metres to you, by the way!'

'Thank you, Vikki. So I chuck a left twice and it's on my left. Yes? I'll pop back here when I've got a Pommy phone number. Cheers.'

As he walked out of the door one of the cashiers behind a glass screen shouted out to Vikki.

'Hey Vik. I've just realised who that was. He's the new Australian cricketer who's going to play for Scarborough this season. I saw his picture in the Scarborough News last week. What a hunk! I wonder where he's staying? Oh, go on, tell me. I wouldn't mind a date with him!

'You're such a tart, Shazza! Get back to polishing your nails. I met him first. I've got first dibs.'

Graeme found the Vodafone shop within a few minutes and walked in. It was quite busy but one female attendant was free. Her name was "Liv" by her name badge.

'G'day, I wonder if you can help me please? I'm working here in the UK for the next few months and I'm hoping you'll be able to advise me on getting a sim-card for my Australian phone.'

'I'll sure try – show it to me please. Gosh, never seen one like this. What's it called a Telstar you say? I thought Telstar was a satellite, not a telephone.'

'No, its a Telstra, not Telstar. It's the biggest phone network in Australia.'

'Just a minute, please Mr er ...'

'Patterson, Graeme Patterson. Graeme's fine. We tend not to stand on ceremony Down Under.'

'Yes I know, you can say that again. I went to visit cousins in Melbourne for Christmas last year. It was far too hot. They took me to the MCG – the Melbourne Cricket Ground – on Boxing Day. It was so hot they had to take drinks breaks every half an hour. Here it's "rain stopped play" not sunshine stopped play. Do you play by any chance, Graeme?'

'Yes, I sure hope so. I'm one of the two new overseas players for Scarborough Cricket Club this season.'

'Wow! I must come and see you play. Anyway, look, about your phone. My advice to you is to keep this Telstra thing quite as it is. Just use it for communicating with your folks back home you know, WhatsApp etc. While you're here in UK I recommend you buy a "Pay as you go phone" which you can top-up easily using a bank debit card ...'

'I haven't got one yet, mate. I've just come from the Dogger Bank down the road. I desperately need a UK phone number. How long will it take to get me one?'

'About as long as it takes you to finish the coffee I'm just about to pour you. Milk and sugar?'

'Thanks – make it a long black please. No Sugar.'

Liv had heard of a flat white but never a long anything, not connected with coffee amyway. Three minutes later she came back with a black coffee which she hoped was 'long' enough and a shiny box with a brand new phone in it.

'Here you go Graeme. You drink your coffee while I set this phone up on our system. Shall we say fifty quid of credit on it for the time being? That should last you weeks, as long as you stick to voice calls and texts within the UK. This is the new number for you. I'll write it down on this card and you can pop it in your wallet. 0 777 etc.'

'Thanks Liv, that's a weight off my mind. Apart from the Bank, the Cricket Club and the Hotel where I'm staying all need to know this number. Actually it will be easy to remember as I flew here on a triple-seven and they're the first three digits aren't they?'

Liv gave him one of those "what the heck are you on about" looks. First there was a 'long black' and now a 'triple-seven.' She worked out the total amount to pay.

'Right, that's exactly ninety-nine pounds please, Graeme.'

He reached into his wallet and lifted out five twenty pound notes that he had just acquired from the Dogger Bank.'

'Oh sorry, I should have said beforehand. This is a cashless branch. We only take plastic.'

'But I've only just arrived, I just explained to you.'

'Go back to the bank and purchase a pre-paid debit card for a hundred pounds. I'm sure they'll do that for you. I'll put it behind the counter for you.'

Graeme sighed, drained the last of his coffee and walked briskly back to the Dogger Bank. Fortunately the friendly Vikki was still on the front desk.

'Hi again, I'm back. I've got a phone number but not the actual phone because they don't take cash – sterling or Aussie dollars. Here's the number look. Now apparently what I need is pre-paid debit card valued at a hundred Pommy pounds please and then I can collect my phone and …'

Vikki tried really hard to keep a straight face but failed.

'I'm so sorry, but as a non-registered alien from the Antipodes and under Section 1234 of the Money Laundering Act of 2024, I'm not allowed to issue you with …..'

Her face cracked and she couldn't keep up the act any longer.

'I'm only joking, Mr Patterson, no problem, I can do that for you. Two hundred pounds did you say? Then you can take me out for dinner one night! Only joking but you do realise that I now have your personal phone number don't you and English girls are not as reserved as you might imagine? Perhaps you can pop back in tomorrow as I need to scan your passport before we can open you a proper bank account. The sooner you do that the quicker we can complete the red tape. Of course we wouldn't have this problem if Australia was still a British colony now would we? Only joking. See you tomorrow.'

Graeme strode back to the Vodafone shop and within a few minutes was once again sat at Liv's desk.

'Here we are, let's hope it works.'

'Well as it's below the sum of one hundred pounds you can just "ping" it. Did you put enough credit on it?'

'Oh yih. Two hundred.'

'Great, that's gone through OK. Here's your shiny new phone. Two hundred did you say? There's more than enough left to buy me dinner one night!'

As he walked up town to find a coffee shop he pondered on the events of the last hour or two. He'd shared breakfast with a friendly groundsman and had already had two invitations to dinner with two members of the fairer sex. He wandered into a COSTA coffee shop which at least was a name that was familiar to him.

'A long black please. Oh yih and one of those blueberry muffins.'

'You what, love? We don't do those whatever it is. If it's not on the board up there we don't do it.'

'Oh right, no worries. A flat white and a muffin please.'

Graeme found a seat in the window and took the phone out of the box. He was about to make his first call in England. He dialled the number from the slip of paper that Marina had handed to him.

'Hi Millie, it's Graeme. I got a new phone not just a new sim-card. Are you still up for a drink tonight as you suggested?'

Millie smiled on the train all the way back to Scarbados.

27.

Back at the Koala, Peter snacked on soup and a sandwich. Everything was going roughly to plan. He was making real progress on his "To Do" list but then he suddenly had a thought. The new "New" sign hadn't yet been delivered to the Hotel Scarbados yet, let alone fixed into place. He decided to give Dave Gibson a call while he remembered. He reached for his phone and hit the speed-dial.

'Hi Dave, it's Pete Fishburn in Scarbados. How are you?'

'Hiya, Pete. Everything OK? Have you actually moved back in yet?'

'Not yet – only a week and a bit to go. Just a quickie. Any chance of fitting the new sign up any time soon? It's just that I'd like it to be in place before I get back from Belgium with the new bit of the family – if you know what I mean.'

''Yes, I heard about that you old snake. Glutton for punishment aren't you? Most chaps I know are over the moon when "her indoors" clears off and now you've voluntarily got another one! Only joking, mate. Hang on a sec, I'm just looking at my calendar. I can do it a week on Saturday if that's OK with you?'

'Actually I'll be in Bruges that day helping Stephanie with the move. Don't worry I'll be leaving keys with the neighbour, Garry Ritson. You've met him before. At least you know where all the electrics are from when you fitted the other new main signs.'

'Yes OK, no problem. Tell him I'll get there around ten o'clock please. An hour should do it. Will you be having an opening do, or should I say a re-opening do, when the time comes?'

'You bet we will. Well after we've settled in of course. It'll take us a while.'

'Will it be run on the same lines as the old Hotel Scarbados?'

'No, definitely not. What I have in mind is a very up-market B & B. No evening meals or lunches. It'll be posh I'm telling you. We'll be sure to invite you and good lady for a weekend as a huge thank you for all you've done for us in the last two years.'

'That sounds great, Pete. Anyway by the time you get back from Belgium it'll all be done my friend. Safe travels and see you soon.'

'Cheers, Dave.'

Not for the first time Peter considered how lucky he was to have made such good friends and connections in the relatively short period of time he had spent in Scarbados. He glanced at his watch. Crikey, it was one-forty five. He was due to pick up Shirley Ritson in fifteen minutes. He'd better get his skates on. He quickly changed into a clean shirt and double checked there was no fruit stuck to the elbows. Grabbing the car keys he dashed outside to the car park and almost bumped into their new Australian guest coming into the back door, by mistake probably.

'Oh, g'day Peter, er sorry Mr Fishburn.'

'Good day to you too. Have you had a successful morning?'

'I should say so. I've made arrangements to open a bank account, got a new UK mobile phone and got a date with a gorgeous girl already fixed for tonight. Not bad eh?'

'Wow, I'd heard you Aussie boys were quick movers with the ladies. Meet a local lass in a coffee shop did you? Let me guess – blonde, early twenties and easy on the eye? Come on you can level with me. Am I right?'

'Two out of three, Mr Fishburn. That's all I'm saying. You look to be in a rush. Heading anywhere nice?'

'Not really. I'm going with a friend to a store that sells household stuff. I need eight new pillows with fancy cases for the new place in sharp order. Me and the youngest daughter, Lucy, are moving back to the Hotel Scarbados in just over a week. Millie will tell you the full story, I'm sure, in the fullness of time. Gotta go, catch you later.'

Graeme scratched his head and thought that but for the dearth of the yellow stuff at this latitude, Peter might have spent too long in the sun. Oh well. He felt tired and obviously the jet-lag hadn't quite worn off yet. He exchanged greetings with Marina on Reception and headed up to his room for a couple of hours shut-eye. He wanted to be bright eyed and bushy tailed for his first ever date in the Mother Country. Now didn't he? Once on his bed he was out for the count after counting only a couple of dozen prime Merino sheep. He forgot to set the alarm on his new phone.

Peter had collected Shirley at the appointed hour and without delay she navigated them onto the main road to York, the A64. It's about another mile on the left, Pete, on the new so-called retail park. Or at least what passes for one in Scarbados. There are hardly any decent shops left in the town centre any more.'

'Yes, so I've noticed even in the relatively short period of time we've been here. How far now?'

'Just up here. Turn left at the lights in the park and then sharp right. There it is! Look, we're lucky it's fairly quiet – you'll be able to park almost right outside. We won't have to carry it far. Did you fold down the rear seats to give more space? Did you?'

Peter frowned and hoped it didn't show to the helpful Shirley. Surely there couldn't be that much to squeeze in. Could there?' They went into the shop whereupon Shirley took immediate charge. She accosted the nearest member of staff.

'Good afternoon. Is Dariel, the Manager, on duty today please?'

'Er yes. Who shall I say is asking for her?'

'Tell her it's Shirley Ritson and that I've got a new customer for her.'

Two minutes later and a smart forty-something brunette wearing spectacles came down the escalator and waved as soon as she saw Shirley.'

'Hiya, Shirl. How are you? Long time no see. How's Garry? Is he still training dogs or is that a silly question?'

'He's fine thanks. We've got three more now. Candy had pups last Boxing Day. Anyway, sorry I'm being very rude. This is our new neighbour Peter Fishburn. He's got the New Hotel Scarbados next door and ...'

'I thought it was called the Wendover, or am I mistaken?'

'What a memory you've got. That was a few years ago now. Peter's family changed the name to the Hotel Scarbados and it's about to become the New Hotel Scarbados isn't it Pete?'

'Er yes it is. I'm looking for a few new pillows, matching cases and just maybe ...'

'Typical man! What he really means, Dariel, is that he needs a complete makeover for three double rooms in the Hotel. One room is for a daughter, Lucy, aged seventeen, a younger daughter, Natalie, coming up to eleven and of course the third is for Peter and his wife, er Partner,

Stephanie. They'll all be moving in in just over a week's time and we want it to be as welcoming as possible.'

'What about the rest of the décor Shirley, you know, carpets, curtains and any soft furnishings?'

Peter was horrified. This was beginning to sound like one of those TV makeover programmes where the television company was footing the bill anyway and the presenter didn't have to worry.

'Yes, I've taken a few photos on my phone. Here look. As you can see the curtains are co-ordinated with the carpets which are different in each of the three rooms.'

In her mind Dariel was already mixing and matching duvet covers with curtains and carpets.

'Shirley, that's what I call planning. Come on over here. We've got promos on a lot of the top of the range Egyptian cotton gear.And what about mattress protectors? Presumably you'll need three of those?

This was already getting a bit too much for the hapless Peter to take in and he decided to play second fiddle, if not third. How had it come to this?'

Dariel came up with a practical if slightly impertinent solution.

'Er look, Mr Fishburn, I can sense that you're a bit discombobulated by it all. Don't worry, you're not alone, most men are. Listen, how about you pop out to the new Cooplands Cafè a couple of doors away? Get yourself a cuppa and a sticky bun and give us half an hour. We should be about done then. OK?'

So Peter did as he was told and disappeared into the world of tea, Chelsea buns and Eccles cakes. The girls started jabbering as soon as he'd gone.

'Men, honestly! Look Dariel, this is just the start. Give him a good deal because I can tell you now that as soon as

Stephanie is back from Belgium and moves in, she'll want the other dozen plus letting rooms appointed to the same high standard. Good business for you! That's why I asked for you personally. Anyway, he'll be enjoying himself right now – he likes cake. Right, now show me the best stuff you've got. You never know, I might just see some gear for me and Garry as well. A little makeover now and again is nice and do you know what – Garry probably won't even notice!' Forty-five minutes later and the stack of purchases were alongside a till at the checkout.

'Right, let's make sure we've got everything. Three mattress protectors, six pairs of fitted sheets, three summer duvets, six duvet covers with matching pillow cases, twelve new pillows, three Egyptian cotton throws, twelve cushions to match curtains – and I think that's about it. Have we forgotten anything? Where's Peter anyway? It doesn't take this long to eat an Eccles cake, surely?'

In fact Peter was already on his his second cup of tea and was eyeing up a second cake. Engrossed in the latest edition of the Scarborough News which was out that lunchtime and had been accidentally left behind by a customer, he had gone straight to the sports pages by instinct. The headline in the cricket section caught his eye in less than a second.

'SCC's two new overseas players expected this week.

Excitement is growing as the Club is about to welcome its newcomers.

Australian all rounder Graeme Patterson is already here and has been seen not only in town but inspecting the wicket within hours of his arrival.

Barbadian batsman, Courtney Morgan, is expected to arrive by the weekend.

Beset by injuries and other mishaps, SCC are hoping that Patterson will be free of jet-lag and sufficiently acclimatised to play against Hull Zingari ...'

Peter glanced at his watch. It was almost three o' clock. Surely the ladies had finished choosing all the stuff by now? He settled the bill in cash and walked out into the car park. He just couldn't believe what he saw. By the still locked tail-gate of his car was a mountain of boxes and cellophane enclosed flat-pack parcels. Jeepers creepers. The shrill but familiar voice of Shirley Ritson brought him back to his senses.

'Ah, there you are, Pete. Time to cough up. Dariel has given you a twenty percent discount as an incentive to come back as soon as Stephanie wants to up-grade the rest of the Hotel's rooms to the same new, higher specifications.'

'You what?'

'Well you did mention that it was going to be an up-market "boutique B & B" as I recall you once said recently. And once Stephanie sets her continental mindset into it who knows where it will all lead.'

'I don't recall saying anything of the sort ... oh well anyway what's the damage? Break the news gently.'

' Eight hundred and forty-nine pounds – after the discount, that is.'

'Good grief. Oh well, where's my wallet? Here's my debit card. Why hasn't it pinged? Don't tell me it's expired. That's all I need right now.'

'No it's fine. Because it's in excess of a hundred pounds you'll have to enter your PIN number. Don't tell me you've forgotten it.'

'No hang on, here we go. He tapped in the Pin No. which was the year of Millie's birth, the only way he could remember it.. Approved! The little till-roll started to spill out the details which Dariel tore off with practised ease and handed it to Peter.

'Your receipt, Mr Fishburn, and thank you. Shirley says you'll be back fairly soon and of course I'll be happy to give you the same discount.'

'Thank you but she's wrong. Shirley and Stephanie will be back. I'll be watching the cricket – if it's not raining. Now, let's get all that clobber into the back of the car – if it'll all go in?!'

They did manage to get it all in but for the first time since the original move from Hull he could barely see using the rear-view mirror. Ten minutes later and they were back at the Hotel Scarbados.

'Thanks so much for your help, Shirley, even if it has cost me an arm and a leg.'

'You're welcome, Peter. Leave all the stuff in the lobby. We'll look at it all tomorrow. I'll give you a hand. And before you ask, I've made another fruit cake.'

28.

Peter and Millie arrived back at the Koala within seconds of each other.

'Hi Dad. How did it go? The shopping I mean.'

'Well OK I guess. Shirley helped me and, well to be honest, she knew the shop Manageress and they did it all for me while I had a snack and a cuppa in a café nearby. It never ceases to amaze me just how many folks the Ritsons know.'

'Dad, you are the limit! So where is all the stuff you bought? The car still looked empty.'

'It's all at the Hotel Scarbados. We'll sort it tomorrow.'

'What do you mean *we*? I've got a half-day off and I've got plans.'

'I mean Shirley – she's going to help me arrange it all.'

Millie just shrugged her shoulders and walked into Reception.

'Hi Marina. Anything happened while I've been out?''

'Yeah, a few things. Firstly, this envelope was hand delivered about an hour ago. It's from the Cricket Club and it's addressed to Mr Graeme Patterson.'

'So if it's not a silly question why haven't you given it to him? I'm sure he's back from town by now. He called me with his new phone when I was shopping in York.'

'He said the jet-lag had caught up with him and he was going to grab forty winks. I didn't like to wake him.'

'You said a few things.'

'Yes, there's another letter addressed to the Directors, also from the Cricket Club, going by the same crest on the envelope. Here you are. Also, an email came in from the travel agents in town confirming your father's flight tickets to Brussels a week on Friday and return tickets forty-eight hours later. I've printed it off for him and put in this envelope here. Do you know where he is?'

'Sort of, he's definitely back from the shopping trip to Dun Elm 'cos I've just seen him. He's getting more flustered by the day as it gets nearer to him and Lucy moving out.'

'When all four of them come back will they spend a few days here before moving in …'

'No, certainly not. If you check the bookings you'll see that I have already allocated their rooms as letting rooms from the Sunday night onwards. Once they've actually left for Leeds Bradford Airport we'll do a proper check of both their rooms. It's all about revenue now and occupancy rates. By the way what time did Graeme, er Mr Patterson, go to his room, can you remember?'

'Yes, it was just after three, so he's had about two hours. Why?'

'I'm taking him out for a few drinks tonight. You know, just to be friendly. We mustn't forget that he's ten thousand miles from home.'

'Well you didn't waste any time did you? Where are you going to take him?'

'He mentioned that he'd like to try some real English ale, so I thought maybe I'd take him down to the Tap and Spile, if I can remember where it is. You took me there if I remember.'

'Great choice. Easy to get to too. Just take the 843 Coastliner Bus to York from down near the Park. It goes through the town and stops almost right outside the Tap. It's only an hourly service but I'll check on my App for you.'

'Thanks, Marina. Meanwhile I think I'll go and give him a shake and pass him his letter. It could be important. And I think I'll open that other letter from the Cricket Club now, while I remember. Pass me the letter knife please.'

She slit open the letter and unfolded the single page inside. It was from Miles Carter.

'We are happy to inform you that Courtney Morgan from Barbados will be arriving tomorrow round about six in the evening, depending on his flights and trains being on time of course. Would it be asking too much if one of you could kindly meet him at the station and take him to the Hotel Koala? As you know his Uncle Malcolm, the former High Commissioner, is fairly familiar with the town but this is Courtney's first visit and he will be more than a little disorientated following his trans-Atlantic flight. Thank you.

I heard from our groundsman, Steve Dodds, that Graeme Patterson has already arrived in one piece and I trust he is settling in and that you are looking after him. I wish I had a UK phone number for him but he probably hasn't got that far yet. I have some urgent news for him so perhaps you could ask him to phone me on my personal mobile number below. Thanks.'

MILES

Millie looked at the date on Miles' letter. It was yesterday! Oh my God, that meant that Courtney would be arriving in just under an hour. Typical Miles. The letter had probably been in his blazer pocket for over twenty-four hours. No wonder it had been hand-delivered instead of being posted.

She chased round the ground floor until she found her father.

'Dad, look sharp, the young chap from Barbados will be arriving at the railway station around six-ish. Miles has only just told us! Can you go and meet him please and bring him back here. It's a jolly good job that you emptied the car of all the stuff you bought this afternoon. Make him welcome please. Jamie will ensure he's well-fed.'

'What? Can't you do the welcome bit. Strictly speaking I'm no longer involved after all, am I?'

'Dad, just do it please. I've got a date.'

Peter just nodded and shrugged his shoulders in mute acquiescence. He was slowly but surely thinking that his time here was ending and the adventure of the trip to Belgium and settling in to the New Hotel Scarbados was a more tempting proposition than looking after dozens of tourists who's main interest was the state of the wicket on two acres of green grass a half a mile away. He checked the Trans Pennine App on his iPhone. Most technology was beyond him but he had at least mastered that. The next train in from York was in just over an hour's time. At least a coloured chap travelling alone with a suitcase and a kit bag full of willow should be easy to spot.

Millie made best speed for Graeme's room on the top floor and knocked gently three times. Was he awake?

'Come in! Oh hi, Millie, it's you. I thought it was a Qantas hostess with my supper.'

'Cheeky! Sleep all right?'

'Yih, raring to go. Where are you taking me anyway, Sheila?'

'Oi, no more of that Sheila lark. I've been called many names but never Sheila. Just watch it you or you'll have a Viking chasing you. Look here, this letter was hand delivered to you a couple of hours ago. It's from the Cricket Club and I know it's urgent. Miles Carter wants you to call him. Here, you'd best open it now, Graeme. He didn't stand on ceremony and read the letter out loud:

'Dear Graeme

I hope you are settling in OK and that the Hotel Koala has met your expectations. The Fisburns are are a friendly bunch and I'm sure they'll look after you for the next few months.

Now, this will come as a bit of a surprise but the Team Captain, Martin Dixon, has asked that you make yourself available to play for the Club this Saturday. It's a home match against Hull Zingari and it's important that we put up a good show after we were thrashed on home territory last year. You'll probably be batting at No. 7 but I'll let Martin fill you in on that.

As regards finances, if you could let me have your Bank details as soon as you have a UK account, I'll arrange for either weekly or monthly credits for you, whichever you wish – payable in sterling of course, as previously agreed. Your accommodation at the Hotel Koala is taken care of as part of a sponsorship deal. Your bar bill is of course your responsibility as are extras such as laundry etc.

The practice nets are available for your use from tomorrow morning onwards – you can't miss them and they're to the left of the Pavilion and the McCain stand. A few Second Team members are only too happy to assist you in the nets. Take it easy on them – they'll be looking to you for some tips!

My office door is always open – it's upstairs in the Pavilion.

Cheers.'

MILES CARTER

'Well that sounds pretty cool to me, Graeme. Listen why don't you call Miles now and make contact with him, then he has your number to put in his phone's address book?' And that Martin Dixon guy too. Always a good idea to keep on the right side of the Captain, I reckon. Hey, give me twenty minutes to change then meet me downstairs in the Bar before we walk down the hill to get the bus. OK?'

'Yer on Shei … er Millie.'

'Just watch it you!'

Millie was actually ready and "good to go" in ten minutes sporting a new smart outfit she'd bought in Coney Street in York that day. Chloe knew all the best shops in York and they would do it again soon. But she also had an eye for a bargain too and if ever she became "Mrs Jamie Fishburn" one day then she knew that her brother's pocket would not be drained too badly too often. You never know!

The Coastliner bus was on time and within fifteen minutes they were inside the pub – the Tap and Spile. The main bar wasn't busy and they grabbed two bar stools. The landlady, Dawn, blondish mid-fifties came to serve them.

'Hi, it's Millie isn't it, from the Koala? You came with Marina last time I remember.'

'Yes, you've got a good memory. It must be months ago. The place was absolutely heaving.'

'Yeah, it always is when we have live music on. Can you remember who was playing that night?'

'Yes, they were brilliant. The Wave! The lead vocalist was always shouting 'come on, give us another wave!' Christopher somebody. Anyway Dawn, meet Graeme. Graeme, this is Dawn.'

They both smiled but the wide bar proved a bit of an obstacle to a handshake.

'Graeme, is that an Aussie twang I can hear? I didn't know you had an Australian boyfriend, Chloe.'

'Well er no, actually Graeme's our guest at the Koala for the next four months. He's here to play cricket for Scarborough Cricket Club and …'

'Wow! Yes I saw it in the paper. So it's YOU! You'll be able to walk to work staying there. When's your first match? Sorry, I'm being a poor landlady. I should be asking you what you'd like to drink. We specialise in real ales here. There's at least six to choose from. We always have lots of guest ales too. Darn sight tastier than the chemical stuff you'll have been used to in WA I can tell you!'

'How do you know?'

'Because I lived in Mullalloo for years when I was married. Things went pear shaped so I came back home to Scarborough. Scarborough girls nearly always return to the same stream they were spawned in. But don't worry about Millie – she's from Hull. Now, what would you like to try? There's Old Peculiar, There's Landlord, there's ..'

It was a mild evening and Graeme didn't even get goose bumps. They took their drinks out into the beer garden and talked and talked and talked. By the time "last orders" had been called at eleven o'clock, Graeme knew almost as much about the Fishburn family and its troubles as he did about his own back in Perth. The one thing he was absolutely sure of though was that this lady was a Bonza Sheila … whoops … a Bonza Millie.

29.

The next morning Millie decided to have breakfast in the main dining room along with the other guests. She was half-hoping that Graeme might be there. He was.

'So I take it you slept well, Mr Patterson? And exactly how many glasses of Old Peculiar did you have? I lost count after five.'

'G'day Millie. You're already sounding like my mother – wanting to curtail my social excesses prior to important matches.'

'Then I have something in common with your mother. What are your parents' names anyway, you never said?

'Marmon Dead?'

'You what?'

'Marmon Dead – my Mum and Dad? It's just Aussie slang.'

'Well it sounds awful, like you've had a bereavement or something!'

'Ha! Well you might have to get used a fair bit of Strine while I'm here.'

'Strine? What on earth is Strine?'

'It's Aussie slang for Australian – the way that most Aussies speak English. I'll teach you some if you like? It's easy once you get the hang of it.'

'So when you were chattering to Dawn in the pub last night did you speak any Strine with each other?'

'You mean the rubidy?'

'The what?'

'The rubidy dub-dub. The pub. It's rhyming slang – probably pinched from Cockney rhyming slang. But anyway to answer your question, Millie, my Dad's name is Leslie and my Mum's is Linda. Oh yih, and my sister is Donna. I call her "Donna Kebab" which doesn't go down well, I can tell you.'

'I'm not surprised. Don't you get on?'

'Not really, no. She got involved with a beach bum and moved to a place called Esperance on the south coast. It's a two day drive and she doesn't come home very often.'

'Two days? Good grief. Maybe you could show me on a map sometime? Oh look, I think this must be Courtney coming in for breakfast. Let's go and say hello shall we? He looks really tired doesn't he?'

'Yih, he looks totally bushed if you asked me.'

Millie raised an eyebrow but said nothing. Quite what a bush had to do with it was beyond her.

'Good morning. You must be Courtney Morgan. Welcome to Scarbados and the Hotel Koala. I'm Millie Fishburn.'

'How do you do and good morning to you too. May I join you for breakfast, Miss Fishburn?'

Millie was taken aback by his overwhelming courtesy. Then she remembered that his uncle and aunt, the former High Commissioner and his wife, were of the same ilk. It showed markedly.

'Of course you may. And can I introduce you to your fellow team mate Graeme Patterson? He's staying here with us for the summer season too, so you'll see a lot of each other I'm sure, apart from being at the cricket club.'

The two men shook hands across the table that was set for four guests.

'So, Courtney, by the strength of your right hand I'm guessing you're a right handed batsman, yes?'

'Correct. One of our tutors at school was none other than Gordon Greenidge, a right-handed opening bat. I try to emulate him but he's a tough act to follow to put it mildly.'

'Crikey, talk about a high bar. Look, have you heard from the club directly yet, the Treasurer maybe?'

'I've just picked up this envelope here. I'll open it now.' Millie stopped him

'Courtney, before you do that let me order you some tea or coffee and what would you like to eat?'

'Well, when in Rome … I'll have the full English please, eggs sunny side up. And may I please have a proper strainer with my tea? It makes so much difference doesn't it? I hope you don't use those awful tea bags.'

Millie skedaddled off to the kitchen to ensure that his eggs were pointing the right way and that Darjeeling's finest was not encased in inch-square meshes. Goodness she hadn't expected this! It was all in sharp contrast to Graeme's – 'yih, anything fried and a mug of tea, no worries.'

Courtney slit open his letter from the Club which proved to be almost a paste & copy version of Graeme's. The only meaningful difference was that he would be batting at No. 3 this Saturday.

'Goodness me that doesn't give me an awful lot of time to acclimatise and adjust my body clock does it? My brain is still on Barbados time, whatever that is.'

'Actually they're quite well organised here in that respect. In the lobby there's clocks that gives you the correct time in all the major cricketing centres.'

'Yes, so my Uncle Malcolm was telling me. He was very impressed I can tell you.'

'Well Mr Fishburn, that's Millie's father, was a mariner for a lot of years and he's a stickler for that sort of thing. I understand he met you at the railway station last night.'

'Yes, he did eventually. My flight from Barbados to London Gatwick was two hours late. Then I missed connections for Victoria, Kings Cross and York. It was tiring and frustrating. I got charged excess baggage for all my extra bats that I brought with me, did you?'

'Yih, 'fraid so. I'm sure that the Treasurer will stump up for it though – excuse the pun!'

'No, I didn't bring any wickets or bails – just bats!'

'They were still laughing when Millie returned with a pot of tea, complete with a silver strainer.

'You two seem to be getting along OK, I must say. Graeme, why don't you take Courtney to the bank where you went yesterday? And get him fixed up with a UK phone while you're at it. I'll leave you to it. Catch you both later.'

'Graeme, what did she mean by "catch you later?" Was it an other cricketing pun?'

'No idea,mate, no idea. I think we'll both have to learn the local lingo. Anyway, are you up for a practice in the nets this afternoon?'

'Well I might be, all things being equal. The jet-lag is far worse when you fly east though. Did you know that? You flew west.'

'No, I can't say I knew that. A flight to Bali was the furthest I've flown outside of Australia before. Look, if we walk into town we can drop into the Club on the way and you can see the set-up for your self, OK?'

'Deal! Let me finish this breakfast then give me fifteen for a brush-up and I'll meet you in the lobby. Yes?'

'That's fine. Oh yes, and bring your passport with you. The bank will need to scan it before they can open you a proper account. The bank will also change your dollars into sterling. Then we'll get you a phone sorted. The girl in the phone shop is a little cutie by the way. Her name's Liv. I'll introduce you.'

A half an hour later and both men were in the cricket ground talking with Steve Dodds, the groundsman.

'G'day Steve. This is Courtney, our new No. 3 bat.'

'Ow do, Courtney. By the way, I hear on the grapevine that one of our openers has pulled a hamstring in training. I'd start think about batting at No. 2 if I were thee.'

By mid-afternoon they were padded up and in the nets. The Second Team players were gunning for them with Yorkers, full tosses and bouncers – all eager to claim a foreign scalp – even if it was only net practice.

Meanwhile, down at the New Hotel Scarbados, Peter and Shirley were admiring their handiwork. The first three double rooms now looked in pristine condition and worthy of any boutique hotel's brochure. Something was nagging Peter though. He had forgotten something but for the life of him he couldn't remember what. It can't have been very important. Can it? In reality there were loads of things that Peter had forgotten. What a good job that he had such an efficient eldest daughter to think and cover for him.

'Well that's all wonderful, Shirley. Thank you. Now did you say you'd made another fruit cake?'

30.

The following morning Millie decided to give Shirley a ring without telling her father. She was keeping tabs on him all the time. Somebody had to – at least until Stephanie was back in Scarbados permanently.

'Morning, Shirley, just a quick call. Thanks ever so much for putting my Dad right with the rooms, bedding etc. He's absolutely hopeless with anything like that. Mum did everything.'

'You're welcome, Millie. Garry's the same. Men just think that bedrooms are just sleeping quarters looked after by others. Anyway we got there in the end. I'll take Stephanie on her own back to Dun Elm when she decides the décor for all the letting rooms. When are they due back by the way?'

'Well Dad and Lucy leave a week tomorrow on the Friday, flying to Brussels then by train to Bruges. I booked them into a budget hotel, the Ibis I think it's called, near the railway station. They spend two nights there and fly back all together on the Sunday. The idea is that they help Stephanie and her daughter do the last minute packing on the Saturday. Something's bound to go wrong though if Dad's involved in the organising.'

'Is he that bad?'

'Oh yes, he hadn't even booked the hotel until I did it online for him. Between me and you, he's had his head up his backside for weeks now.'

'Well he has had a lot to think about hasn't he? Are the school arrangements finalised yet? And didn't the head teacher say that he wanted Natalie's residency status clarified before …'

'You're scaring me now. By the way did either he or Lucy ask you if you would kindly look after Sebbie and AlfieBoy for those two days until they get back?'

'Er no, but it's no problem. What time on the Sunday, roughly, will they get back? Any idea?'

'About five ish I think. The Airport Taxi is booked and will take them straight to the Hotel Scarbados. Once they leave here on the Friday, that's it. They won't be coming back. In any case their rooms will be totally emptied the minute they leave and anything left behind I will take in the car to the Scarbados Hotel – which hopefully, by the time they return, will be the *New* Hotel Scarbados. I keep giving him an amended "To-do" list but he just seems blind to it.'

'Millie, what about food? Should we stock up for him on the Saturday and put a few days supplies in the fridges and freezers?'

'Damn! That's something I forgot to put on his list. I can't believe I forgot that. I remember the horrible day we arrived here in a snowstorm and stopped at a Sainsbury's Express for some frozen Chinese food. You helped us out do you remember? I don't know what we'd have done without you, I really don't. This time should be a doddle by comparison. Let's go down to the cash and carry shall we as soon as Dad and Lucy have left?'

'Yes, that's fine. At least there's only two adults and two girls to worry about – oh yes and two dogs now not one! Why is Lucy going anyway? Isn't it just more expense? Not that it's any of my business.'

'Not at all, Shirley. Lucy hasn't ever been on a plane before and nor has Natalie. It's all part of the bonding process and building memories together, so Dad says anyway. If I had my way they'd all be coming back in the back of Clayton James' truck – you know, like illegal immigrants! Only joking of course. The other thing is that Dad and Lucy are travelling out with almost empty suitcases so that leaves some extra capacity for Stephanie and Natalie. You know, just in case. Excuse the pun!'

'Stephanie struck me as being a very well organised lady. I'll bet you everything's tickety-boo and good to go as soon as your Dad and Lucy arrive. And Clayton is the most marvellous removals man he probably won't need anything like the several hours turnaround time he's allowed for in the itinerary.'

'Crikey, is that the time? I'd better go. I've got those two young cricketers to see to this morning before they go off for nets practice.'

'I saw that young Aussie boy's picture in the paper. He looks quite a dish. Have you given him …'

'Just watch it you. Don't get any ideas. Don't get any ideas about buying a new hat!'

'Ha ha! Bye, Millie. You know where I am, love.'

31.

The next few days absolutely flew by and Graeme and Courtney both played their début games for Scarborough Cricket Club. Neither of them exactly covered themselves in glory. Scarborough won the toss and elected to bat first under a cloudless sky of early summer. They put a respectable two hundred and ten runs on the board in the allotted fifty overs. Batting at Number 2 as expected, Courtney scored a dashing sixteen, all in fours, before carelessly getting run out in only the fourth over. He'd mistaken the other batsman's cry of "no" for "go" and, realising his error, turned back only to be run out by a sharp fielder. Oh well, sixteen runs on his first outing wasn't too bad. It could have been worse. Graeme fared marginally better. He hadn't needed to bat so when the skipper chucked him the ball to bowl the first of his six overs he should have been fresh. He thought he'd taken two wickets LBW but sadly both proved to be "no balls" which added to his frustration. He redeemed himself with a marvellous "caught and bowled" in his fifth over and then he clean bowled their Captain in the sixth. Scarborough won by thirty runs. For the new boys it was a relief just to be on the winning side. Songs were sung and beers drunk in the Pavilion Bar afterwards,

Graeme and Courtney walked back to the Koala together at around six-thirty, both carrying their kit bags through the lobby towards the lifts. Courtney was decidedly sleepy, yawning as he pressed the button on the panel.

'You know what Graeme, I think I'll go straight to bed if you don't mind. The jet-lag's catching up with me again. What about you?'

'Not sure, mate. I seem to remember Millie say she was taking me out somewhere for supper. I can't remember where though,'

A shrill female voice suddenly sounded out behind him. It was Millie who had appeared out of nowhere.

'Well, boys, how did you get on? Did you start your Scarbados careers with a win? I jolly well hope so,'

'We did, we beat Hull Zingari by thirty runs. I took two wickets, including their Captain.'

'Well don't tell Dad you did that. He used to watch Hull Zingari when he was a lad. His own father used to take him. Right, you've got half an hour to shower, change and smarten up. Meet me in the Bar at seven OK?'

'Sure, but where are we going? And what do mean by smarten up?'

'Well, no shorts or trainers for a start. You're in England now and in God's county to boot. I can see that Courtney might have to give you lessons in etiquette before long. Obviously culture and manners reached the Caribbean before Western Australia.'

She exchanged a wink with Courtney a fraction of a second before the lift door opened with a loud ping. Saved by the bell. Men-only banter continued as the lift ascended.

'Crikey, Courtney, I've only been here a few days and already Sheila here is trying to make me speak the Queen's English and dress like a tailor's dummy. It's just not right, mate.'

'Graeme, I'd just go with the flow if I were you. It's obvious that she's got her beady eyes on you.'

'Oh yes, without a shadow of a doubt, mate. You know her Dad and her younger sister Lucy are moving out soon, don't you? To the old Hotel Scarbados where the family started out here. That will free-up accommodation on the top floor where all the family's rooms are.'

'What are you getting at, mate?'

'You Aussies are a bit slow on the uptake. I'll bet you as soon as her Dad's gone she'll come up with some excuse to move you to the top floor. I'll bet you two pints of English ale that I'm right.'

'You're on, mate. But only if it's a brew called Old Peculiar. It's very nice. I had a few scoops the other night.'

'What's a scoop? You use some strange words.'

'Well they don't seem to drink schooners here do they?'

'A schooner? I thought that was a boat, you know, like a ketch.'

'You've totally lost me, mate. Anyway look, you get some shut-eye while I get a Tyrone Power and get spruced up. Lord knows where she's taking me. See you tomorrow.'

Graeme was in the Bar just after seven o'clock, as arranged. He ordered a half a litre of local ale and wondered why he got a funny look from the girl serving him.

'We don't serve litres, Sir, only pints or half-pints.'

Graeme settled for a pint and when it was poured from the pump he thought that it was as close to a half a litre as he was going to get. He wondered why on earth the Mother Country hadn't gone fully metric a half a century ago when Australia did. Oh well.

When Millie finally appeared, ten minutes later and thus ten minutes late, she looked radiant in a flower pattern, below the knee, summer frock with white strappy sandals without heels. They were yet further purchases resulting from her expedition to York with young Chloe. There was a reason for the choice of footwear.

''Wow, you scrub up quite well, Miss Fishburn, I have to say.'

He gave her a peck on each cheek, most un-Australian. Perhaps Courtney had already had words with him.

'You look smart yourself too. Well, are you going to buy the lady a drink or what?'

'Of course, what can I get you, Miss, for an aperitif? A sherry perhaps? Or would madam prefer a cocktail? May I recommend the Margaritas in this establishment ...'

'OK, Graeme, I can't take much more of this. A half a lager and lime will be fine. You've been practising that line haven't you? I'm impressed.'

'Right, where are we going tonight? If we need a cab I kept a card from the bloke that first picked me up – a Charlie somebody. He gave me a free ride around the drive to here when he brought me from the train station to here.'

'No, we can walk down a load of steps to the seafront to where we're going. That's why I've got sensible shoes on. No heels tonight.'

'So exactly where are we going? Is it far?'

'It's called the Saltwater Café and it's only a half a mile away as the crow flies. It's mostly local seafood but there's other stuff as well. You won't starve, trust me. Come on, drink up, let's go. I booked a table with a sea view for seven-thirty. I know the owner, Luke. He knows which table I prefer.'

'Do you know everybody already in the short time you've been in Scarbados?'

'No, but I know a lady who does! Come on, let's get a wiggle on.'

That last expression was lost on Graeme. Ten minutes later and they started descending the hundred plus steps that would take them to the complex known as the Sands. The steps were old and worn due to Council neglect since they had sold off the Victorian funicular which had stood proud for decades. Despite his flat loafer shoes, Graeme somehow managed to misjudge the last three steps, all of which seemed to be of different heights and widths. He landed awkwardly on the scuffed, unkempt tarmac pavement.

'Ouch! That hurt. Aorta build some new proper steps.'

'What do you mean, aorta. There's no sign of any blood.'

'No, I'll explain. "Aorta" is a generic name for any Government or Council department that isn't looking after the public's best interests. So here, for example, "Aorta" build some new, even steps or better still build a new twenty-first century tram from sea level up to where we came down from. Don't you think?'

'I know somebody who would agree with you. She's called Pamela Hesketh and she lives in one of those fancy apartments over there – Sandpiper Heights.'

'Do you know her? You seem to know everybody else!'

I certainly do. Actually she's a Director and on the Board of Best Eastern Hotels plc who own half of the Hotel Koala. Her and Dad had a fling a while ago. It's all history now. I get on with her well now. We can meet her for a coffee one morning if you like.'

'Sounds like a plan. How far is this Salt place? My ankle's starting to throb a bit.'

'Don't be such a wuss! It's only about another two hundred yards.'

'How many metres is that?! Only joking.'

'Gosh, you are limping a bit aren't you? Hold onto my waist to keep in a straight line.'

Five minutes later and they were seated upstairs at the table Millie had requested with a superb and direct view of Scarborough Castle in the distance.

'Wow. You don't get many views like this in Perth. Apart from in a 'plane the only good way to get a view of our coastline is from a place called Observation City, which speaks for itself really, doesn't it? Now, what do you recommend from this menu, Millie? You'll have to advise me.'

'Sure, but tell me, what exactly is Observation City?'

'It's a very tall building in the Scarborough Beach area.'

'So it's not really a city then is it, if it's a building? That's a bit odd isn't it?'

'I suppose when you look at it like that, it is. It was built by one of your mob though – a Pom called Bond, Alan Bond.'

'Don't you mean James?'

They both laughed out loud, something they did easily together with increasing frequency.

'No, it was definitely Alan. He went to prison for corporate fraud but he had his good points too, I can tell you that.'

'Like what? Well for a start the Bond Corporation was the main sponsor for the America's Cup, or rather the Australian team that won it. We're talking millions here. He was never really replaced from a sponsorship point of view. By the way, Millie, on the subject of sponsorship the letter I got from Miles Carter said that my hotel accommodation was sponsored. Is that right and by who? I'd like to say thank you.'

'Graeme, yours and Courtney's hotel accommodation is courtesy of the Hotel Koala.'

'What, no way. Why didn't you say?'

'It wasn't relevant. It was an arrangement we reached a long time ago, in fact last year, but neither you nor Courtney were able to take up your contracts until this year.'

'I don't get it. So what's in it for you?'

'Business, it's that simple. We have a free link on the Club's website pointing straight to the Koala. The spin-off has been tremendous.'

'Well, I'm pleased for you but it makes me feel a bit guilty. So that means that Courtney and I are taking up rooms that you could otherwise let out for profit?'

'Yes, but looking ahead beyond Friday, we might be able to mitigate that loss substantially.'

'Don't tell me you're kicking one of us out into a grotty B & B?'

'No, on the contrary, on Friday, Dad and Lucy leave the Koala for good. Firstly they go to Belgium and then return direct to the Hotel Scarbados. That frees up two double rooms on the top floor – the owners' accommodation, one for you and one for Courtney.'

'Heck, so which one's going to be mine. The biggest one? The one with the best view?'

'No, Graeme, the one next to mine.'

The smile on Graeme's face was almost as wide as Scarborough Beach was long. If only Courtney could have been a fly on the wall. He was right! The locally caught haddock with tartare sauce and mushy peas was a revelation for Graeme whose previous seafood experience had been limited to snapper, red mullet and flake – all with chips of course. They were just about to settle the bill when Millie's mobile phone buzzed in her purse. She pressed the green button without checking the caller ID.

'Hello, Millie Fishburn.'

'Who's that gorgeous hunk you're chatting up then, Millie?'

The southern lilt swiftly betrayed the callers identity. It was Pamela Hesketh.

'Oh, hi Pam. Where are you … how did you know I'm …'

'I'm in the café. Look at the far end of the window tables. I'll stand up and wave.'

'Gosh, I'm sorry I never noticed you.'

'No problem. You were obviously otherwise engaged! Listen if you two haven't had coffee yet how about coming up to my apartment for one? It's Suite 410. Just give me ten minutes OK?'

'That sounds lovely, Pam. See you in a bit.'

32.

'Wow, what a bonza view from up here. Hi Pam. I'm Graeme.'

'Hello, Graeme, I'm Pamela but I answer to almost anything. Has Millie told you about me – warts and all?'

'Well only a little bit. You're a Top Brass member of Best Eastern Hotels and ...'

'I was persona non grata for a long time but it all seems to have worked out for the best. Now, can I get you both coffee? And maybe a little brandy to help it go down? Why don't you two take a seat out on the balcony while I fix the drinks? I won't be a tick.'

The view was indeed spectacular and Graeme just stared at the vista before him. The twilight was fading fast and the twinkling lights marking the Marine Drive had come on. Amazingly there were still a few surfers at the water's edge but it wouldn't be long before they headed for their camper vans and drove away. The Council had recently tightened up the overnight parking regulations. Graeme opened the batting, even if he normally batted at Number 7.

'So, Pammie, you mean you actually live here, in this Apartment?'

'Sort of. I'm renting it from the Management company for a few months until I can buy one of the penthouses up top which aren't actually finished yet – another couple of months should do it.'

'How lucky are you? I'd love my Mum and Dad to see this view.' Millie interrupted him.

'You mean your Marmon Dead!'

Pam looked puzzled and raised an eyebrow.

'Graeme's been teaching me some Strine. It's quite easy once you get the hang of it. Anyway, Pam, while I'm here maybe you can give me the low-down on the company. What's the state of play with regard to acquiring more businesses in this region?'

'There are a few possibilities we're looking at, most are confidential at the moment for obvious reasons. Although we have lots of liquid cash in the bank we're only interested in the bigger stuff now. There are quite a few smaller businesses for sale, you know, cafés, restaurants and the like but too small for us to consider. It's also been decided to put funds aside for promotional or sponsorship deals. On that point, I'd like a chat with your young colleague from Barbados. Has he arrived yet? I saw something in the paper?'

'Oh yih he has. We've already played our first game. The poor chap was still jet-lagged though and he'd have scored more runs if he wasn't so bushed.'

Millie mouthed "tired" at Pamela and winked.

'Yih, it wasn't terribly well planned by the Club to be honest. We should both have been given a week to settle in. Can I ask why you want to speak with him?'

'Please keep this under your bush-hat but we are looking at the possibility of sponsoring a whole Barbados Team visit to Scarborough, maybe next year. We've been looking at it for a while. I used to go to Barbados on holiday and I often took in a day or two watching cricket. My Dad once took me to the Oval in London when I was a teenager and I guess I got bitten by the bug. A few years ago I Googled Barbados hotels and the search engine came up with Hotel Scarbados.

That's how I came to Scarborough in the first place! Covid was still badly affecting international travel so I came here instead. The rest is history, as they say.'

Millie was as much taken aback by this news as Graeme.

'You mean a Barbados Eleven could all come here? Wouldn't that be expensive, like mega-money?'

'Well, we're looking at it. Is Courtney's Uncle, Malcolm Morgan, visiting here soon? I was thinking about asking him to act as a go-between. If it comes off then the possibilities are endless. "Scarbados versus Barbados" has a great ring to it doesn't it? Sponsored by Best Eastern Hotels plc. They could even play a Yorkshire Eleven too couldn't they, perhaps at Headingly even? Anyway that's all in the future and, like I said, keep it to yourselves please.

Getting back to the present, we'll be putting together some management accounts for the Koala next month to mark the half-year. They're going to look very good I think. Well done. More coffee you two? By the way I suppose I'd better ask about your Dad. How is Pete? I'd heard he's moving back into the old Hotel Scarbados. That's good news – a fresh start for him.'

'Yes, you're right, Pam. He and Lucy are flying off to Belgium in a few days to help Stephanie and Natalie make the move. It's huge for them too. Natalie is so excited. She and Lucy WhatsApp each other every day it seems. And of course she's fallen madly in love with Sebbie and AlfieBoy. Jamie seems to already have taken on the role of Big Brother and he even calls her Nattie which is a name that only he uses. It's all looking good. Natalie's going to Scarborough College in September.'

'How is Jamie doing? I've not seen him in ages.'

'He's fine despite the responsibilities of catering for guests and running the Four Seasons as a separate entity.

When it get's a bit too much he jumps on a train to see Chloe, his girlfriend.'

'Millie, I've got something for Jamie. I was going to drop it into the Koala but I'll pop it into an envelope and give it to you. It's a cutting from a trade publication. Ask him to give me a call when he's got a few minutes please.'

'Gosh, that sounds ominous.'

'Tell him to keep an open mind on it. You're his Big Sis, so he will take notice of you. He always did didn't he?'

'Well some of the time he did. Not always though. We all like Chloe though, so whatever happens between those two is OK by us. Even our mother liked Chloe!'

'What?! How is the old dragon?'

'She's on the high seas again I think – this time with one of your Chinese colleagues.'

'It won't last, believe me. He'll tire of her after a cruise or two!'

Millie glanced at her watch. It was ten o'clock now and almost fully dark.

'We'll have to order a taxi. Graeme twisted his ankle on those horrid steps over there …'

'They might not be there much longer. If our plans come off we're going to redevelop and have a twenty-first century electric tram installed. It's not just hotels we're going to invest in. Watch this space. I've got a number for a taxi here somewhere – hang on a mo.'

Graeme fiddled with his wallet and fished out the card that Charlie Wagstaff had given him when he first arrived in Scarbados.

'I'll call him now. No worries.'

'Hello Graeme. You're where? Sandpiper Heights? Give me ten minutes mate.'

Charlie was as chatty as ever.

'I see you won your first game, well done. When's the next one?'

'Saturday – away to Harrogate. Where's that?'

'About eighty miles west, mate. It's posh over there. It's fillet mignon with petit-pois instead of fish and chips. You'll like it though. Just make sure you win. By the way you were lucky to catch me tonight. I was taking the wife to the Neptune Café in the Old Town but they had to cancel the booking. Seems like the proprietor is unwell. There have been rumours for a while about him and his wife moving to warmer climes on health grounds. Bloomin' shame if it closes. The food is great and it's always busy. You've got to book at least a week in advance. Have you been there, young lady?'

He glanced at Millie in the rear view mirror. She was almost wrapped around Graeme like a Boa constrictor.

'Er no, I haven't. My dad has though and he spoke very highly of it.'

Five minutes later and they were in the lobby of the Koala. Jamie was just about to turn in.

'Ah, Jamie, glad I caught you. Believe it or not we went out for supper and guess who we bumped into? Pamela! We ended up having coffee and brandy in her apartment above. It's just fab! Anyway she asked after you and asked me to give you this envelope. Don't ask me what it is, I have no idea. She said please give her a call. Don't forget.'

'Thanks. Night, Sis.'

Five minutes later and Jamie was in bed and re-reading the contents of Pamela's envelope for the third time. It was a BUSINESS FOR SALE ad.

The Neptune Café.
A small but successful seafood restaurant in
Scarborough's Old Town. Twenty-four covers.
Owners accommodation included.
Five years accounts available. POA.

33.

After breakfast the next morning Jamie collared Millie. He hadn't slept too well, images of the ad in the trade magazine kept leaping into his subconscious. What was this all about? What was the real reason that Pamela had sent him the cutting? She was still a bit of an unknown quantity, he thought.

'Jamie, I honestly don't know the reason Pam has sent you this. You'll just have to ask her. I'd call her if I were you. Why don't you suggest meeting her in the Watermark Café? I think she often pops in there. By coincidence the taxi driver last night just happened to mention that the Neptune Café was closed last night. Don't dilly-dally like your father. Call her now and fix a meeting.'

Half an hour later and Jamie and Pamela were sitting in window seats looking out over a wide expanse of sand with the water's edge at least eighty yards distant.

'OK Jamie, I'm going to have to put some cards on the table here, in total confidence you understand.'

'Sure, go ahead, I'm all ears.'

'I'm hearing noises at Board level that Best Eastern aren't happy at only owning fifty percent of the Hotel Koala. It's only a matter of time before they will want to own it all.'

'Oh heck, did you tell Millie this?'

'No, it's confidential, and of course she wasn't alone last night. She had the Aussie cricketer with her. Are they an item, by the way? They seemed awfully close. She's even learning how to speak Strine.'

'What's that? Strine?'

'It's colloquial Australian. It's a bit like Cockney rhyming slang.'

'My goodness, he's only been here less than a week and you're telling me that she's fallen head over heels for a bloke from thousands of miles away?'

'Look Jamie, you've got involved with Chloe, your Dad's back with Stephanie and well, maybe it's her turn to settle down. She hasn't found anyone in Scarborough has she, let's face it.'

'Now you put it like that. He seems a nice bloke – even if he does speak funny! But anyway, what's the real reason you sent me that ad for the Neptune Café?'

'I think you should consider buying it.'

'What? Yeah right, what with? Brass buttons. Come off it!'

'Jamie, if and when Best Eastern buy you and Millie out, and depending on the amount of course, you might have enough to buy it. Think about that. Your own restaurant! And don't forget, you're an award-winning chef now. That accolade seems to have fallen by the wayside in recent months. Well doesn't it? The timing could be just right when you think about it.'

Jamie swallowed hard on his Cappuccino. This was almost too much to take in.

'I need some more coffee, do you? I'll get them.'

Jamie's head was in a spin as he queued up for refills. There were two ladies he needed to speak to. One was in York at Uni, the other God knows where on a ship with an Oriental gentleman, or so he thought anyway. He would sent them both a WhatsApp message and hope that both would get back to him. He rejoined Pamela in the window, only narrowly avoiding being tripped up by the lead of a Jack Russell terrier that had suddenly shot across the isle between tables when he spotted a visitor proffering what looked like half a sausage in his direction. On some days the place was like Battersea – no wonder Lucy was always coming here. It would be even worse when sisters Lucy and Nattie returned to Scarbados from Belgium.

'Pam, what should I do now? What do I do if I want to explore it a bit further?'

'You reply to the ad. Do you remember what POA actually means?'

'Remind me, price something.'

'Price on application. Shall I do it on your behalf? Strictly between us?'

'Thanks, Pam, that would be good. But if I sold out and left, what would happen to Millie?'

'She would stay on for the foreseeable future with a good contract. She wouldn't want to leave yet anyway, would she? Not while Aussie Boy's here. Take my word for that – womens' intuition!'

'OK Pam, let's leave it at that for now shall we? I need a bit of fresh air so I think I'll walk back the long way round through Peasholm Park. If I had some bread I could even feed the ducks.'

'Well if you look sharp the lady on the next table has left most of her toast untouched. Grab it before the waitress comes to clear the table.'

Fifteen minutes later and four mallards, a Mandarin duck and two coots were happily munching on some Hovis leftovers. At least they didn't have to make any decisions. Life as a duck must be beautifully uncomplicated. He was almost back at the Koala when his phone pinged in his jeans pocket. It was a text from Pamela.

'The asking price is £550k including all fixtures and fittings. All equipment is almost new. The agent is

emailing me the accounts this afternoon. Let's meet again tomorrow, same place same time. OK? Pam x

It was time to make contact with the two women in his life.

34.

Supper for the guests was over and Jamie was chilling just watching some TV. It was a repeat of an old episode of 'Vera' that the whole family used to enjoy back in Hull. He hadn't seen this one before but somehow he just couldn't concentrate on the plot. His mind was on King Neptune and the café named after him. Could it work? This place was big and getting bigger. The Four Seasons' identity was already getting overshadowed, even swallowed up, by the corporate marsupial – the Hotel Koala. His mind was in turmoil. His father Peter came into the room.

'Hi Jamie, you look miles away. What's up?'

'Hi Dad. How's it going? Down at the Hotel Scarbados I mean? How's that "To-do" list coming on?'

'Don't you start! Although I love her dearly, my first-born is driving me nuts. Every time I think I've finished this list a new amended one appears. Where is she anyway? I've hardly seen her since Aussie Boy has arrived. And where is Courtney? I've barely said hello to be fair. Do you have any plans for the rest of this evening?'

'Nope. I've a couple of quick messages to send then I'm done. Why, what's on your mind?'

'Tell you what, see if you can find Courtney and we'll take him up to the Albert pub. He might appreciate a pint and a game of darts. What d'ya reckon.'

They found Courtney in his room speaking on his cellphone, as he called it, to his fiancée in Barbados. He was feeling very homesick.

'A beer and a game of darts? You'll have to show me how to play properly. Why does the score start at "501" for a start? Why doesn't it start at zero and it's the first one to reach 500?'

He had a point. Why did it? Neither of them knew.

'Meet you downstairs in the lobby in fifteen minutes. It's only a ten minute walk up past the cricket ground.'

Jamie went alone to his room and called Chloe direct. She was busy writing up an assignment on the latest water pollution data for the North Sea. He filled her in on developments that day.

'Jamie, that sounds absolutely amazing. But how can you make it happen, rather than just wait to see if it does?'

'I can't. That's the problem. There are no guarantees that Best Eastern will definitely make the offer and even if they do will it raise the five hundred and fifty thousand asking price?'

'What does your Mam think? She's always had your best interests at heart you know, whatever the differences between her and your sisters. She was so proud of you at the opening night of the Four Seasons. She almost had a little weepy. I liked her, I really did. We had quite a chat I can tell you. Where is she now?'

'On a cruise ship somewhere. Frankly she could be anywhere – the Mediterranean, the Pacific, anywhere. I can only guarantee where she won't be.'

'Where's that?'

'In the North Sea. She doesn't like the cold any more.'

'Look Hun, send her a WhatsApp message and tell her what you've just told me. I'm sure she'll be thrilled just to hear from you. She's only got one son, you know.'

'You're right Chloe. I'll send it now. Then I'm going for a game of darts with Dad and the young cricketer from Barbados. His name is Courtney and he's homesick for his fiancée back home. I think he said her name was Florence.'

'No way! You're joking!'

''You've lost me. What's so funny?'

'Don't you ever watch "Death in Paradise" on TV? It's brill. This English Police Inspector is madly in love with a local girl called Florence but he always fluffs it! You know, gets cold feet at the last moment.'

After the call ended Jamie wondered if that last bit was a hint from Chloe about their own relationship. No matter. He left a long message in his mother's voice-mail and kept his fingers crossed that she picked it up soon whether she was in Valletta or Vanuatu. He left his phone on charge and went downstairs to rendezvous with his Dad and Courtney. It was a fun evening.

Returning shortly before eleven it was time to turn in. Now fully recovered from jet-lag Courtney was eager for net practice the following day. Graeme was less so. His ankle still wasn't a hundred percent and he thought that maybe the Club's physio should be consulted. After all, they both wanted to be at their best for the away match at Harrogate on Saturday.

Jamie unplugged his iPhone from the charger. To his surprise a message from his mother had come in. Maybe she wasn't on the other side of the world after all. He pressed "play" and waited.

'Jamie love, I'm so pleased to hear from you. What amazing news. If Best Eastern come up with the offer you MUST go for it. You could end up like that Stein chap who has restaurants in Cornwall or some trendy spot. By the way I'm not on the Seven Seas at the moment. It's a long story. I came back to 'Ull last week. Sell your shares to Best Eastern at the earliest opportunity, love. You'll be better off on your

own now. But you won't be alone now will you? That girlfriend of yours, Chloe, is absolutely lovely. I hope I see her again. Keep in touch. Mam xxx

Jamie's mind was made up. He would go for it, just as his mother said. All he needed now was for Best Eastern to come up with the brass.

Down in Hull, Mandy Fishburn didn't waste any time. She knew exactly what she needed to do. She put out her own WhatsAppp message to Albert Wong.

'Hello Albert

I hope this finds you well, wherever you are. I hear you now have a lovely Italian lady as your travelling companion. Italians and Chinese have always got on well. Marco Polo did all right didn't he? Anyway, further to our agreement I am pleased to report that I have finally persuaded my son, Jamie, to sell his shares in the Koala to your company. He will be seeking a sum of no less than five hundred and fifty thousand sterling and will be looking for an early completion to the transfer of the shares. You have my bank details already for the transfer of my own "arrangement fee" in the sum of one hundred thousand sterling, as agreed. Sincerely, Amanda.'

35.

The next morning, as arranged. Pam and Jamie met for coffee at the Watermark. This time Jamie was totally chilled.

'So, Jamie, have you had time to chew it over? What are you thinking?'

'Well, Pam, it's all green lights as far as I'm concerned. Chloe and I had a long chat and although it'll be a year or so before she finishes Uni, I can see her helping me no end in the long term. I think my Mam's thinking along those lines too. You know what mothers are like!'

'Indeed I do but mine tried to marry me off to boring stock brokers and bankers. She failed of course! Your Mam is probably more perceptive than you give her credit for. Look, I'll keep my eyes and ears skinned for any development. There's a Board Meeting in London next week and of course I'll be there.'

'That's great Pam, thank you. But what do I do in the meantime, if anything?'

'Two things actually. Firstly, you get someone with knowledge of accountancy to look over the last five years accounts. I've brought them with me. Take them. Secondly, you make an appointment to look over the premises and check everything against the Sales brochure. Again, I downloaded a copy for you.'

'That is so kind of you but Pam, if you don't mind my asking, what's in it for you?'

'Nothing, is the honest answer. I still feel slightly guilty at what happened in the past so maybe it's a little bit of remorse but all of you, in your own way, are lovely people. And if it wasn't for you guys I'd probably still be sitting at a desk in Mayfair instead of looking at these beautiful waves in front of us.'

'Yes, it's a funny old world isn't it? And if Dad hadn't asked me to go and buy you some of that "Odour Toilet" perfume I would never have met Chloe, now would I?'

'Ha, well I've learnt something today!'

'I'm going to pass these accounts on to Clive White. He's Millie's course tutor and our family adviser. He'll give me his honest opinion.'

'Good, let me know how you get on OK? Don't forget to make that viewing appointment. And take somebody else with you. Millie maybe?'

They parted company and Jamie set off uphill towards the Hotel Koala. He was almost walking on air and hardly noticed the steep gradient. He found his sister in the lobby attending to some guests who wanted to make a repeat booking for the next Yorkshire game in town. It was all getting very hectic.

'Hi Sis, can you do me a favour please? Can you scan these accounts and then email them to Clive for me?'

'Good grief, what have you been up to?'

'I'll fill you in later but can you just do it for me please? It's urgent.'

'Let me take a look. If you want Clive to look forensically at these then all he'll really need is the Profit and Loss accounts. The Balance Sheets won't really matter at this stage. I'll do it now, just give me five. Then, little Bro, you owe me an explanation later. There mustn't be any secrets between us. Agreed?'

'Agreed, thanks Sis.'

'You realise that these figures will be in Clive's email inbox in a few minutes time so you'd best call him as soon as possible or he won't relate to them. Do it now – go!'

Jamie called Clive White in Beverley to put him in the picture. Clive agreed to call him back within the hour with his thoughts. It would prove to be a very long hour for Jamie. It goes without saying that Clive made a pot of tea before donning his reading glasses to carefully peruse the figures in front of him. Not for the first time he mused over the adventures of Millie's family, their ups and downs and the incredible speed at which events seemed to move. If he ever put pen to paper one day to record their family and corporate history, then there was only one title he could think of to do it justice – "The Fishburn Saga.' It would make a change from the Forsyte Saga. As always he decided to take notes. Once a bank manager, always a bank manager.

'Hi young, Jamie. It's me, Clive. Right, let's start at the beginning shall we …?

Right, going back to the earliest year, let's call it Year One, it was of course a disaster.'

Jamie's heart sunk to the floor, in fact almost a hundred feet to sea level.

'Oh no. Please don't tell me that. Why?'

'Well, it's obvious isn't it? Covid! You must remember what the then Prime Minister, Boris, said. "You must stay at home!" It was the start of the first lockdown. That's why you couldn't trade when you first bought the Wendover Hotel before you changed its name. Don't tell me you don't remember! Well of course the proprietors of the Neptune Café had the same problem. They had to close down for months. Every business had to, unless it was essential to the nation. Anyway to move on, the turnover was low for Q1 …'

'Huh? What do you mean Q1?'

'The first quarter of the year – January, February and March. It was winter and turnover would have been lowish anyway. Who knows, they might even have taken a winter break. Lots of folks in the hospitality industry do. It's normal. Anyway, again moving on, Q2 and Q3 were virtually zero due entirely to lockdown, with Q4 seemingly picking up again until another lockdown which shortened everybody's Christmas holiday. How it compared to Q4 in previous years we'll never know. Are you listening, Jamie? You're very quiet – and I hope you're taking notes at your end too?'

'Er, well actually, no I'm not. Should I?'

'Tut tut. It's just as well you're a star chef and not one of my junior bank clerks, I'd have … I'm only joking. Look, I'll plough through this. Just listen OK? So moving on once again to Year Two, Q1 was almost non-existent but after Easter, when the country opened-up again, it was boom time. Half the country wanted to come to the coast and spend all that furlough money. Turnover shot up for the rest of the year. Year Three ….'

Ten minutes later and Clive had reached Q4 of Year Five.

'So, towards the end of Year Five it seems to have become somewhat erratic, in fact pear-shaped to put it bluntly. There seems to have occurred a serious, almost catastrophic, downturn in trade. It could have been one of a number of factors at play. Maybe a rival setting-up and undercutting their prices – a sort of turf war if you like. Maybe bad reviews on Trip Advisor, possibly instigated by a rival. It can be very cut-throat you know. But something certainly happened. You could maybe ask around and do a bit of fishing – excuse the pun. Maybe ask your girlfriend's father?'

'Clive, I don't have to. I already know the reason.'

'You do? Well it's not obvious from the accounts I can tell you. Enlighten me, young man.'

'It's ill-health. The proprietor's wife has a chronic medical condition and they're selling up and moving to the Canaries apparently. That's why the business is on the market.'

'Mmm, well that throws a slightly different complexion on matters doesn't it? You might get a lower offer accepted if you were a quick, cash buyer. But I can tell you, beyond question, that this business is basically sound with good net profits.

'Well hopefully, I will be a cash buyer. Best Eastern Hotels seemingly want to buy me out. They want my shares. In fact it seems that they want buy out both Millie and myself.'

'My goodness me. Since when?'

'It's not official yet but seems like it's only a matter of time.'

'OK look, don't do anything just yet, promise me. You, me and Millie need to talk. And soon. What about this coming Saturday?'

'That sounds good to me. Graeme will be playing away at Harrogate and …'

'Graeme who? Who are you on about?'

'Oh of course, you're not up to speed are you? Sorry. I mean Graeme Patterson, the Aussie cricketer who's staying at the Koala for the summer season. Sis has fallen for him big time. She's even learning to speak Strine and …'

'Oh dear, I'm sorry to hear that. A beautiful English rose about to be nobbled by an Antipodean bush-wacker. Look, just keep Saturday afternoon free and I'll take the train up to you this time. How's your Dad by the way?'

'He's OK I guess but the move back to the Hotel Scarbados is going ahead and he'll actually be in Bruges this weekend with Lucy. All four of them will be back in Scarbados by Sunday evening.'

Clive just sighed. If indeed he was writing the "Fishburn Saga" he would be on Chapter ninety-nine by now with no end in sight.

36.

It was the following Friday and the day of departure for Peter and Lucy. A specialist airport taxi was taking the pair of them to Leeds Bradford airport about ninety minutes drive away. Peter was in a tizz, as usual.

'Lucy, you don't need to take all those clothes, darling. It's only two nights and we'll be back on Sunday, The reason for us both taking almost empty suitcases is to leave some space, not to mention baggage allowance, for Stephanie and your little sister. I hope they're organised at the other end. Now, please take the two extra pairs of shoes out of the case …'

'But Dad, we'll be going out to eat tonight and tomorrow night won't we and I want to look good. Natalie's been telling me that Bruges is a smart place with great boutiques. OK, I'll do a deal with you. I'll almost empty my case if you agree to buy me two new tops in a shop in Suidstraat that sells Herme...'

Pete was in no mood to argue. Who on earth did she think she was? A deal? She hadn't even been to Bruges let alone seen any shops there. Natalie must have put her up to it, that's all he could think. Mobile phones, WhatsApp and Instagram had a lot to answer for. There was lots of talk these days about protecting youngsters from the evils of the internet, trolling, grooming and the like, but nothing about protecting parents from spendthrift teenagers. Why Millie had acquired a state of the art phone for Lucy he could never

223

understand. He still had to make do with his old one. Still at least the cost of Lucy's expensive phone was down to the Hotel Koala and no longer his responsibility. Five minutes before they were due to leave an email came in on the main PC in reception. Marina spotted it quickly.

'Mr Fishburn, an email for you. It's got the Scarborough College logo on the footer and it's from a Mr Guy Merrett. I'll print it off for you. It's quite long. I'll pop it into an envelope for you then you can open it later. Here you are. Safe journey. Come here and give me a hug Lucy and I'll come and see you all when you've settled in at the New Hotel Scarbados.'

Lucy was only going to be away for two days but it was a special day for her – her first trip away on an aeroplane and with her own passport too. The dogs could sense that something was up when Lucy gave them each two hugs and carried her own bag, weighing only three kilos, out to the waiting taxi. A final wave and they were gone. Millie gave a huge sigh of relief. Phew! Now it was time to check their bedrooms. No doubt there would be a mountain of stuff still to move to their new home. She wasn't wrong. Her father's room wasn't too bad, considering. Several pairs of shoes still occupied the wardrobe floor and his old Stewards uniform, which had so attracted the amorous Pamela, was hung up in its protective polythene cloak. Maybe, just maybe, he wanted to move on mentally and had deliberately left it there? Who knows. The en-suite bathroom was as clean as a whistle – not even a razor or a half-empty tube of toothpaste remained. It was spotless. Mariners were like that. The expression "ship-shape and Bristol fashion" must have come from somewhere. She moved on to Lucy's room. Good God! By contrast it looked as if Imelda Marcos had just left in a hurry after a bomb scare. Two pairs of doggie-walking boots were on the floor, still with muddy soles, eight more pairs of shoes were in the wardrobe, half a dozen tops were hung up on rails and, horror of horrors, her iPhone charger was still plugged into the socket alongside her bed. It immediately brought back memories of when Pamela Hesketh and done that deliberately to test the efficiency of the old Hotel Scarbados. It seemed a lifetime ago. She went downstairs to sort a large box to put her father and Lucy's clobber into. Then she would take it down to the New Hotel Scarbados along with the two dogs to hand over to Shirley and Garry Ritson. Then she suddenly remembered that she and Shirley were going to go to the Cash & Carry to stock up with food supplies for the new 'family of four' and she called Shirley a few minutes later.

'Hi Shirley, it's Millie. I'll be down in about half an hour. Dad and Lucy departed a short while ago. They've left some stuff behind, clothes and stuff, which I'll just plonk in their rooms. I hope you've got keys by the way, because I don't have any.'

'No problem, Millie. Then we'll have a coffee before we set off shall we? Have you made a list of what we should buy, by the way? I've seen how efficient you are with your Dad's "To-do" lists. You almost drove him bonkers.'

'You won't believe this, Shirley. I forgot. See you soon. I'll just organise the dogs. Is Garry at home, you know, while we're out? Not that we'll be long.'

'Yes he is and he's just shouted out – tell Millie not to forget their baskets, bowls and leads.'

Millie sighed yet again. There seemed to be no end to it all. On the way out, with both dogs and their paraphernalia safely on board the estate car, she set off for the short journey to the New Hotel Scarbados. Only then did it occur to her that, up until then, they had somehow managed with only one car, albeit a fairly substantial family estate. Her father would want to take it with him. She knew little or nothing about cars. Maybe Graeme did. Yes, she would ask him this evening. The Club physio had cleared him to play against Harrogate tomorrow which was one less thing to worry about. Then she remembered that she intended to move Graeme into her father's old room. The blue tooth clicked in on the hands-free phone.

'Hi Marina, it's only me. I almost forgot. Can you ask Housekeeping to sort Dad's old room out please? Graeme's moving into it later today. Thanks.'

'I've already seen to that Millie. I said you were a quick mover, now didn't I?'

Both dogs started to bark profusely as soon as they drove into the drive. Somehow they just knew they were coming home. As soon as Millie lifted the tailgate they shot off to their respective default destinations. It was almost like they were pre-programmed. Sebbie headed off to the eucalyptus tree for a pee and AlfieBoy to the Ritsons' front door where Shirley was already proffering one of his favourite treats.

'Right, Millie, lets put their stuff into the Hotel Scarbados first shall we? I've got the key. What a contrast to when you all arrived more than two years ago, remember? It was freezing, two inches of snow on the ground, no food apart from what you'd just bought at that Sainsburys Express just before it closed and no beds made up. Remember?'

'Shirley, how could I forget? We would not have survived without your and Garry's kindness. Looking back, I don't think Mam settled here from day one. If we'd arrived in the middle of summer maybe things would have worked out differently.

'Oh well, that's life, Millie, that's life. Come on, let's make a start on that list of provisions. I've switched their freezer and fridge on last night, by the way. Now then, there's tea, coffee, milk, fruit juices, frozen family sized vegetarian Lasagnas, various vegetables, ice cream and …'

'Listen, it's on the way, so why don't we pop into Dun Elm en route? Their manager, Dariel, tipped me off that there are some fab offers at the moment including a new range of Egyptian cotton duvet covers and …'

'You're on Shirley, let's do that.'

'I've pinched Garry's debit card. Don't tell him! I'll swap "old for new" while he's out with the dogs this afternoon. A pound to a pinch of the proverbial he won't even notice.'

Two hours later and Millie was back at the Hotel Koala. Marina was just about to finish her shift.

'All present and correct topside and ready for your inspection. Does he know he's moving rooms yet?'

'No, I'll tell him when he and Courtney get back from nets practice.'

'They're back already! Apparently he had to go steady after his misadventure with a pavement. He's in the main lounge watching something on TV. He seemed a bit down about something.'

'Hi babes, what's up? Feeling homesick or something?'

'Sort of. Dad left a message on my Telstra phone. Mum's feeling a bit crook again it seems.'

'You've lost me. Crook?'

'Yih, You know, not well.'

'I'm sorry, Graeme. Is it serious?'

'It's a heart condition called tachycardia. It flares up now and again. She'll be right soon enough. She's had it a while. That's why I was a bit mad when Donna Kebab zipped off to Esperance. They had hoped that she and I would run the place when they retired. You know, so it could stay in the family. They've already bought a retirement condo down the coast in a place called Mandurah. It overlooks a lagoon – it's beaut.'

A message soon pinged on her own phone. It was her father.

'We've arrived safely in Bruges. No delays and we are now in the Ibis Hotel near the train station. Stephanie and Natalie are joining us for supper. She says there are a "few things" still left to pack tomorrow. Bye for now. Dad x'

Meanwhile the ferry MV Pride of Hull had slipped her moorings on the River Humber and was now heading south-east on a heading of 125 degrees towards Spurn Point and the North Sea. Safely board were Clayton James, his son and the three ton truck with the electrically operated lift. So far so good.

After a joyous reunion in the Ibis Hotel they all had a fabulous supper at a nearby bistro. An early night followed. All being well, Clayton would arrive mid-morning. Just before retiring for the night Peter suddenly remembered the email that had come in for him from Scarborough College. He opened the envelope and unfolded the printed message which was spread over two pages. He put on his reading glasses.

'Dear Mr Fishburn

The College is delighted to confirm Natalie's place in Grade Six as from September. As discussed we would like her to attend for the last two remaining weeks of the summer term which will help her to familiarise herself with her new surroundings.

Unfortunately, an unwanted fly has landed in the ointment. You may have heard recently that HMRC are now applying VAT to all private school fees. This means that the previously quoted fees will now be increased by twenty percent.

Accordingly, I am attaching an amended Fee Note and Invoice for the first term.

Digressing, did you, as I asked, clarify Natalie's residential status with the Home Office? If you haven't it is important that you do so without undue delay.

We look forward to seeing you soon.

Sincerely
Guy Merrett
Head Teacher'

Poor Peter, as if he hadn't got enough on his plate. This could prove to be a serious problem. Finances were already tight. He didn't sleep well.

37.

Peter and Lucy were up in good time for an early breakfast – Continental of course. Not a fried egg or fried sausage to be seen. Just as well Sebbie didn't live here. He hadn't even broached the subject of the New Hotel Scarbados' breakfast cuisine with Stephanie yet. All in good time. It was a warmish morning with no need for the anoraks they had brought with them. That's the trouble with living in Scarbados – you had to be prepared for anything at any time of the year. They took the short walk to the taxi-rank that Stephanie had pointed out and gave the driver instructions. The two empty suitcases went into the boot.

'Good morning. Number 15 Kartuizerstraat, Sint-Kruis please, driver.'

Peter's attempts at the Flemish version of Dutch brought forth a broad smile from the driver, in his early thirties.

'Actually my English friend, that's not bad! Most of your fellow countrymen make a complete hash of our tongue. You must have been here before, I'm just guessing?'

'Er yes, you can say that again. Many, many times. Although I'm not sure where this address actually is. Is it far?'

'Not really, about two kilometres. You said many times.'

'Yes, I worked on the ferries from Hull to Zeebrugge for twenty years. The route doesn't exist any more, sadly.'

'No, that was terrible, axing those ferries. The hospitality trade suffered badly since that happened – and of course it took a long time to recover from the Covid epidemic.'

'So, is Bruges back to normal now? You know, business wise?'

'I would say almost but not quite. We have less Brits but more Eastern Europeans visiting these days. And more Chinese of course. More's the pity. You guys spent a fortune on tobacco and booze. Apart from the missing ferries, we were also affected by the Brexit carry-on. Actually most people living here in Flanders would like to leave Belgium, let alone the EU. Anyway, who are we to argue? We're just taxpayers.'

'It's the same back home, my friend. You never get what you voted for.'

Peter instantly thought about Natalie's school fees and the unexpected added tax.

'Anyway my friend, we're almost here now. It should be just down here on the right. Yes, there it is – number fifteen. That's just twelve Euros please my friend. I'll get the cases out of the boot for you.'

Within seconds Natalie came dashing out of the front door. Her English was getting more parochial by the day.

'Morning Papa, morning Lucy. Sleep well?'

She kissed them both on the cheeks as they stepped into the hall of the smart but modest terraced property which was three storeys high. Peter was horrified at the sight before him. Boxes after boxes were piled on top of each other as far as the eye could see right through the long hall to the back room. Peter started to count them up in twos – ten, twelve, fourteen, sixteen, eighteen, twenty, twenty- two, twenty-four! Stephanie, you told me, and I told Mr James, that you only needed ten boxes.'

'Peter, I said ten boxes each. OK so it was twelve each in the end. Who cares?'

'Oh no you didn't. I heard you distinctly. Anyway, we

are where we are. Fortunately Mr James is bringing a larger truck than originally planned so we should be OK. The bigger truck has a lift at the back to handle the two heavy items of furniture. Where are they, can I see them?'

'Of course they're in the front room, just through here. Come and see.'

To be fair they weren't quite as big and ungainly as Peter had imagined. In fact they looked quite smart and highly polished. The bureau was flat against one wall and was probably used as a writing desk from time to time – the original purpose for its manufacture. The so-called "sea chest" was under a bay window and by the rings in the wood's surface had probably seen many vases of flowers placed on it over the years, if not decades. Unwisely Peter decided to move it slightly to test its weight. Big mistake.

'Owch! You didn't tell me it was *that* heavy. Anyway, any chance of a coffee whilst we're waiting for Clayton James? He sent me a message about an hour ago to say that the Pride of Hull was on schedule and that all being well he would arrive here by around eleven o' clock. They'd left the motorway to stop at a McDonalds breakfast. Why on earth they didn't eat first on board before they disembarked I just don't know.'

Natalie smiled and looked up at her father.

'But Papa, everybody loves McDonalds for a breakfast McMuffin, don't they?'

Peter couldn't think of a suitable reply so said nothing. The sudden twinge in his lower back was a timely reminder not to touch either of those pieces of furniture. His phone pinged. It was Clayton James.

'Hey up, Peter. Slight delay. I borrowed a Euro Tom-Tom from a mate who holidays over here quite a lot with his campervan. He didn't tell me it spoke in Dutch! We've taken a wrong exit somewhere. When we saw a sign saying Brussels so many kilometres instead of Brugge, we knew we'd taken a bum steer. Any road, we're pointing in't right way now. It'll be nearer to twelve before we get to you but it'll be fine. No worries.'

'Thanks Clayton. By the way there are twenty four boxes not ten. Is that OK?'

'Yeah, no problem. Where women are involved I always double their estimate. A few years ago I moved a lady called Melanie, in a village near Scarborough, who had over a hundred boxes of clothes. Can you believe that? And she was only moving houses about two hundred yards. She could easily have got a wheelbarrow and moved them herself, one at a time. See you soon.'

'So, Stephanie, is there any chance of that coffee? And Clayton and his lad will probably need one when they arrive too.'

'Sure, no problem. I left a few mugs and stuff for coffee out and unpacked. Then it can all go in the one box I've left open which can be the last one put onto Clayton's truck. Is there anything else you've left out of the boxes?'

'Only enough clothes for tonight and the flight tomorrow plus some toiletries and stuff like that.'

'So you won't really be needing all the empty space in our two cases which we brought with us then?'

'Not really, no. Everything else is packed in the boxes and I've stuck a note on each box to tell me what is inside each one for when we start to unpack at the other end.'

Pete smiled. It was all in stark contrast to the original and nightmare move from Hull, thank goodness. Natalie interrupted him.

'Papa, you didn't forget to put Yorkie, my new teddy-bear, in my new room did you? You promised.'

Oh heck, so that's what was nagging him when they left the Hotel Koala. He knew there was something. He decided a white lie was called for in the circumstances and that a follow-up call to Millie was going to be essential.

'Natalie, I'm quite sure that Yorkie is already in his new home and quite happy.'

As soon as the truck was loaded and on the way back to Europort, he would send an urgent message to Millie and keep his fingers crossed that all was well. As if he hadn't got enough to worry about. Coffee was served and within ten minutes the front bell rang and a voice boomed out.

'We're 'ere! It was Clayton & Son. Just as well it wasn't Steptoe & Son collecting "any old iron!"

'Sorry we're slightly late, Peter. Ow are ya any road? I had a funny feeling we'd cross paths again.'

They shook hands and both of them sported great smiles of relief that, thus far at least, things were going roughly to plan. Clayton took charge like a Clerk of Works but without a clip-board and a hard hat.'

'Right, let's see, so you've got twenty-four cubic metre boxes. I know just what you ladies are like. I even brought ten spare flat-pack boxes, just in case. He repeated the "Melanie story" for Stephanie's benefit and she instantly responded.

'Oh, I wonder if she's who Millie called "Mel from Licensing" at the Town Hall? She's got a black Labrador and …'

'Yes, that's the one. She still holds the record for the biggest number of boxes I've ever moved for a person. Well, we're certainly not going to beat that record today are we? You are so well organised it's not true. And all the boxes are numbered too. Marvellous. Now, on the basis that what goes into the truck last comes out first, which boxes do you want to have immediately available when we get to Scarbados tomorrow afternoon? Any idea?'

'Yes, boxes one to six are my clothes and personal stuff, seven to ten are Natalie's and the rest is general household effects. So the first ten need to go upstairs first then the rest …' Peter intervened.

'Into the conservatory, to get emptied and sorted. It's fairly empty, thankfully.'

'No palm trees this time then, Peter?! I seem to recall we moved half of Kew Gardens on that first move. It was worthy of a "Carry On film" that was. Never again – and it was snowing like that disaster movie wasn't it, you know, the "Day After Tomorrow." Anyway folks, the day after tomorrow and all this will be in the past and in a week, ancient history. Right, two more things please. Where are the two electric bikes and where are the two very heavy items of furniture? I want to load them first and secure them immediately behind the drivers cabin. They'll be lashed to secure fastening points so they can't slide around. Then the boxes after that and then lastly the two bikes. In the unlikely event of a full HM Customs inspection they might just lift off the bikes to check the batteries and ..'

'I've removed them completely, Clayton, and packed them separately. They're in Box No. twenty-four.'

'Wow. If only all my clients were as efficient as you. Now, where are the two heavy items?'

Stephanie led them into the front room and pointed.

'That's the bureau against the wall and …'

Clayton strode towards it. Built like the proverbial silverback gorilla, Clayton looked it up and down as if he was going to value it for the Antiques Road Show.

'It's not as big as I thought it was going to be but an old client with similar stuff told me that Rhodesian teak made oak feel like balsa wood. Let's try and move it out away from the wall a tad shall we?

A minute later and he had managed to move one end of it about six inches away from the wall and just sufficient to notice a square piece of paper seemingly glued to the back of it. He'd seen similar things before stick to items that had been shipped from abroad. He shouted to his lad.

'Right, bring the skateboard from't truck. We did bring it didn't we? God help us if we didn't.'

'Yes Dad, we did, I'll go and get it.'

The skateboard, as they called it, was about the same size as your average domestic door. The top side was completely flat but the underside sported no less than eight large brass castors, four down each side and reinforced by steel spars. If any castor was damaged it could be replaced without affecting the other seven. Clayton had designed it himself and was very proud of it. Between them they brought it into the lounge and pondered their next move. Once they had manoeuvred it about a foot clear of the wall they managed to lift one end of of the bureau sufficiently clear of the floor to slide the "skateboard" almost entirely underneath it. Another two minutes of brute muscle power and the bureau was almost in the centre of the skateboard.

'Phew! That Mr Abbott bloke was right. You can read all of that label now – look. Stephanie glared at it, transfixed. After all it was part of her family's history. She felt obliged to read it out loud to the others who all crowded round.

MENEER LOUIS VAN GELDER

Societé Anonyme Belge d'Expolitation Navigation Aérienne

COMPAGNIE MARITIME BELGE S.A.

SS JADOTVILLE

MATADI – ANTWERP

30 JUNI 1960

Stephanie was absolutely ecstatic at retrieving this previously unknown information and she immediately reached for own iPhone to photograph it before it disappeared into the truck. That operation alone took a full fifteen minutes as it was slid out through the front door and onto the now lowered platform. Fingers crossed the electric motor would do its job. It certainly took its time as the platform rose at an agonisingly slow rate of about a centimetre a second. Neither of the two men travelled vertically with it to save weight and strain on the motor. Once at the truck's floor level they jumped in and easily slid it to the front. Then, horror of horrors, they suddenly realised that they might need the skateboard to perform the same operation for the sea chest. Dear God! Clayton shouted out to Stephanie.

'Is that chest empty or full, love?'

'It's full of old books and journals I think. Why?'

'Get it emptied quickly please to lighten its weight then between us I think we can get it out here to the lift. Look sharp, please.'

It took Stephanie a full ten minutes to take out endless SABENA Flight Manuals, maps and thirty of what looked like hard backed diaries. They weighed a ton – well probably about thirty kilos – enough to make the chest manoeuvrable by the men anyway. Three minutes later and it too was safely tucked into the truck and safely lashed.

'Right, now pass them boxes up here one at a time in reverse order starting at Number twenty-four. Get on with it. We've lost enough time already. I want to be on't road

237

in fifteen minutes. Have you repacked all them books into say two empty boxes. Don't put them all in one as the boxes might split or burst open. Here, use this duct tape. Look sharp now.'

Ten minutes later and both items of furniture, twenty-six sealed boxes, two electric bikes and the final opened one with the coffee making stuff, were safely aboard and secured. There was only about a metre of space left, if that. What a good job they had brought the biggest of their vans. With a final mop of his perspiring brow with his T-shirt, Clayton jumped into the driver's seat, started the engine and re-set the Tom Tom. Next stop Europort.

Once again, the Satnav gave them a "bum steer" and almost took them to downtown Rotterdam instead of Europort and the ferry terminal. They were the last truck to board the MV Pride of Hull with only a few minutes to spare before the gate was closed. The load-master was not amused.

'You only just made it, pal.'

'Yeah I know, it's these foreign Tom Toms. It's all double Dutch to me.'

38.

Back in Bruges, Lucy had reminded her father of the deal they had re the empty suitcase and her wish to buy some glossy tops in smart boutiques. It was almost like the conversation had been plotted by Lucy and Natalie.

'Stephanie, where is the shop called "Chez Hermes" in town? I can't find it any more as my iPhone's run out of charge and I think I must have left the charger at the Hotel Koala before we left.'

Peter didn't miss the chance to get his own back.

'Well that'll teach you not to be so careless, young lady. And if you don't have an adaptor for a continental plug it wouldn't be any use anyway, would it?'

'Well next time I won't forget. And tomorrow morning at the airport I'll buy one of those adaptors. No problem.'

Peter raised an eyebrow. Next time? What next time? This was a one-way trip as far as he was concerned. Was something going on that he didn't know about? Stephanie broke the awkward silence.

'Come on, a final check around here and we'll order another taxi to take us to the Ibis Hotel. From there we can walk into town and do those last minute bits of shopping, can't we Lucy? Your father can stay in the Hotel if he doesn't want to join us, can't he?'

Peter sighed. If this was the way things were going for the next decade then he wouldn't get a look-in. Still at least Garry would be there and the two male dogs. And Jamie was only a ten minute walk away through the Park and up the hill.

The taxi soon arrived and it was time to say a fond farewell to both sets of next-door neighbours. There were lots of hugs and kisses but no tears. The last words that Stephanie spoke to one of the neighbours stuck in Peter's ears like an ear worm.

'See you in August, Anna. We'll keep in touch by email.'

Peter then knew for certain that something was going on. Having dropped all their luggage off at the Ibis Hotel, they all walked into town. Lucy was the keenest to find the shops she wanted to visit.

'Dad, there's a lot more room in my case than we thought there would be, so can I buy say four new tops please? It won't be long before it's my birthday after all will it and …'

Peter just wasn't prepared to argue at this point. All he really wanted to do was get back to the New Hotel Scarbados and start preparing for running a viable business again. The letter referring to the increase in school fees was hanging over him like the Sword of Damocles. He knew that soon he would have to address the situation, not to mention discuss it frankly with Stephanie. This 'next trip in August' was irking him too. It all added up to a Sword and a Dagger of Damocles. He needed to talk with Stephanie alone and as soon as possible. The opportunity to do so was not long in coming.

Right Dad, this is Suidstraat and Natalie says that "Chez Hermes" is about a hundred metres up the road. You and Stephanie don't have to come with us. You can catch up with me and Natalie in a bit. So how much can I spend?'

'Er well, how about two hundred and fifty Euros. OK?'

'Dad, that'll barely cover two Hermes tops. And if I choose a Versace one for my birthday present then I'll need a bit …'

Peter needed a way out of this and the chance to speak with Stephanie. He took the easy way out.

'OK, three hundred tops.'

Then he realised he had carelessly used the wrong words.

'Dad, you're a star, but three will be fine and …'

'Little monkey, you know what I meant. Meet us in that coffee shop over there in say half an hour. And have you got enough money, by the way?'

'I don't use Euros. I'll use the Apple Pay on my phone … oh heck it's out of charge. Have you got any cash?'

Peter peeled of six fifty Euro notes from his rapidly depleting wallet and handed them to her.

'Here, start getting used to using real money again. Just remember "Cash is King" now that we have one on the throne again. See you two soon and don't be late. We've got a few other things to do. Life's not all retail therapy you know, Lucy. When we get back home I'm going to …'

But the two youngsters had already gone and Peter found himself speaking to fresh air. The two remaining adults walked to the swish-looking coffee shop and soon found an empty table. The Cappuccino and Mocha arrived, delivered by a waitress who addressed Stephanie in Dutch and himself in English. Did he really stick out like a foreigner?

'Steph, honey, we need to talk. Seriously, I'm worried and a little bit upset to be honest. I distinctly heard you say to your neighbour, Anna was it, that you'd see her again in August? I thought you and Natalie are moving to Scarborough permanently, you know, the four of us to live as a proper family. Plus the dogs of course. I simply couldn't stand the thought of you changing your mind. Please tell me I'm thinking along the wrong lines. I'm in mental agony right now, honestly.'

A smile almost as wide as the cup her Mocha was served in illuminated Stephanie's face. She found it hard to suppress a grin but she knew immediately that she had to put Pete out of his misery. She reached into her handbag for an email that she had printed out and read it out loud to him. It was in English already so there was no need to translate it.

Dear Stephanie Van Gelder

I hope this finds you and Natalie well as you make your final preparations to leave Bruges and make the journey to Scarborough.

Once you get here we will do all that we can to make the transition of schools as seamless as we can.

Digressing, after our last meeting I dug out a file marked "School Trips" and one in particular caught my eye. Much planning had been done five years ago (by my predecessor) for a four day trip to Belgium. It would be part geographical and part historical. Sadly, when the Covid epidemic arrived, the whole idea had to be cancelled. Natalie's imminent arrival here at Scarborough College has prompted me to reopen the file.

It is early days yet but I am pleased to tell you my colleagues are keen for the matter to be explored once again. We have approached some of our students' parents to "test the water" as it were. The response had been most favourable although "testing the water" is probably not the best analogy, bearing in mind that the Hull to Zeebrugge ferry route no longer exists.

We are hoping that, should the trip go ahead this August, both you and your daughter would accompany the party – perhaps as guides as it were, or even interpretors?

Once Natalie has settled perhaps you would be kind enough to join us over lunch here at the College and we can discuss this in more detail.

Wishing you both a safe journey.

Guy Merrett
Head Teacher

Poor Peter didn't know whether to laugh or cry.

'Oh, Stephanie, how could I have ever doubted your intentions? I'm so sorry.'

He leant across the small tiled table top and kissed her on both cheeks.

'But darling, on the subject of the College and the fees involved, I am genuinely concerned, worried even. There is no guarantee that we'll be able to fund it all after the Sixth Grade. What if the New Hotel Scarbados doesn't generate the profits and …'

This time it was Stephanie's turn to lean across the table. She put one hand over his and whispered almost silently, as if it was top-secret, like a meeting of spies.

'Darling, don't worry. I'm sure something will turn up.'

She left it at that and resumed sipping her Mocha. There was a commotion at the door as Lucy, holding the lead of a tiny Maltese Terrier, walked in closely followed by Natalie carrying no less than three designer shopping bags – advertising two different fashion houses. Who needed Harrods when you had Hermes and Versace within walking distance?

Hi Dad. We did it within budget but only just – a Hermes top each and a Versace one for my upcoming birthday.'

More in hope than expectation Peter's next question was almost perfunctory.

'Any change?'

A sly smile was the only response so he took that as a "no" and moved on.

'Why are you holding somebody else's dog lead?'

'The lady owner saw us coming out of the shop with these designer bags and decided to pop in there herself. Actually she was English but Natalie interpreted for her. She won't be long.'

It looked as if Mr Guy Merrett's ideas were already proving more than a little prophetic.

'OK we'll wait until she comes back for her dog and then we'll move on. Where next, Stephanie?'

I want to buy some nice chocolates for Shirley Ritson as a thank you for all she's already done for us. We'll go to my favourite chocolate shop, Verheecke's. It's just down the road. I've known one of their staff, Maxime, for years. I wanted to say cheerio to her anyway before we left but now I can also say "see you soon" can't I?'

In her mind's eye she was already planning ahead. Taking twenty plus school kids into Verheecke's shop in August would be quite an experience.

'Pete, let's fill the girls in on what might happen shall we, you know, re a school trip. I think Natalie already knows! You read that email didn't you? I told you, Peter, that she was a little minx when you met us in London didn't I?'

Natalie started laughing and immediately spilled the beans to her sister. It was just as well that Peter was not telepathic. Lucy was already plotting ahead to add to her up-market wardrobe on the next trip to Bruges.

'Yes, OK, well while we're at it, I think I'll pop into Jerry's Cigar Bar and buy Garry a nice box of Cuban cigars, you know in one of those beautiful hand-made wooden boxes made in Havana. He loves a cigar.'

'Are you sure? I've never seen him smoke!'

'Shirley doesn't approve, so he only smokes when he takes the dogs out for a long walk on his own. Now you know why he walks to Scalby Mills a lot.'

Stephanie didn't know whether to believe him or not. It sounded a bit too far fetched to her.

'Right, you lot, here's the lady to collect her dog. Let's be off – and, Lucy, try not be a Battersea Dog's Home attendant wherever we go will you please. There'll be time enough for that when we get back to Scarbados.'

A hearty meal of Coq au Vin or Moules Mariniere soon followed at the restaurant of the same name – Moules & Poules – in the Square named after the famous Belgian navigator and mathematician, Simon Stevin. Like the Portugese and British before them, the Belgians had been formative in making possible, international travel to unexplored parts of the world, so taken for granted today. If Mercator had not developed maps to accommodate the spherical orthodoxy of the globe, then many a sailor would have ended up in Torquay instead of Trincomalee.

The next morning was all about time keeping and schedules – Peter's forté. The plane was only five minutes late into Leeds Bradford Airport where their Nippy Taxi driver was waiting for them for the last leg to Scarbados. He had to wait a bit longer than anticipated. The Fishburns and the Van Gelders were more than a little delayed when they got to the Immigration desk – the official UK Border. It was just as well that they were the last in the queue, thanks to Lucy wanting to show off her Hermes carrier bag to fellow passengers. Oh well. The Immigration Officer was more than a little confused.

'Let me get this right, Mr Fishburn. Both of these young ladies are your daughters, correct? So why have they got different surnames?'

Peter was more than a little flummoxed and it showed. Stephanie tried her best not to grin, let alone laugh.

'Well, young Natalie here is definitely my daughter – but she's Belgian and being only ten years old is travelling on her mother's passport. Surely that's permitted isn't it?'

'Well yes it is, Sir. But since Brexit both Natalie and her mother are now subject to the ninety day rule. They'll then have to return to Belgium or there will be consequences.'

Suddenly it dawned on Peter why the Head Teacher at Scarborough College had stressed the importance of sorting out Natalie's residential status. The Immigration Officer obviously had a terrific sense of humour and scratched his chin to give the impression of deep thought.

'There is, of course, a solution but it would prove very, very expensive.'

Peter's heart dropped through the floor as he mentally added the cost of expensive immigration lawyers to the cost of school fees and the Value Added Tax. His youngest offspring was going to cost him a bomb and a half.

'Can you recommend a suitable lawyer …?'

'Good Lord, no Sir. I'm not allowed to get involved in that sort of malarkey.'

None of them could possibly guess what was coming next. The Officer looked him straight in the eye and said:

'Get married, mate, I would. Your family is beautiful. Take my advice and invite me to the wedding remember my name. It's Arkwright, John Arkwright. And don't forget – you've got ninety days. Through you go!'

39.

The ninety minute drive back to Scarborough was uneventful save for one thing – the incessant chatter from the two girls sitting in the back seat. The taxi was one of those "airport specials" – half van and half people-carrier. In the event they could easily have managed with just one case between Peter and Lucy but both chocolates and cigars had been taken aboard the plane as hand baggage. The rules had changed since Brexit and long since gone were the days when you could bring in almost as much tobacco as you could carry, as long as you could establish that it was all for personal use. The polished box of fifty "Romeo and Juliet" cigars would be well received by Garry. They would have to arrange an illicit meeting so that Shirley didn't see them. Unfortunately for Peter and Stephanie, both girls had overheard the Immigration Officer's advice on marriage as the best and quickest solution to the problem of Residency. Initially, the girls spoke in whispers but then decided to start a proper conversation so that both adults couldn't help but overhear them. Lucy started first.

'Did you hear that, Natalie? A wedding! Oh, how lovely! We'll both be bridesmaids won't we?'

It didn't generate any response from Peter and Stephanie. Not yet anyway. They tried to pretend they hadn't heard. So they started to speak louder and louder, almost shouting over the tops of the seats that separated them by a couple of feet. Then it was Natalie's turn.

'We'll have matching dresses of course.'

'Yes, a nice pale peach I'm thinking.'

'Who do you think Dad will pick as his Best Man...?'

It was too much for an exasperated Peter and Stephanie just couldn't stop laughing. She had warned Peter that his third daughter was a minx. There was an awkward silence for about ten seconds and but for the noise of the diesel engine you could have heard a pin drop. Peter was on the spot and didn't he know it. He hadn't done this for a quarter of a century but finally he drummed up courage and cleared his throat. There wasn't enough room in the taxi to perform the customary going down on one knee.

'Stephanie, will you marry me please?'

'Of course I will Pete, of course I will. When?'

Both girls shouted out – 'soon, soon! We want a wedding!'

The taxi driver was totally bemused.

'Well, I guess I'd better offer my congratulations. I've seen many things happen in the back of my taxis, some I couldn't possibly describe in front of minors, but I've never in thirty years seen or heard a marriage proposal. Would you like me to stop in the next lay-by so you can go go down on one knee properly?'

'Er, no thanks. We'll celebrate properly when we get to the New Hotel Scarbados. I'll text Millie to give her our rough ETA.'

Peter had an ulterior motive for doing so. His last few words on the text were:

'Did you find that flippin' teddy-bear that Natalie won at the bingo?'

Her reply took only thirty seconds to ping through.

'A warm Prosecco welcome awaits you all at the New Hotel Scarbados. I hear that Clayton James has only just arrived – delayed at HM Customs apparently. Bear sorted. Millie x'

Thank goodness for that. The bear issue had been nagging him. Natalie's, not to mention Stephanie's, residency status was seemingly solvable by a wedding but at what cost? John Arkwright, the Immigration Officer, had jokingly said that the solution would be expensive. He wasn't wrong, the girls would see to that. And there was still the massive issue of the school fees. It was all very well for Stephanie to have whispered in the café 'Don't worry darling, I'm sure something will turn up."

Yeah right. Like what? A Lottery win? Six years fees at a cost of mega-bucks a term had the potential to reduce the hotel's net profits to zero and all the "creative accounting" in the world by Clive White wouldn't save his bacon. The nearer the taxi got to Scarborough and their new home, the more he tried to put it out of his mind. It was late afternoon by the time they arrived. The taxi driver was slightly irritated.

'Crikey mate, there's a bloomin' great truck backed into your drive and an estate car parked right in front of it. It looks as if they're still unloading – look at all those boxes being lifted off the back platform!'

'Thanks driver, how much do we owe you?'

'Nothing mate, it was prepaid by the Hotel Koala. A Miss Millie Fishburn.'

'Oh wow thanks. That's a bit of good news. Here, have a few beers on me mate.'

Pete slid a twenty pound note from his wallet.

'Cheers and don't forget to invite me to the wedding when you get it organised. I want to tell folks that you proposed in the back of my taxi. Here's my card. We do wedding cars as well by the way, when you come to planning the details.'

'Cheers. I'll bear it in mind.'

And that reminded him. Where was the bear?

The front door was open and in stark contrast to their original arrival from Hull in the midst of a snow storm, everything was totally organised. The girls walked in first to be met by howls of barking from Sebbie and AlfieBoy who almost licked Lucy and Natalie to death. Natalie was overjoyed with happiness and bawled her eyes out. Millie took her in hand and grabbing her suitcase led her upstairs.

'So Natalie, welcome to your new home.'

The late afternoon sunshine poured into the room and directly onto the mass of pillows and cushions. Atop the bed-head was "Yorkie" the teddy bear.

'I told you we'd look after him.'

Natalie cried again. This was her first real home with a real family.

'Oh yes, Natalie. There's a little gift here, just from me to you, OK? It's a little bedside DAB radio and I've already pre-tuned it to BBC Radio York. When you wake up in the morning just press the little "on" button here and wait a few seconds. When we first came to Scarborough I found it very welcoming – you get all the local news and the weather forecasts. In no time at all the presenters will become like family members. There's Georgey who can't stop chattering all the time, there's Katerina, the weather girl, who can't stop talking about food and there's Emmanuelle who .... well anyway, you'll find out for yourself.'

They went downstairs to join the rest of them. Clayton and his son had finished with the all the boxes, twenty-six of them that had all been lifted into the almost empty conservatory.

'Well Peter, at least we didn't have to lift half of Kew Gardens in this time did we? I'll never, ever forget that. You lot hadn't even arrived when we set off home. Listen, Peter, a quiet word in the corner while the girls are all yacking.'

'Anything wrong, Clayton?'

'Yes and no, but I've got to tell you. It seems that we got singled out by HM Customs for a random check. This was the first time my van had been on the route and their cameras probably picked out my registration number as never being seen before. Anyway, after driving onto dry land we were signalled to pull into this Customs shed and told to open the rear doors but only sort of half-open. This bloke with a machine, about the size of a cornflake box, arrived and stuck the end of a plastic pipe into it and other end right into the van over the top of all those boxes. When it wouldn't go any further he asked me what was stopping it.'

'Gosh, what did you say?'

'I told him the truth, that it was the two bits of furniture – as detailed on the manifest and the Customs Declaration. There were two customs blokes – you know, good cop bad cop sort of set up. The younger one was probably a trainee, you know the type, eager to impress and tick boxes. I asked him what this was all about.'

'It's illegal immigrants mate. We were tipped off by the Dutch authorities that big trucks like yours might be carrying up to a dozen without the driver even knowing it. This piece of kit is very sensitive and can sniff carbon dioxide levels if even just one human was aboard.'

'So what happened then?'

'He said "all clear" but then the young smart-ass one wanted to know what was in all the boxes. I told him he was welcome to open any one of them if he wanted to.'

'And did he?'

'Yes he did. He picked one at random. About ten pairs of your good lady's shoes fell out of it. His colleague laughed his socks off and said "come on, I want my Sunday lunch at lunchtime not at tea time" and that was the end of it. Anyway, the last job now is the hardest. Where do you want that bureau and sea chest? Can I suggest in the conservatory? We'll manoeuvre the bureau in on our homemade skateboard to wherever you want it. Just bear in mind it could be there for a while until you unpack whatever's in it. Then we'll bring in the chest. What was in the chest is now packed separately in two of those boxes. Stephanie will know which ones – she numbered them. What an efficient lady you have there. Then we'll be off home to Brid. I'm starving. Hopefully her indoors will have some nice scran ready.'

Back in the dining room they were very well prepared. It was like a mini reception party. There were nibbles on the big table that Shirley had prepared and two bottles of champagne. Garry joined them with hugs for Stephanie and Natalie. It was almost as if they had just returned from holiday, not arriving at their new home collectively for the first time. Peter collared Stephanie and signalled for everybody to pipe down. He emulated Bob Dylan –

'Come gather round people wherever you are.'

Only Garry was old enough to remember the lyrics and he too was a fan of the American folk legend.

'Firstly a huge thank you to those of you who have made our return here so memorable. I've noticed the new NEW sign and we'll test it out as soon as it's dusk. I must remember to call Dave Gibson and thank him.

These are for you, Shirley. A box of Bruge's best from the Verheecke family. Don't eat them all at once. I know you don't have a sweet tooth, Garry, so I'll buy you a few pints later.'

He managed a surreptitious wink in his direction.

'And now, you good people, I have a special announcement to make. Stephanie and I are getting married as soon as we can arrange it.'

There were cheers all round. Millie was especially pleased. It would act as a softener to the news that Jamie and she were going to impart to their father. It would perhaps be best to wait until tomorrow when the three of them could be alone.

Some of the boxes were unpacked in a very orderly fashion but the bulk were left until tomorrow. Sebbie and AlfieBoy were asleep and it was almost as if Sebbie had never left. The Hotel Koala would fade into a doggie dream. Snuggled up in bed with his now new fiancée, Peter reflected on what a lucky guy he was. There was just one massive question he had to ask his betrothed.

'OK Stephanie, you can level with me now. What's really in that bureau and chest?'

40.

Breakfast the next morning at the New Hotel Scarbados was a leisurely affair. Millie and Lucy's purchases had included some Continental-style butter croissants with a variety of preserves in those little jars that you always got in hotels. When the time came for them to trade again as a hotel, they would ensure than boxes of every flavour were on hand. It looked so much more professional for a guest to have their own little jar on the table. Sebbie and AlfieBoy were not amused. The proprietors had returned but where oh where were the sausages and scraps of bacon. If they were literate then a written complaint to the RSPCA might be in order.

After coffee and yet more coffee it was inevitable that the subject of conversation got around to the wedding. Lucy started first.

'Dad, you mustn't dilly-dally. One of the girls at work who is getting married next month said that she and her fiancée had to wait almost six months to get the date booked that they wanted. They had to be very patient.'

'Well look, if they wanted to get married at St. Mary's Church, with buglers, harpists, a silver coach with six grey horses and the Archbishop of York officiating then I could understand it. We'll be looking for something a bit less grand with an early date to avoid the trap of this ninety day rule.'

He looked towards Stephanie for some back-up. She managed to force a half smile only. After all, she hadn't been married before and she wanted it to be special. Lucy was quick to retort.

'No, Dad. That was for a Registry Office wedding. Nothing particularly special.'

Peter gulped to the extent of almost choking on the last curly bit of a croissant. The end of it fell onto the carpet and laid there for less than two seconds before an eagle-eyed AlfieBoy snaffled it.

'Seriously Dad, you need to make enquiries as soon as you can. We don't want to see Stephanie and Natalie deported – the Government's as keen as mustard on all of that sort of thing now.'

'You're right of course. I'll call up the Registrar of Births, Marriages and Deaths straight after breakfast and see what the score is.'

'Dad, just drive up there. The office isn't far away on Burniston Road on the way to the Sea Life Centre on the left hand side. You can't miss it, honestly.'

'I'll call first to make a proper appointment and …'

Lucy had already fiddled with her iPhone and before Peter could even reach for a replacement croissant the phone was already thrust into his hand. She had obviously found her charger. It was ringing already.

'Good morning, Registrar's office. How may I help you?

Within a minute an appointment was made with the Registrar herself – a Mrs Christine Copland.

'Mr Fishburn did you say? You're in luck, an appointment scheduled for twelve o'clock has just been cancelled. The lady in question was in tears when she called me as she couldn't face coming in.'

Peter assumed that it was a case of a bereavement and that the informant was too upset to attend in person. He could not have been more wrong.

Leaving the girls alone to continue the systematic unpacking of all those cardboard boxes, Peter and Stephanie dressed fairly smartly and went out to the car. They had forgotten that Millie had driven back to the Koala in the only vehicle they currently jointly possessed. Plainly, the purchase of another set of wheels was a priority. Garry came to the rescue once again and gave them a lift. Thinking quickly, Peter took the opportunity to put the box of cigars in the back of Garry's car and tipped him off.

'Don't let Shirley know we brought them back from Bruges for you. Mum's the word, mate.'

'You're a star. Wow, Romeo and Juliets! I'll savour each and every one of them. Not had one for over a year now. Here we are, I'll drop you off here outside the Registrar's. I'll think I'll drive straight down to the Sea Life Centre car park, sit on the wall facing the sea, and enjoy one.'

'But have you got a light?'

'No, but all cars have a cigar lighter don't they? Even if nobody smokes cigars any more!'

Peter and Stephanie didn't have to wait long in the nicely appointed Reception area of the Registrar's office. A door soon opened and a smart, pleasant bespectacled lady in her sixties appeared.

'Mr Fishburn and Miss Van Gelder?'

'Yes, that's us. Good morning.'

'It's actually just a minute after twelve o'clock so I'll say good afternoon instead. Please, come into my office. Take a seat please. You look far too happy to be registering a death so can I take it you want to arrange a wedding?'

'Yes please. Do we look that happy?'

'Indeed you do. Now firstly, do you have a date in mind, perhaps in the Autumn?'

'Gosh no! It has to be within ninety days, Mrs Copland.

We have inadvertently fallen foul of the new rules, post Brexit. Stephanie and our daughter Natalie are Belgian nationals and the quickest way around a potentially disastrous situation is to get married as soon as possible and …'

'If you'll kindly let me finish please. I was just about to tell you that the lady who cancelled her appointment has also had to cancel her wedding which was scheduled for four weeks today.'

'Oh no. I hope it wasn't illness or even worse?'

'No, her fiancée got cold feet and it's all off. I've seen it before but usually cancellations like this are within a few days, not weeks. You are both very, very lucky.'

'Er, why is that exactly?'

'Because twenty-eight days is the minimum notice time by law. It used to be twenty-one days but a while ago it was increased to twenty-eight. That would make it a Monday. So we have just enough time to comply with all the rules and regulations. So, the sixty-four thousand dollar question is – do you both want this date?'

Peter and Stephanie turned to face each other, smiled and almost as one voice answered.

'Thank you so much. Of course we do, that's awfully kind of you.'

Twenty minutes later and they were outside and on the phone to Millie. It was only right that Millie and Jamie were privy to their plans as soon as possible. Millie was almost as excited as them.

'Dad, I'll come and fetch you in the car and then we'll need to have a long chat with Jamie. We have news for you too and it's urgent. We can drop Stephanie off at the New Hotel Scarbados on the way back. She'll probably want to oversee the young ones unpacking.'

Peter had switched his phone onto "speaker" mode and Stephanie nodded in agreement.

'Right, stay where you are. I'll be down in ten minutes OK?'

In fact it was substantially less than ten minutes and within a quarter of an hour Stephanie was unpacking Box number sixteen. The boxes were not the problem but the two pieces of furniture would be another problem for another day.

Peter, Millie and Jamie were in the smaller of the two lounges and alone. It was just like the old days.

'Dad, Jamie and I are over the moon with your news. Have you got a date fixed yet because …'

'Yes, it's exactly four weeks today – a Monday. At twelve noon.'

'You have to be joking, Dad.'

'No, there's been a wedding cancellation and we've booked the slot as it were. How shall we play it? The New Hotel Scarbados will be in no fit state to hold a reception by then? Can we do something here at the Koala?'

Jamie was first out of the blocks.

'Of course we can, Dad. If an award-winning chef can't do it, who can?'

Peter gave his son a giant bear hug. Millie reached for a pen and paper.

'Oh no, Millie, not another one of your famous "to-do" lists!'

'Of course! There's no time to lose. Let's see now – guest list, menus, wedding cars, flowers, dresses ...'

'And Dad, don't forget you'll need to have a Best Man to hand over the ring and make a sober speech.'

'Of course, I'll have to give it some thought. We must make it a memorable day for Stephanie. Her girlhood dream of a big church wedding in Bruges simply can't happen. I'm a divorcee don't forget. But hey, I have some other news for you too. Scarborough College are going ahead with a school trip to Belgium in August, towards the end of the holidays and they want Stephanie and Natalie to act as guides and interpreters. Isn't that great news?'

Millie was thinking out loud and came up with a terrific idea.

'I've got it. You go with them, Dad, and treat it like a delayed honeymoon. Hey, and think about this too – maybe you could retake your wedding vows in Bruges Cathedral? That might make up for a civil ceremony here. Tell you what, why don't you suggest it to her as your own idea? I promise not to let on.'

'Promise?'

'Of course I do. Come here and give your daughter a hug – Jamie just had one.

Now, Dad, we don't want to dampen the mood and wonderful news but Jamie and I have some news for you that you need to know. After all, although you're no longer directly involved here, you are still the head of the Fishburn family and it's only right that you should know OK?'

Peter looked worried, almost crestfallen. Millie acted as joint spokesperson. She was good at it.

'Dad, this has all happened fairly quickly. In a nutshell Best Eastern Hotels have made Jamie and I offers for our shares that we simply cannot afford to turn down. The offer is straightforward – it's a half a million pounds each with completion of the transfers by the end of September. After that the offer will lapse – probably for ever. On Saturday, while you were in Belgium with Lucy, Clive White came up to see us to give us his thoughts.'

'I can't believe I'm hearing this.'

'Dad, just bear with us please. Jamie will have his turn in a minute.'

'OK, I'm listening, go on.'

'Best Eastern Hotels are slowly becoming more involved with every week that goes by. To put it bluntly, Jamie and are are rapidly getting sidelined – and of course they control the purse strings. Long term, we're both on a loser. I don't think my long-term future is best suited by staying here. Graeme's contract with Scarborough Cricket Club finishes mid-September and he's asked me if I fancy going back to Australia with him – just for a holiday you understand. I've said yes. The timing all fits in. But now, let Jamie give you his absolutely brilliant news. Go on Jamie, go for it.'

'Thanks, Sis. Dad, a couple of weeks ago Pamela Hesketh asked to meet me for a chat so we met in the Watermark. She wanted to tip me off about the forthcoming sale of a small restaurant in the Old Town called the Neptune Café. It's a small but nicely appointed place …'

'I know it! It's really nice. Stephanie and I went there together. That was the night we agreed to stay together and make a go of it. So, go on.'

'Well, Chloe and I went to have a look at it. It's got twenty-four covers as it's presently set out. Clive has put the last few years' accounts through the mincer and he says it's a sound little business. It's on the market for five hundred and fifty thousand but Clive reckons there's a deal to be done. I might only be a few grand short. It's within reach anyway. What do you think, in principle anyway?'

'You've got to go for it, both of you. But, Millie, just make sure that you come back in one piece. I'll speak to young Patterson later to make sure he looks after you. Now, any more of that coffee in the pot?'

41.

The next twenty-one days simply flew by. So much was happening it was hard to take it all in. Millie's latest "To-do" list was slowly but surely being ticked off. It wasn't chaos by any stretch of the imagination, just very busy. The wedding day was referred to as "W-Day" and at W minus seven they all gathered at the Hotel Koala for a "round robin" chat. Everything seemed to be in hand. Millie glanced down at the guest list, the invitations having gone out two weeks earlier.

'So, Dad, looking down this list, who's responded? You know, yes or no thank you.'

'Everybody on that list has responded in the affirmative either by telephone, text or email. It's not like years ago is it, with fancy cards printed:

'Mr & Mrs Van Gelder request the pleasure of the company of John Smith on the occasion of the marriage of their only daughter Stephanie ...'

'Er well no, I suppose not, Dad. I have to say though I'm wondering why some of these people are on this list. Fred and Babs Coates from Skipton for a start. We only ever see them ...'

'Millie, they were amongst our first guests when we took over the Hotel Scarbados. They remained loyal to us when we moved here. Well, didn't they? The wedding reception will be an ideal opportunity to do a bit of networking. After all the New Hotel Scarbados will be up and running and trading as a boutique B & B in the not too distant future. Stephanie is already making plans for a complete makeover. It's looking as if all the guest rooms are going to have a name, not just a number. I saw her drawing up a list the other day. She caught me peeking at it and whisked it away.'

'What sort of names?'

'Place names, you know, the Liege Suite, the Ostend Suite, the King Leopold Suite …. I can't remember any more.'

'And a lot of the names on the guest list are just trades people who …'

'Yes, Millie, but those good folks are the people who helped us the most. Just think, where would we be without Dave Gibson? He must have got sick and tired of us by the end. He put up the new "NEW" sign for us while we were in Bruges three weeks ago and he still hasn't even sent us an invoice.'

'And Clayton James for goodness sake. Why are he and his wife on the guest list? He got paid didn't he?'

'Yes, but to be fair, Stephanie also requested that both Dave Gibson and Clayton were on the list.

'OK Dad, I take your point. It's not my wedding after all. There's almost fifty people on the list. Jamie, what about the catering? Are you up to speed? What are your plans anyway? Sit-down or a buffet?'

'Oh definitely a running buffet. We'll set all our tables out in fours, sixes and eights and just leave it to folks to sit where they want and with who they want. The food is all ordered and Chloe's dad, Frank, will be delivering all the seafood fresh on the morning of the wedding.'

'And Dad, don't forget to bring the clothes you'll be wearing on the wedding day here to the Hotel Koala the day before.'

'What on earth for?'

'Because it's the tradition that you don't spend the night before the wedding with your bride, that's why. And that's the end of it. I've already booked you a single room. At least you'll look very smart. I can't believe you even considered wearing your old suit. You probably last wore it at Aunt Mary's funeral. I remember you buying it in a Burton's Sale just for the occasion. No, that was a brilliant idea of Chloe's to take you to that Designer Centre the other side of York. Macarthur Glen.'

'Macarthur Park, I call it. "Someone left the cake out in the rain."'

'You're showing your age now, Dad. And speaking of cakes the wedding cake is all sorted. It's a surprise design following a chat between Stephanie and a girl called Val Smith who she met by chance in a coffee shop. She works in a Care Home, makes cakes for a bit of pin-money and they are just sensational.'

'Go on then, give me a clue,'

'Nope, sworn to secrecy. Now, what else have we got to tick off the list?'

Seemingly only one item on the list hadn't even been addressed.

'Right, Dad, I think that leaves just one item remaining on the list – the Best Man. Who is he, for a start?'

'You don't need to know, Millie. He's my Best Man, not yours. And that's the end of it. Right then, if we're done here I'd best be off. Will one of you give me a lift back to the New Hotel Scarbados please? You, Jamie, if you're not too busy. We've ordered the new small 4 x 4 like the one that Garry's got but in silver not white. But it won't be here until just after the wedding.'

Millie raised both eyebrows. Where was the money coming from for the car, let alone the wedding? She rather wished she had volunteered to take her father back. She would have grilled him for information, nicely, but grilled him nonetheless.

They were half-way down the hill towards Peasholm Park when Peter turned sideways to his son.

'Jamie, will you be my Best Man please?'

'What?! Me? Are you sure?'

'Yes, of course. You didn't think I was going to choose Sebbie did you? That was your sister Lucy's idea by the way. As if! I hear she's already ordered a white carnation for each one of the dogs to fix to their collars on the day. Bonkers, mate, just bonkers. So what's your answer then, yes or no?'

'Dad, I'd be honoured. Wow! Just wait till I tell …'

'No, Jamie. It's our secret. Until the day no-one is to know. Promise me.'

'OK Dad, I swear.'

Back at the Hotel Koala, Millie was wondering just who her father had chosen to be his Best Man. She day-dreamed through an imaginary list. It wasn't very long. She just hoped that it wasn't going to be Miles Carter, the Cricket Club Treasurer. He was very personable, had a good speaking voice but, oh dear, if he had a bottle of Presecco and a few pints on board then he could get a bit raucous, not to mention a bit unsavoury, with his jokes. Millie racked her brains until she almost got a headache but she just couldn't come up with a name. Oh well, she would just have to wait until the day arrived, like everyone else.

That day did, of course, arrive. On the Sunday evening the Hotel Koala looked absolutely splendid. There were sprays and mini bouquets of flowers everywhere in the public rooms. It looked like the Chelsea Flower Show. Down at the New Hotel Scarbados Stephanie had her wedding dress all laid out in one of the guest rooms – the one she intended to name the King Leopold Suite in the fullness of time. Lucy and Natalie were so excited too. Their matching peach-coloured dresses had been tailor-made by Mr Armani in Bar Street. It had cost Stephanie an arm and half a leg but the cost didn't matter. This was going to be *her* day and she wanted her daughter and step daughter to look like Cinderellas. She had made sure that Pete's suit was perfectly pressed and the white shirt ironed to perfection. She had packed him off to the Hotel Koala with his clothes in perfect order.

'See you tomorrow, darling. Just think, this time tomorrow I'll be Mrs Stephanie Fishburn.'

'And this time tomorrow our daughter will effectively be Miss Natalie Fishburn.'

They embraced and briefly kissed before Peter got into the white Nippy Mondeo.

'Hotel Koala please.'

The driver looked curious. Do you want that suit hung up mate or laying on the back seat and you can get in the front. It's a posh-looking whistle and flute, I must say.'

'Yeah, the thick end of five hundred quid mate. None of your Burtons stuff. I got it at that Macarthur Park Place …'

They both started singing

"Someone's left the cake out in the rain …'

'Special occasion is it, mate?

'You could say that. I'm getting married tomorrow at "high noon."

'You're kidding! You've hired our wedding car, a Merc. I'm the designated driver!'

The beautiful sunrise over the North Bay bade well for the occasion. Everything and everybody was on time. No words were fluffed. Mrs Christine Copland personally conducted the ceremony and had tears in her eyes when she became the first person to congratulate them as man and wife.

'I'm sorry I'm so emotional but I officially retire today. This is my last ceremony and this time next week my hubby and I will be be living in Tenerife. So today is a mixture of joy and sadness combined.'

Without hesitation, they invited Christine to join them for the wedding breakfast at the Hotel Koala and she accepted with alacrity. What a lovely way to finish her career too.

The buffet was superb. Jamie had absolutely excelled himself. He felt that he had to. After all, this would be the last major function he would cater for before leaving and taking over the Neptune Café. The deal with Best Eastern Hotels was going ahead within just a few days. As he had foreseen, he was short of the sum needed by some twenty thousand pounds and he needed some working capital too. Inside the breast pocket of his suit was the envelope postmarked "Humberside" containing a short hand-written note and a cheque that was now nestling in his bank account. He would keep the note for the rest of his life – he just knew he would.

'Dear Jamie

I am so happy for you. To own and operate your own restaurant at such a young age is marvellous. I just know it's going to be great success. The cheque enclosed comes with my love and best wishes. It is not a loan, I gift it to you absolutely. Today is your father's wedding day and although I won't be there for obvious reasons, I wish him and his new family well. Who knows, I might even have to buy a new hat to attend my own son's wedding one day. I hope so.

All my love to you and Chloe.

Mam xxx

He was awoken from his daydream by Chloe digging him in the ribs.

'Jamie, just concentrate will you. Your Dad's coming to the end of his speech. He'll be giving you the nod in a minute. Get ready....'

'Ladies and Gentlemen without further ado I would now like to ask my Best Man to say a few words. Would you please welcome …...Mr James Fishburn.'

Everybody was stunned, except Jamie and Chloe. She had helped him write his speech – not too short and not too long. Chloe had been to a few weddings of friends recently and she knew the format. No rude jokes. There were a few youngsters present and he didn't want any of them, especially Nattie, getting the wrong impression. After all he was "big brother" now and he had to act accordingly.

Millie was glued to her beau, Graeme, who had also had to purchase a new suit for the occasion. He wasn't family, at least not yet, There was a huge cheer when the wedding cake was wheeled in on a tea trolley. It was covered in a white table cloth and after a countdown from five it was flipped away to reveal a massive sponge cake about two feet across and four inches deep. It was covered in white butter icing and bore a colourful and spectacular design – the crossed flags of the United Kingdom and Belgium. There were no words. They were simply unnecessary. The flags spoke a million words. Millie simply couldn't take her eyes off it. She day-dreamed about how it might look with another nation's flag instead of Belgium's. The six stars of the Southern Cross always looked beautiful.

The ceremonials over, the bride and groom mingled amongst the guests. Without being noticed, Stephanie managed to have discreet words, first with Dave Gibson.

'Yes that's right. I've written it down on this card, Mr Gibson. And do it whilst we're away in Belgium please, between those dates. Thank you, now can we get you and your wife some more champagne?

'Good afternoon, Clayton. A little job for you please. At least you know the way now don't you? No, I promise you it's nothing heavy. Just some paintings and other objects d'art that need to come here – the same collection address as last time. Meet me at the same address as before in Bruges please on the date on this card. Say 2PM? Thank you. Now, can I get you and Mrs James some more champagne?'

The afternoon turned into evening and folks started to drift off. The Ritsons had already taken Lucy and Natalie back to the New Hotel Scarbados as they were keen not to leave all the dogs alone for too long. In any event they would all be needing a pee before long.

Another taxi came to take the bride and groom back home and as Peter ceremoniously lifted his bride across the threshold he said:

'Darling I've just had a wonderful idea. When you go on the school trip to Belgium, why don't I go with you and we can renew our vows in Bruges Cathedral. It would perhaps make amends for not getting married in church. What do you think?'

'That would be perfect Darling, just perfect.'

Only she knew how perfect.

Natalie was already in bed, not asleep but curled up reading. One at a time, she had been reading the many journals that her great Grandfather had packed into the sea chest before his final departure from the Belgian Congo. She was now on the last one dated 30ᵗʰ June 1960. She read it several times to make sure it was real. Had her mother read this? Perhaps not.

'It is with a heavy heart that my wife Natalie and I leave the country today. This will be my last entry. Our departure as the colonial power has not been a happy one. In fact it has been fraught with danger and difficulties. Sadly, many people have lost their lives. Normal financial and banking arrangements have been impossible for months. Along with some of my colleagues at SABENA we have therefore made alternative and irregular arrangements of our own. Several one-kilogram bars each of copper and gold have been purchased and carefully hidden into items of furniture before being shipped home to Antwerp. Our consignment is set to leave the port of Matadi today on the SS Jadotville bound for Antwerp – a voyage of some sixteen days. Natalie will be a passenger on the ship but my contract obliges me to fly the company's planes back to Belgium. I chose gold and copper rather than diamonds. I think both metals will be in huge demand in the years ahead and will prove to be a sound investment. Perhaps one day they will be used to provide for the education of my descendants about whose existence I can only speculate at the time of writing. Please, God, may we all have a safe passage home.'

Now Natalie knew where her name had come from. She was named after her great-grandmother.

EPILOGUE

It was Day Four of the school trip to Bruges. The official itinerary: " A canal tour followed by a visit to Bruges Cathedral" was still strictly speaking true but had been slightly amended. The precise time of twelve o'clock was given for a Special Ceremony. Natalie was the only school child who was privy to the secret. She was to act as both presenter and interpreter. She felt very honoured. It wasn't just the school party either. At any given time Bruges Cathedral was rammed with foreign tourists from all four quarters of the globe. A priest appeared clad in all the finery and regalia demanded by his status. He rose slowly to the top of a massive pulpit, seemingly made totally of wood. A hand-held bell rang which brought forth silence to the assembled gathering. He addressed everybody, speaking in Dutch. As he did so, Natalie translated his words into English, a sentence at a time.

'Dearly beloved, we are gathered here today in the sight of God to bless the marriage of Peter and Stephanie. They will repeat the vows made at their wedding several weeks ago, Stephanie in Dutch and Peter in English. Their daughter, Natalie, will translate the words for Peter to speak in English.

Then let us begin …'

The ceremony over it was time to return to their hotel for a light lunch before taking the train to Brussels and the connection to the London-bound Eurostar.

'Peter darling, you go back to the hotel with Natalie and the kids. I promised to pop back to the old house to see a couple of the neighbours who were on holiday when we left before. I'll catch you at the Hotel, no problem.'

Fifteen minutes later and and she was talking with Clayton James whose smallest van was parked outside on the kerb.

'Right, Mrs F. where's all these paintings and stuff. Nowt heavy you said. My back's still not right, you know.'

'No, just a couple of dozen items, mostly works of art – a couple for each room when we get back home. They're valuable but not heavy. Thanks for coming.'

Three hours later and they were all safely on the Eurostar – next stop London St. Pancras. The kids were all playing with iPhones and tablets. Peter and Stephanie were just chilling with a coffee and a cognac. What another wonderful day it had been. Stephanie nestled into Peter's shoulder, composed herself and whispered:

'Darling, I've had a brilliant idea. Let's change the name of the hotel to Hotel Belgique. What do you think, darling?'

* * *

BY THE SAME AUTHOR

Novels
Your Country Needs You
A Very Special Relationship
Her Place in the Sun

The Takeaway
The Maltese Mandarin
Hocus-Pocus AUKUS

Hotel Scarbados
Hotel Koala

Non-fiction
MALTA My Island
One Thousand Days in Hong Kong
From UK to Belgium and Back
Sunburnt Pom's Tales of Oz

www.hotelscarbados.com

www.mvhbooks.com